A SPIRIT OF SUMMER

BOOK THREE OF THE PERTH PARANORMAL SERIES

A.B. HOOSER

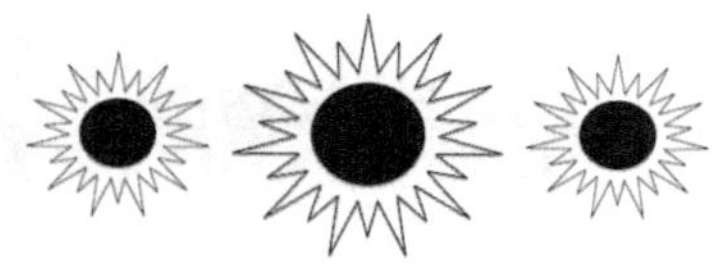

PRINTED IN THE UNITED STATES OF AMERICA
FIRST PRINTING, 2025
PAPERBACK ISBN- 978-1-962019-16-3

THE HENLO PRESS
P.O. BOX 1694 ASHLAND, KY 41105
WWW.THEHENLOPRESS.COM

1

If this was a John Hughes movie, the rain would be gentle and the multicolor lights of open shops would reflect across the sidewalks of Main Street. I'd be soaking wet with my makeup still perfect, and a boy I'd had a crush on since junior high would run toward me to proclaim his love. But this was not a teen movie from the eighties. The rain was torrential, the shops were all closed because nothing in Perth stayed open after nine, and I was dead. Never needing an umbrella didn't balance out the fact that I would never fall in love with the perfect guy, have a career, or get married. My sister, who had been by my side since our birth, had crossed the graduation stage without me a few short hours ago and I was throwing myself a pity party.

It wasn't Pansy's fault that I wasn't joining the Class of '96 as they matriculated from Perth High School. It wasn't even her fault I'd died in a car crash, although she'd been driving and still blamed herself. It was maybe her fault that I'd come back three days later, although that was like, a total bonus. She couldn't see or hear any of the other ghosts we'd met, but recently there'd been a glimmer of hope on that front. A few weeks ago a real, honest-to-god psychic medium had helped us dispatch a corrupted spirit to the great beyond, wherever that may be. Christine was impressed with the promise Pansy had shown at Medium work. It wasn't exactly a skill one could put on their college admissions application or anything, but we thought it was pretty cool.

Perth was a small town and our senior class consisted of about ninety kids, most of whom did not, in fact, find Pansy cool in any way, shape, or form. She'd been in the papers uncovering too many dead bodies for them not to take notice. First had been Christopher, who we suspect had been drowned by his mother. Then there was the body of missing country music star Stuart Mayes. My friend Lee, also a ghost, had actually found the body, but Pansy and my best friend Bagel had "discovered" it for legal purposes. We hadn't known the body was someone famous at the time, so the news coverage she and Bagel received shocked us all. Then there was Doctor Welling. Pansy hadn't even been present when the Perth Paranormal Society had dug up the grave of Mister Evil Doctor Dude who'd been haunting our last case. That didn't stop the local news from slapping her photo up on the screen every time they talked about the burned pit of bones and shoe leather they'd filmed after the PPS had set fire to his grave. It was like they loved to make her look as crazy as possible.

I was thinking about ways to haunt the reporter when I noticed something moving from the corner of my eye. I'd been staring at the reflection of a neon sign in the growing stream of water backing up on Main Street and I couldn't figure out, at first, what had caught my attention. A crack of lightning lit up the street and I saw a scraggly orange tail disappear around the low brick wall surrounding the elementary school. What self-respecting cat would be out running around in the pouring rain?

I floated across the street, through the wall, and with the next flash of lightning located the orange ball of sopping fur curled under a metal playground slide. One green eye stared me down as I drew closer. Only one eye, I realized, because Harvey was missing the other one. This was Summer's cat who lived a life of leisure batting at suncatchers and wind chimes in her shop across the street. Sarah, Summer's twenty-something assistant, had been running Wild Harmony since Summer had left—had Harvey escaped earlier in the day without her noticing?

"What are you doing out here, buddy? Don't you know that it's raining? How'd you get out?"

Harvey gave a plaintive meow, which in no way answered my questions. Had Summer returned home? She'd been gone for almost six weeks with no word about where she'd gone or when she'd be back. It wasn't like her. She'd told Chandra, our fellow PPS member, that there was a family emergency and that she had to go home. She hadn't left a phone number and it wasn't until after she'd gone and the group started talking amongst themselves that they realized that no one knew where her family lived or even where she'd grown up. It was straight up like an episode of Unsolved Mysteries. What could we do but wait for her to call or come back home?

Despite Summer's mysterious disappearance, Harvey was my immediate concern. Even though I could now pick up small objects and make things move for short distances, there was zero chance that I could drag a fourteen-pound cat out from under a playground slide and carry its unwilling butt all the way across the street.

"Hey, buddy. I'm going to go get Pansy. I need you to stay put so we don't have to look too hard for you, okay?" He stared past me and I wondered for the hundredth time if he could actually see or hear me. Either way, I hoped he stayed where he was.

I floated back out to Main Street and was so distracted thinking about Harvey that I waited on the sidewalk as a pickup truck drove past. Some habits are just hard to break. I crossed the street to Wild Harmony and up to the second floor to see if maybe Summer was home or if Pansy would need to call Sarah to get the key. I hoped she was home. She'd missed out on the conclusion of our last investigation and we had, like, a metric crap ton of stuff to tell her. I hoped to float into her apartment to find the electric kettle steaming and maybe some Stevie Nicks blasting from the ancient stereo system, but the lights were off, and the only illumination came from the security light in the back parking lot. The sheers covering the window over-looking the lot were billowing in the breeze on a curtain rod that was bent and hanging by only one bracket.

I searched the area around Summer's end table, finally locating one of her lamps—now on the floor—and pushed the switch. The light cast crazy shadows since it was leaning at a strange angle, but the scene before me would have been bad even in normal lighting conditions. The whole place was trashed. It looked like a scene from one of those aforementioned teen movies where the parents go out of town and the kids throw a wild party. Everything was either knocked over, broken, or both. *What had happened?*

"Strange things are afoot at the Circle K," I muttered to myself.

The curtain sheer blew into the room again, and the shards of broken glass scattered across the floor caught the light. Well, this answered the question of how and why Harvey was outside in the rain. *Poor baby.* The storm must have seemed less fright-ening than whatever had gone down in here. I floated out the back wall to check the parking lot and found it empty. I booked it over the ravine that ran behind the shops on Main Street and across our neighborhood until I came flying through our front door. Like, literally.

"Pansy!" I yelled at the top of my lungs. I could hear voices in the living room, but that was just the parents entertaining Grandma and Aunt Bev who'd driven up from Red River for graduation. It was exactly where I'd left them two hours ago, and I considered having Pansy enlist their help for a second. I thought better of it, as it was a little after midnight and Mom rarely saw her mom and sister. Besides, this shouldn't take long, Pansy just needed to alert the police and then they'd take over from there. Fifteen minutes, tops, I estimated.

Floating upstairs, I headed straight for our bedroom, the large room at the end of the hall we'd shared since birth. Pansy was still wearing the pink slip dress she'd worn under her graduation gown, the knee-length scrap of satin shimmering as she danced to Walk Like an Egyptian. Someone must have broken out the Greatest Hits of the 80s CD after I'd left.

"Pansy," I yelled again to be heard over the music.

She froze in her Egyptian pose, one arm up, the other down.

"I need you to call the cops."

"What?" she asked out loud before remembering she wasn't alone. But the music was loud and since Amber, Anne, Chrissy, and Jenny were all still singing and dancing along, her outburst went unnoticed.

I moved closer to yell in her ear. "I just found Harvey running around outside in this storm, and when I went to see if Summer was home I found the whole apartment trashed. You've got to call the cops."

"Gotta go pee girls, give me a minute," Pansy said to the room as she made her way out of our bedroom and hustled toward the upstairs bathroom.

"How am I going to call the cops?" she hissed as she closed

the bathroom door. "I'm here and there's a room full of witnesses that I haven't left all evening. How would I know what's going on at Summer's apartment?"

"I don't know, but we've got to call it in. The window is broken and her carpet and drywall will be ruined if they don't cover it up."

"Is whoever broke in still there?" she asked.

"I... I don't know. I didn't hear anyone moving around, and the back parking lot was empty. I didn't notice anyone parked in front of the shop, but I didn't look down the street. It's possible someone was out there and I didn't see them."

"Crap," she said, tapping her pale pink fingernails against the bathroom counter while she did mental gymnastics. "Okay, I'll say, I don't know, uh... that I need to go get more ice. I'll drive over and say I was on my way to the gas station when I thought I saw something."

"I told Harvey to stay put, for what that's worth. He's under the big slide on the elementary playground. You could say that you saw him and stopped to see how he got out."

"Okay, but what if he's gone by the time I get there?"

"Does it make a difference? He's out and no one can prove you didn't actually see him. But if you need something else I also left a lamp on in Summer's apartment," I offered.

"Okay. Okay," she repeated to herself as she mulled it over. "That's good. I can work with that. I'll say I was driving by and saw Harvey run across Main Street and behind the building. So, I drove back there and saw a light on upstairs. Since Summer's Bug wasn't there, I stopped to look around. I'm assuming it's the window off the fire escape?"

"Yep."

"Then I'll tell them I saw the curtain blowing and realized the window was broken." She tapped her nails twice more in confirmation, nodding her head in response to some internal conversation. "That should be believable. Crap. Why tonight? Why can't we just have one normal evening?"

I wanted to tell her that she was the only one having a normal graduation evening, but I bit my tongue. I needed her and she didn't need the guilt. Summer also needed her, even if she didn't know it yet.

"Okay, let me go get my keys and my purse. I'll meet you there."

"Don't forget your cell phone."

I watched as she went back into her room and made some excuse about needing to run out and get a bag of ice. I heard several offers for some company, but she finally convinced the others to stay dry and continue having fun without her. As she darted from the front door out to the street where her bright yellow Geo Tracker was parked against the curb, it occurred to me that I should have told her to make sure she had an umbrella and maybe even a towel. *Yeah*, I thought, watching her climb into the Tracker already looking like a drowned rat, *she was definitely going to need a towel.*

Can I help it if that gave me my first real smile of the evening?

2

I flew back to the elementary school to check on Harvey who'd moved out of the growing puddle under the slide to shelter in a recessed doorway of the school. I left strict instructions for him not to move, receiving a slow blink in response. As I moved across the street I noted that there was only one car parked across from the Firefly Cafe. A more thorough search of Wild Harmony was needed to assure myself that whoever had broken in wasn't still there. I might be feeling petty about the unfairness of our situation, but I would never want Pansy to walk into something dangerous. I floated through the plate glass display window and could instantly see that the entire downstairs was also trashed. Light from the street lamps along Main Street glinted on the bits of broken glass and reflected from the ruined wind chimes that were sticking out of the piles. No display had gone untouched. But there was no movement, no shuffling sounds, no one knocking anything over. Whoever had done this was long gone.

I went back outside, waiting under a street light for my mortal half to catch up. Traffic was nonexistent so when I saw the familiar headlights heading my way, I waved my arms in the air, flagging Pansy to stop at the curb in front of the school. When she jumped out of the Tracker her feet immediately disappeared into what looked to be about two inches of water pooling along the curb on Main Street. The Perth stormwater system couldn't keep up with this much rain.

"Ugh, this is going to be a long night," she grumbled, staring at her submerged feet. Thrusting a hand behind the driver seat, she pulled out a dark blue golf umbrella from the floor and pressed the button, the edges shooting out and pulling the fabric taut. She was already drenched, I don't know what she thought she was protecting at this point. Her long dark hair was soaked through, running in black rivers across her chest and snaking down her back in three separate sections. At least wet underwear was something I never had to deal with again. "Where's Harvey?" she asked, striding down the sidewalk towards the playground. Her pink ballet-style slippers splashed up dirty water with every step.

"Over here." I led the way to one of the side doors of the school and Pansy collected the wet mass of orange fur in one arm, settling the big boy across her chest and shoulder under the umbrella.

"It's okay, Harv, I've got you. We're going to get you in the truck and then I'm calling the police, okay Buddy?" She received a meow in response and Pansy splashed back toward the Tracker where she struggled to open the door while holding both a beefy cat and a giant umbrella. "Hold on, don't you dare take off on me. No, don't jump yet. I've almost gerrrrt it." She was leaning over sideways with the umbrella handle wedged between her chin and shoulder so that she could open the door. I enjoyed her dilemma for maybe a second or two too long before jumping in to catch the umbrella when it finally slipped.

"Thanks," she said half a second before dumping Harvey into the passenger seat, directly on top of her purse. After making sure that his tail wasn't in the way, she slammed the door and sloshed back around to the driver's side. Wrenching the door open, she climbed into her seat before snapping the umbrella closed and pulling her own door shut. The rain-slicked nylon was tossed into the black hole that was her back seat. Pansy sat still for a moment, the drumming of the rain on the vinyl soft top filling the silence while she stared down at her ruined dress and shoes. Her moment of reflection was ruined when Harvey stood up and gave a full body shake, slinging water everywhere. "Holy crap," Pansy grumbled as she turned on the cabin light. "Is there a towel back there?" she asked, holding up both arms to block the next wave of cat tsunami.

"Uh, no towel, but there's a spare tee shirt on top of the pile directly behind your seat." Pansy reached blindly behind her, eventually grabbing hold of the discarded tee with some minor assistance on my part. She immediately rubbed it over her face, smearing her mascara everywhere. I decided not to mention it —she'd figure it out eventually. The tee shirt was soaked by the time she wiped down her arms. Turning the key, she started the Tracker and backed out into the street, turning down the alley and into the small parking lot behind Wild Harmony that it shared with the four other shops on that block.

"911, what's your emergency?" I could hear the tinny voice coming from the speaker of Pansy's cell phone. She'd dialed as soon as she'd put the truck into park.

"Yeah, this is Pansy Bellafini, I was just driving down Main Street and saw Harvey, Summer Hopkin's cat, outside."

"It's after midnight... are you calling about a cat right now, Miss Bellafini?" asked the bored female voice on the other end of the line.

"No, no, I caught the cat. Umm, the problem is that Summer has been gone for a few weeks and so I thought she must be back, but when I pulled into the lot behind Wild Harmony her

Bug isn't here. There's a light on in her apartment and I can see that the second-story window at her fire escape is busted out. I think someone broke in."

"You think someone broke in because there's a light on?"

"Well yeah. I've knocked and called but she's not answering and her car isn't here and now there's a light on and a broken window."

"Maybe the storm broke the window," the less-than-helpful voice replied.

"While I guess that's possible, but the storm didn't turn on a lamp." Pansy's tone was losing some of her default politeness. I snort-laughed and she shot me a look.

"Tell her you can see the shop through the front window and everything downstairs is broken."

"I can see through the front window that everything inside is broken, can you just please send someone over here to check it out?"

"Fine. I'll notify patrol in Perth and they should be there shortly. Please don't leave, I'm sure they'll have questions for you."

"I'll wait for them," she bit out, gritting her teeth, "thank you ever so much for all of your help." She stabbed the end call button and tossed the cell phone into her cup holder. "Great," she said, turning to me. "Now we have to wait for the cavalry to arrive."

"You'd better call the 'rents. You know they worry when you're gone too long." Not that their worry wasn't without cause, there was that whole car crash thing, after all. I figured the entire family was going to have some hang-ups about Pansy driving at night by herself for at least the next decade.

"Hey, Mom. No, no, I'm fine. Yeah, I went to get ice. No, no, I'm calling because while I was driving, I saw Summer's cat out in the rain, so I caught him, but her place has been broken into and she's not here, so I called the cops." There were many words that I couldn't make out on our mother's end. "No, I'm fine, I told you. I've just got to wait for the police. Can you let everyone know that I won't be back for a while? Yeah, the slumber party is still on, I'll just be late with the ice." This was followed by many more words from our mother and finally Pansy was allowed to say goodbye.

Pushing her hair out of her face with a sigh, she turned the key in the ignition and the radio flared back to life. "What are we going to listen to while we wait?" She pulled the purple nylon bag of tape cassettes from the center console and started flipping through her options. "GNR? The Forest Gump soundtrack? Oh, nope, here we go, Shakespears Sister."

"You've got the eye makeup for it," I said as she popped the tape into the cassette deck.

"What? Oh no," she said, horror dawning as she pulled down the visor and opened the lighted mirror. "Oh my god, why didn't you say anything? I look like a raccoon!"

"A rabid one. Dude, did you forget that you used a crap ton of mascara tonight?"

"Oh my god," she mumbled again, pulling the soaked tee shirt out from under the cat who'd decided to use it as a bed. She made a valiant attempt to undo the damage before anyone saw her, unfortunately, the police station was just two blocks away. In the time it took for two officers to remove themselves from behind their desks, make it out to one of the three patrol vehicles the Perth Police Department owned, and drive over, Pansy's scrubbing had only made it worse. She still looked like a raccoon and I was still feeling very pleased about it. Maybe this was a sign that I should also start attending the weekly therapy sessions with the rest of the family.

A black and white Yukon pulled in next to Pansy and we waited for the officers to get out. The pair seemed reluctant to exit their nice dry vehicle as the rain was driving sideways. A gust of wind rocked the Tracker.

"Hang on," I told my sister before floating over to the four-door SUV to see what, exactly, they were doing. The ability to be really, really nosy was one of the few perks of being dead.

"Dispatch, this is Patrol 22, we've arrived on location and can see the busted window. Can you try to call Sarah and have her come over with the keys so we can search without breaking down the door?" The cops were both young, Officers Stevens and Bias, which I knew because I hung out at the police station with my friend Lee entirely too much. They were both good guys, maybe not especially bright, but friendly and not power-hungry jerks like you see in the movies. If you were speeding in Perth, these were the guys you wanted to be on patrol; they almost exclusively handed out warnings because they didn't like doing paperwork. They'd picked the wrong call to make a run on tonight, this one was definitely going to involve writing up some reports.

Bias leaned forward to get a view of the window. "Well, the window wasn't busted before and I don't remember the light being on when we've made rounds." He brushed a hand over his dark crewcut as he leaned back in the seat.

"Yeah, it's been dark since she left. Maybe Sarah turned it on earlier today and then the house panther knocked something into the window and busted it. I mean, why would anyone want to break into her apartment? Anything worth stealing would be from the store." Stevens replied.

"Well, maybe they thought breaking the downstairs shop window would be noticed and that no one would see this one. Once they were inside, they could have unlocked the back door, loaded up a whole van with stuff, and left without anyone seeing."

"We probably should have checked to see if the door was still locked before Mindy called Sarah."

Bias shot him a look. "Feel free to get out and check it."

"I'll wait for the keys, thanks. You know, maybe they don't have a vehicle at all and they're holed up in there," Stevens said, squinting like that was going to help him see through the brick wall. Unless his Coke bottle glasses were the x-ray kind, it wasn't going to help him much.

"I mean, maybe they heard us or the Bellafini girl pulling into the lot and ran, but then again, with this storm, maybe not. Hit the siren, give it a whoop, and see if there's any movement." I floated back over to Pansy to let her know who was there and that they were currently trying to avoid getting out in the rain.

"I'm going over," Pansy said, reaching into the back for the umbrella.

"Just wait a second, they're having the station call Sarah so that she can bring the keys. Let me see if she's coming or not before you get soaked. Again."

"I'm already sitting in a pool of water over here, I'm not sure it matters at this point."

She was certainly going to have to leave the roof off for a few days to dry everything out. I floated back over to the Yukon where Bias was busy explaining his methods of making home-made risotto to Stevens. I was taking mental notes when the radio squawked to life and the dispatcher confirmed that Sarah was on her way with the keys.

"Sarah will be here in just a minute," I told Pansy who was now running the heat at full blast in an attempt to dry out.

"Good, I'm tired of sitting here twiddling my thumbs." We weren't quite finished singing along with the next track when the scrubby weeds that lined the edge of the parking lot lit up.

"Here come headlights, it's got to be her." I pointed to the splash of light and sure enough, Sarah's black Durango came flying around the corner on two wheels. She jerked to a stop in her usual spot, the driver's side door flying open even as the vehicle was still shuttering from the force of her braking. Keys in hand, she was across the few feet of gravel and under the tiny canvas awning that covered the back door in less than five strides. Stevens and Bias scrambled out of their SUV in tandem, yelling for her to wait.

"Sarah, hang on! There might still be someone in there."

She already had the key in the lock and the door wide open but stood back as the two patrolmen rushed to secure the doorway. Bias was carrying a flashlight the size of a small baseball bat, its beam flashing across the yoga studio and highlighting absolutely nothing in the large, empty space. The three stepped inside as Stevens radioed dispatch to let them know that they'd entered and would advise as soon as they found anything. Sarah hit the overhead lights, the recessed can lights illuminating the studio and reflecting off of the expanse of highly polished wooden floors. There was nothing amiss in the room, an open box with nowhere to hide. The yoga mats were still rolled and stacked against the back wall; the sound system next to the mat storage was untouched on its shelf. The table in the corner that held the thirteen-inch TV/VCR combo that Summer used to watch the PPS investigation tapes sat by itself—there hadn't been any tapes stacked next to it since Summer had left.

"Clear," I heard Bias yell, followed by a soft 'duh' from Stevens.

"Police, is anyone here?" Bias shouted before pushing through the beaded curtains that separated the yoga studio from a small office space. Summer typically stored boxes of extra inventory there, and the room held a small desk that I'd never seen her use. It was also where the interior staircase leading to the apartment above was located.

"Holy crap," I heard Bias mutter a second after the beads

swept closed behind him. He hit a light switch at the bottom of the staircase and I could see that every drawer of the old-fashioned roll top desk had been thrown into the floor, the contents dumped everywhere. Boxes of inventory, books, candle holders, and what looked like a collection of moon and star-themed sun catchers littered the floor.

"Be careful, there's broken glass everywhere," he warned.

"What? Why, what's broken?" Sarah asked from behind Stevens. Her short black hair was sopping wet and she tried to squeegee her forehead with her equally wet arm. It didn't look like it worked.

"Looks like pretty much everything," Stevens replied, poking his head through the beads.

"Is she here?" I heard Pansy ask from the doorway. She must have gotten tired of hanging out in the Tracker while the patrolmen 'secured the scene.'

"Bellafini, wait right there, do not come any closer. We don't know for sure that whoever was here is gone. Give us a few more minutes." Bias pushed his way through the empty boxes and crushed merchandise and into the main area of the retail shop. The beaded curtain that normally hung there had been pulled down and I could just make out a few strands of beads buried under a pile of wind chimes. Hitting another light switch, the disaster area that was the front shop was revealed by the one pendant light behind the counter that had not been destroyed. Of the big lights—a pair of old brass chandeliers— one hung at a drunken angle from a single wire and I spotted the other half-buried under some books. The weak light was enough. Bias whistled under his breath.

"Yikes," I muttered. The upstairs was bad, but whoever had destroyed the shop had left no item unbroken. It had looked like a mess in the dark, but now, with the light on, I could better appreciate the level of devastation that had gone on here. It was like a tornado had gone through the place. A very, very angry tornado.

Stevens was starting up the stairs and Bias quickly waded through the debris to catch up while informing dispatch of the situation.

Sarah and Pansy waited in the yoga studio while the cops searched upstairs. I followed them up. The duo had some choice words for whoever had done this to Summer, but they cleared the area quickly, confirming the intruder wasn't still lurking in a closet or something.

"I have Harvey in my car," Pansy was telling Sarah when I came back down. "He wasn't happy about being out in the rain, but whoever did this must have scared him out of the apartment."

"Oh, thank goodness. I'll take him home with me when we leave," Sarah said, clutching one hand to her chest. "I can't believe this is happening. Who would want to steal from Summer? And what would they steal? I don't get it. I haven't even ordered new inventory since she left because I have no idea when she's coming back or what she wants done with the shop. What's going to happen now?" The panic was rising in her voice as she looked around the studio.

"I'll help clean up. Dario will want to help, too, and I'm sure the rest of the PPS will be more than happy to pitch in. We've all been worried about her." Despite years of sniping at one another, my best friend Bagel, or Dario as Pansy referred to him, had become friends with Pansy since my death last October. He'd joined the PPS after our first few months of investigations and was now a part of the team. They would all happily help out a fellow member of our merry band of weirdos.

"I'm worried about that window," Sarah said, staring up at the floor above. "I don't know what to use to cover it. The hardware store is already closed and I don't think we have a sheet of plywood or anything like that at home. Maybe I could duct tape some garbage bags together until we can do something more permanent tomorrow."

Pansy still had her cell phone in her hand and held up one finger to Sarah as she hit a speed dial preset. "Hey, Randy, it's Pansy. I'm sorry to bother you, but I need a favor." Randy was the President of the Perth Paranormal Society. He worked as an exterminator at his real job and lived just outside of town on an old ranch that had been in his family for generations. If anyone would have a random piece of wood lying around, and the tools to hang it up, it was Randy. Pansy had explained the situation and was disconnecting as the two patrolmen came back down the stairs.

"There's no one here," Bias said as he pushed through the remaining beaded curtain. "We'd like to check everything over tonight and see if there's anything here resembling, I don't know, a clue or something, I guess. I didn't see a security camera or anything."

"No," Sarah said, "we didn't have a security system. Just the bell on the front door and the deadbolts. Will I be able to start cleaning up the place tomorrow?"

"I don't see why not. I don't think we'll find anything, but they'll want to fingerprint the place and take photos of the damage, first."

"It's, like, a store and yoga studio," I said, waving my hands around. "There will be fingerprints from a hundred different people in here."

Pansy just shrugged at me before turning to the patrolmen. "I just got off the phone with Randy, he said he'll be here in about ten minutes with a sheet of plywood to block off the window. Can we go ahead and, like, soak the water up out of the carpet, at least?"

"Well, luckily the rain is hitting from an angle that isn't

coming in through the window, so there's no water mess," Bias replied. "When you say Randy, you mean Randy Martinez?"

Pansy nodded.

"Okay, I'll keep an eye out for him. I'll wait here to get the window secured and Stevens can go ahead and get you two to the station to get you fingerprinted and take your contact information. Get statements, you know. All that stuff."

"Fingerprinted? Why do I need to be fingerprinted?" Pansy whined. Her hopes of being home soon were about to be dashed.

"It's just procedure, Miss," he said. His adrenaline must have been wearing off because as I watched, his facial expression changed from stone-cold serious to a smirk as he took in her whole drowned rat appearance. Her pink slip dress was stuck to her body and her hair was plastered to her head and shoulders. With her messed-up eye makeup and ruined dress, she looked like an extra from a horror movie.

Pansy finally noticed that Bias was trying not to laugh while looking at her so she turned to the wall of mirrors lining the front of the room and caught an eyeful of herself. I heard her muttering under her breath as she turned back to the cops and shot them both a dirty look.

"It's fine, Miss Bellafini. Trust me, we've seen worse," Stevens said, turning his flashlight off. "I'll come back with the detectives in a bit," he said to Bias. "Ladies, if you can follow me back to the station, we'll get your statements and hopefully back home where you can get dry and cozy as soon as possible."

The rain had slacked off to a steady drizzle but the back parking lot was flooded with about half an inch of water. Pansy opened the door of the Tracker and lost a shoe as she was struggling to haul herself up into the seat. Jumping back down, she fished the slipper out of a puddle, took the other one off, and threw them both into the passenger floorboard. A very startled

Harvey came flying up out of the floor, screeching like his tail was on fire, causing Pansy to scream as well. I may or may not have completely lost it.

"Oh my god, your face," I wheezed.

"I'm glad someone is enjoying this evening," she muttered before climbing back into the driver's seat barefoot. She slammed the door and started up the engine, following Sarah and Stevens out of the parking lot. They made a sad little parade as they drove the two blocks down Main Street, turning left into the lot that backed up to the police station. Not even bothering with her shoes or the umbrella, she jumped out and sloshed across the paved lot to the back door.

An older man with a shock of white hair that swooped back from his gaunt face was coming down the hallway as we entered. "Were your spidey-senses tingling?" I asked as he came to a stop beside me.

"Not quite. I overheard Stevens calling in to dispatch," Lee said. He shook his head as he took in Pansy's appearance. "Poor kid looks half-drowned. I'd offer her my robe, but..." he shrugged. Lee wore a pair of blue pajamas with a coffee stain down the front and a ratty brown terry cloth robe that must have been two decades old when he'd died in his sleep. "So, Junior Investigator Bellafini, what do we know?"

I filled Lee in on the evening's events while Pansy and Sarah got comfy in a pair of metal folding chairs. It took forever for someone to fingerprint them and then finally take their statements. Once they'd finally been cleared to leave, Pansy handed over a very cranky Harvey to Sarah. It was a little after two before they left the station.

She went home alone. Lee and I still had work to do.

3

I'd met Lee Bradley, or, I suppose, the ghost of Lee Bradley, shortly after my death. Although I'd originally nicknamed him Mister Jerkface, the grumpy old fart had grown on me. He was now one of my favorite people, breathing or not. Plus, his years of experience as an investigative journalist had proven invaluable as Pansy and I seemed to stumble over one mystery after another.

I'd caught the tail end of a conversation between the dispatcher and the detective on duty while Pansy had been waiting at the station, enough to surmise that no one was going out to investigate until morning. Since no one was hurt and the window had been boarded up, Summer's case wasn't a high priority. Lee and I had decided to take advantage of those hours and look for any clues. Was anything missing? Had any messages been left behind? Our list of questions included: Who would do this? What were they looking for? Why bother destroying everything? When had it happened and where did they go afterwards?

After some quick snooping to reassure ourselves that Summer was the only victim of a break-in on Main Street, we turned our attention to her upstairs apartment. I was now able to turn on lights and shuffle through debris just as well as Lee, but Bias kept driving by, shining his spotlight into the front windows of Wild Harmony. I ended up doing lookout duty while Lee searched room by room. Despite our best efforts to remember what had originally been where, there didn't seem to be anything missing. There were no notes scribbled in lipstick on a mirror, no spray-painted warnings, and nothing that answered any of our questions. The only thing we knew for certain was that whoever had done this had been in a rage.

We moved to the bedroom where every item of clothing left in her closet had been ripped up and thrown on the floor. Even the bed had been torn apart, both the mattress and the box spring sliced to shreds and thrown against the wall. "I'm not seeing anything that looks like a clue, are you?" I asked.

"There has been a definite lack of clues. Which is kind of weird in itself."

"What do you mean?"

"Well, look at your bedroom. Both of you kids have photos everywhere, whole albums of them, filled with memories of school friends and family events. You have special outfits saved in your closet even if you only wore them one time. There's not even an old prom dress stuffed into a forgotten corner." He motioned to the empty closet. "Pansy's graduation is what started me thinking. There's no graduation gown in the closet. No cap stored on a shelf, no old sports sweatshirts or ball caps, not even a tassel hanging from a mirror. Summer was barely in her thirties but she doesn't have any kind of high school memorabilia that I can see. Everything in here is relatively new," Lee said from behind me.

I looked around the bedroom again and took note of what I was seeing. Under the clothes and debris, the hardwood floors were covered in a scattering of colorful rag rugs that were sold at the hardware store next door. The toiletries that had once lined her dresser were drugstore brands. The crumpled jewelry box full of costume jewelry had been a papier mache affair covered in colorful paper scraps, something she sold downstairs at Wild Harmony. The colorful comforter was the kind you could buy for twenty dollars at Walmart—there were no family quilts or chenilles in sight. Generic clay pots and the crushed plants they had held were jumbled under the window sills and the artwork knocked off the walls had been cheap prints in poster frames. There were no heirlooms, no photos of her family, nothing that looked like it had been lovingly passed down.

"New and pretty cheap. Maybe she lost everything in a fire," I said, still looking around. "But there's nothing... personal in here, is there?" Even her collection of coffee cups had been thrifted from yard sales. I'd heard her tell Pansy once that buying anything new that you could buy secondhand was a waste of resources.

"I didn't really pay attention when she moved here a few years ago, yoga and hippie stuff isn't a special interest of mine," Lee said. "But I don't remember her having a U-Haul. That kind of thing always gets people talking, usually because people think they can drive a big truck and then they end up blocking traffic or getting it stuck. They just let every lunatic off the street rent one. Anyway, my point is, don't you think it's odd to move here with enough money to buy this building but not actually owning anything?"

"How do you know she bought the building?"

"Because that is definitely something people talked about at the time. She had the bank manager all worked up. Paid cash."

"So, what, you think she robbed a bank or something?"

"I mean, not necessarily, but something like that? Maybe. Could she have had some opportunity to take a bunch of money and run? But run from what? There's not even a pile of clothes that don't fit in here. Everything that I see on the floor is something I have seen the woman wear. If there's one thing that I learned from being married, it's that a woman will pack up things she hasn't been able to wear for twenty years when she moves, just in case. Diane was almost fifty before she finally donated her old skirts from high school."

I could only nod in agreement as I had tee shirts from middle school stashed in my closet that I was loath to give away. *And I was dead.*

Downstairs it seemed that while all of the inventory that had been left was still there, it was crushed and broken. A rack of snow globes had been thrown or stomped into the wooden floors hard enough to wedge shards of glass into the boards. I made a mental note to warn Pansy to be careful where she stepped.

"How many calories do you think they burned tearing this place apart?" I asked Lee. Before our wreck, Mom had always been trying out new aerobics tapes and from what I could see, no amount of crunches and squats could have equaled the energy that had gone into this destruction.

"I don't know, kiddo. A lot. And was it just one person or several? I can't get over how thorough they were about smashing every last breakable thing. What was the point?"

We both turned to look at the cash register on its side on the floor, the change drawer sticking out. The sun was coming up across the high plains, the first rays of light streaming through the front windows and limning the giant mess on the floor in a soft orange glow. It highlighted the arc of coins that had been flung across the floor when the register had been thrown.

"Sarah said she takes the cash home at night, just leaving the change. There wasn't any money to steal." It didn't make any sense. I looked at the sad piles of books and broken candelabra strewn together with suncatchers and what had once been elaborately dipped and cut candles that were shattered into pieces. *Such a waste.*

"Well," Lee said, hands on his hips as he surveyed the damage. "I guess you can let Pansy get her beauty sleep. I can almost guarantee you that neither Starsky nor Hutch is even out of bed yet. They won't finish with the place until the afternoon." He was referring to Detectives Crane and Billings, the only investigators the department could boast, for what that was worth. "I'm going back over to the police station and see what their plan of attack is here."

"Okay, I'm going to go make my morning trip to check on Mrs. Garcia, then I'll swing by and see if Pansy's still sleeping. I'll also try to signal Bagel and let him know what's going on."

"Sounds like a plan. You know where to find me."

"Peace out, dude," I said, shooting him two fingers in a peace sign. I swear I heard his eyes roll from across the room. I laughed at his disgust as I floated through the front window.

Ever since Christopher had poofed and Mrs. Garcia had been left alone in her big pink house, I'd been trying to visit her at least once a day to make sure she was okay. I worried about the old lady—she needed more human interaction than just the church ladies who came to collect her every Saturday for trips to the bank and grocery store. The rest of the week she stayed home by herself without even a cat for company. Her family didn't live close and to hear her tell it, she'd outlived all of her friends.

Mrs. Garcia was in the kitchen making a pot of coffee when I came in, the crocheted coffee pot cover that was shaped like a barn lying on the counter. She had the radio on, her ancient hips swinging back and forth in a motion so jerky it was painful to watch. Her hands were no shakier than normal as she filled the carafe with water and measured out the coffee grounds. She seemed to be perfectly capable and in good health. I wasn't sure, exactly, what signs of ailing health I should be looking for. It wasn't like I'd ever met anyone with dementia, but the old girl seemed to be perfectly happy with her yarn, large-print magazines, and the reruns on cable. Andy Griffith was her favorite—she never missed an episode as far as I could tell.

Reassured that the old woman was still kicking, I floated back home, stopping in to see if Pansy was still in bed. The red LCD numbers on the alarm clock beside the bed read seven twenty-three and my twin was still face down in her pillow. She hadn't pulled her hair back into a braid before falling asleep and it lay in tangled knots across her purple comforter. I was surprised to find her alone, but everyone must have gone home last night when she took so long getting back from the police station. Our room was still a mess, empty bags of Doritos and Oreos scattered across the end of the bed, the contents of both of our Caboodles spread over the carpet and a pair of socks that didn't belong to either of us had been left under my desk. I considered turning the stereo on to scare the crap out of her, but figured she'd had a long night, so I could let her sleep for another two or three hours.

Bagel Boy would be up, though. After a quick flight across town, I found Bagel sitting on the end of his bed wearing a pair of orange and blue basketball shorts, a Sega controller in his hand, and a cartoon hedgehog bouncing around on the TV screen. I gave him three taps on his arm and he screamed, throwing the controller directly into the wall behind him and knocking down his movie poster of The Crow. He lay back on the bed, one hand still clutching his chest as the beautiful figure of Brandon Lee draped over his face.

"We need a better warning system. I'm going to buy one of those little bells, you know. The kind that they keep next to cash registers that say 'ring for service.' Holy crap." He sat back up, shoving the poster to the side. A bell wasn't a bad idea. I'd hate to be the cause of a premature heart attack.

I gave him three more taps, and he took the hint.

"Okay, okay, hang on. Why are you here so early? It's Sunday and you know I have the day off."

I waited for him to pull out the Ouija board that he kept hidden under his bed and immediately moved the planchette to the word 'call' that Bagel had written in Sharpie in one of the blank areas. We'd also added the words 'Pansy,' 'go,' 'work,' and 'write.'

He grabbed a dirty tee shirt off the floor and was pulling it over his head as I moved the planchette to the R, followed by the A.

"Okay, Call R A, got it."

I only had to move it one more time to the N before he figured it out and gave Randy a call to get the low down.

"We're going to meet in the lot behind Wild Harmony around two." Randy's booming voice came through clearly even several feet away. Heck, Bagel's mom and dad in the bedroom next door could probably hear him. "Bring good leather gloves and thick-soled boots if you have them. There's a lot of broken glass downstairs."

"Yeah, I've got stuff to wear. Okay, I'll meet you there."

I gave a little fist pump. My breakfast pastry, as Lee liked to call him, was on the case.

4

I watched Crane and Billings as they fingerprinted some door knobs and light switches, took photos of nothing in particular, and poked around in the mess for about half an hour. After all of that *intensive* searching, they'd concluded that a wild pack of roaming teenagers must have gotten bored after graduation and broken into the store to smash things. Like, whatever. After this disappointing attempt at police work, they'd released everything back to Sarah for cleanup and headed down the block to The Firefly for breakfast. Sarah had started with a broom and dustpan but had quickly graduated to a snow shovel loaned from the hardware store next door. I'd floated home to wake Pansy up and by the time she'd crawled out of bed, dressed, called Bagel, and located her keys, Sarah had already been working for a good hour. She was carrying a load of broken merchandise out to the almost full dumpster when Pansy pulled in.

"Oh, no. Is there anything that can be saved?" Pansy asked her as she exited the Tracker. She was dressed in paint-splattered sweatpants that had been pushed up to her knees, white Keds, and a stained red tee shirt that had a rip under the left armpit. Her long dark hair was pulled back in a ponytail that stuck out the back of an old ball cap that she must have stolen from Dad. Although I knew she was planning to work and get dirty today, I marveled that she'd actually left the house looking like this. The Pansy of even six months ago would have been terrified that someone would see her looking less than perfect, but we'd been through a lot in the last year. This Pansy was less interested in impressing anyone and I was liking her more and more.

Sarah didn't even notice Pansy's clothes, as she was dressed in an old pair of basketball shorts and an equally ragged tee. She'd opted for a red bandana tied over her hair to keep the dirt and dust out. Sarah was explaining her plan of attack to Pansy when Bagel pulled up in his Bronco.

"Hi. Hope you don't mind me pitching in," he said to Sarah. His dark hair was held back with a Broncos ball cap and not hiding half of his face for once.

"Of course not, I'll take any help we can get. I'm trying to set up the studio as kind of a staging area," she said, leading them back into the room. "I want to put things that aren't broken over there," she gestured toward the yoga mats, "and I've got some cleaning supplies set up over there," she waved a hand at the corner table. The TV/VCR combo had been pushed into the far corner and a giant box of garbage bags, a box of latex gloves, and two hand brooms sat on top of the table. "Mr. Trujillo next door donated some supplies from the hardware store."

"I called everyone before I left the house," Pansy told her. "Shawn should be here soon but Chandra has to open the cafe. Her manager is coming in at eleven so she'll be over then. Randy and Greg should be here about noon and they're bringing Greg's trailer so we can haul stuff to the dump. He said that Greg had to run to the laundromat to look at their air conditioning first, but they're hoping that it won't take too long. I called Blake but he didn't answer. I left a message on his answering machine."

"Thank you. I'm so glad Summer had all of you with the PPS as friends. I don't think I could do all of this on my own. One thing before we start—if anyone spots a purple leather address book, please let me know. Summer kept the phone numbers for all of her suppliers in it and I want to let them know that the store is closing. It's got to be in this mess somewhere but I haven't found it yet."

"Well, let's take a look at what we're dealing with," Bagel said. "But first, let's move these out of the way." He reached up and pulled the remaining beaded curtain down, rolling it around his arms before depositing it with the yoga mats. "At least she'll have something that isn't broken." He walked back towards the office/storage space between the studio and the store and let out a low whistle. "Wow, you weren't kidding when you said someone destroyed the shop."

"No, they seemed very determined. They even ripped out the light fixtures," Sarah said, pointing to the chandeliers.

By the time Shawn arrived, we'd barely made a dent in the mess. And by we, I'm including Lee and myself as emotional support because it was heartbreaking to watch everything that Summer had built and curated be carried out as trash.

Shawn stood in the doorway, one hand brushing through his short dark curls as he assessed the damage. He disappeared for a few minutes to walk next door and finally returned with a wheelbarrow that held a big roll of heavy-duty paper, masking tape, and more dustpans. After explaining his plan of attack, Pansy grabbed a broom to sweep her way across the studio floor while Shawn and Bagel taped the paper down behind her. Together, they created a path from the shop to the back fire door that would protect the hardwood floors. With that task complete, Shawn shook out two tarpaulins, one to collect the items that could be saved, and a separate one for paperwork and documents that would require Sarah to sort through one by one.

Everyone chose a place to start, Pansy moved paper from the desk to the tarp and Bagel started on books. It was a painstaking process, shaking bits of glass and wax from each one before either stacking those that weren't ripped back onto the shelves or tossing the damaged ones into the wheelbarrow. Shawn had already carried the busted register out to the dumpster and was working on reconnecting the lights. As the electrician of the group, the exposed wiring dangling overhead had made his eye twitch. Sarah tried to clear the space behind the counter where all of the smaller items, mostly incense, incense holders, and a crap ton of CDs had been pushed off into the floor. She had a handful of jewel cases and was sorting them into stacks on the counter: Enya, Chant, Yanni, and at least five different sounds of nature CDs, when Chandra came in the front door carrying two giant paper bags.

"Wow," she said, stopping dead to survey the mess. Her hair was lit up from the sunlight as she stood gaping in the doorway, giving her a cranberry halo.

"Yeah," Bagel agreed, setting another book on the shelf.

"I come bearing food and drinks from the Firefly," she said, lifting the bags and giving them a little shake.

"You're the best, babe. I'll have this done in another minute or two," Shawn said from atop the ladder.

"Be careful where you step," Sarah told her, pointing at the broken snow globes. "You can move the cleaning stuff off the table in the studio and we can eat back there where there's room."

"Yeah, I think I need to re-up my tetanus shot before I come back in here," Chandra said as she began to pick her way across the room. Bagel jumped up to take the bags from her and help her across.

Chandra was passing out drinks and everyone was sitting on the floor with a burger in their hands when we heard someone drive into the gravel lot behind the building. It sounded like they were splashing through every puddle twice. "That will be Greg and Randy," Chandra said, digging into the bag for straws.

I floated out to see Greg's truck with a huge flatbed trailer attached, blocking most of the lot. The two got out, dressed in their standard dark jeans and worn work boots. Even though it was June, Greg still wore what I liked to refer to as lumberjack chic—a flannel shirt over a white tee. Randy had opted for a polo, although, with the amount of black pelt it exposed around the collar and on his arms, I wasn't sure he'd be much cooler.

"Eat first," Chandra told the pair as they entered the studio. "Then we'll get to the work part."

As they were grabbing their burgers from the bags I turned to Pansy. "While everyone is here, get a piece of paper and start making a list. How to find Summer. What do we know?"

"Good idea," Pansy said, turning to search the tarpaulin behind her for a crushed stack of printer paper. She pulled a purple marker from the pile of pens and pencils she'd been tossing onto one side of the tarp before turning back to the group.

"Since we're all here,"

"Except Blake," Bagel interrupted.

"Except Blake, I want to make a list before we start cleaning again. I want to find Summer but we need somewhere to start. What do we know? Did she ever mention anything to anyone here about her family? Any old boyfriends or BFFs?"

Everyone looked at one another, shaking their heads. "She never talked about herself," Randy said. "She'd ask about my family, talk business, talk about an investigation, but I don't remember her ever saying anything about her family."

"Somewhere south, maybe?" Sarah offered. "She's always slathering on sunscreen and saying that she was dumb for not protecting her skin from the sun when she was a kid."

"South doesn't exactly narrow it down, now does it?" Shawn replied.

"And too much sun could be any direction, not just south," Randy said as he squeezed ketchup on his burger.

"If we could find her hometown," Pansy said, writing 'hometown?' on her paper, "we could call the local library and have them look up everyone named Hopkins listed in the phone book"

"What if she was married and that's not her maiden name?" Greg asked.

"What if she was in witness protection and Summer Hopkins was a completely made-up name?" Shawn asked.

Chandra shot him some side-eye. "You watch too many spy movies."

"What about her mail?" Lee asked. "Has anything ever been delivered in a name she doesn't recognize?"

"Anything addressed to an alias?" I repeated the question to Pansy.

"Sarah, what about her mail? Was there anything that ever came to her in a different name?" Pansy asked, not mentioning that it was the ghosts who wanted to know. While the rest of the group was aware of Pansy's connection to me and by extension, Lee, now was not the time to drop that bomb on Sarah.

"Not that I ever noticed. I always open everything and just throw away the junk mail. You know, sale circulars and credit card offers? Everything else is for the shop." She paused to take a drink while she thought back. "I've been opening the mail for years and you know, she doesn't ever get, like, birthday or

Christmas cards from anyone outside of Perth. That is kind of weird, isn't it?"

Everyone agreed that it was.

Chandra pointed a toe towards the pile of paperwork. "Maybe there's something in her bills and mail that will give us a clue. A credit card statement or something? If she's used the card since she left it may give us some idea of which direction she went, at least."

"Summer didn't have any credit cards—she said they were a scam," Sarah advised. "I've been paying the utility bills as they come in but I haven't seen anything unusual."

Pansy wrote, 'no credit cards' on her paper under 'no personal mail.'

"What about the building?" Randy asked. "Did Summer own it outright or did she have a mortgage?"

"Umm, we don't pay anyone monthly so I guess she owns it? All of the papers were in the filing cabinet."

"Lee said she paid cash for the building," I told Pansy. She wrote 'no mortgage' on her list.

"I put all of the stuff from around the filing cabinet in that corner of the tarp," Pansy said, pointing to the general area. "I have no idea what a deed would look like so I can't tell you if there was one in that pile or not."

"What about insurance?" Greg asked Sarah. "Have you had time to call them yet? Surely they'll pay for the damages."

"Crane said he would have a duplicate set of photos developed for me to send to the insurance company, but I don't know if they'll even let me file a claim without Summer here to sign things. I've never had to do anything like this before."

"Are you going to try to reopen?" Chandra asked.

"No. I was thinking about it last night, without her here to run the yoga classes or to authorize more inventory..." She waved a hand towards the front of the building. "I've just been selling whatever stock we had left. There's no way we'll be able to recover from this. I'm just going to have to shut the store down until she comes back."

"If you have leftover stock that needs to be stored, one of my cousins owns a block of storage units. I know he'll give me a really good deal and I don't mind paying for it until Summer comes back," Randy said.

"If she comes back," Shawn muttered.

"You know," Pansy said, staring at her list of questions. "While I was waiting at the police station last night, I started thinking about how Summer started acting weird around the time of the Chivington Investigation. You remember? She left early that night."

"Yeah, she said she had a migraine coming on," Randy said. "I offered to drive her home but she insisted that she could make it even though it was an hour's drive. My wife gets migraines and let me tell you, Angie only has like ten, maybe fifteen minutes to lay down somewhere dark. I mean, maybe Summer has a different kind of migraine, but it stood out as strange to me at the time."

"Maybe she didn't want to pull you away from the investigation. It was just getting good when she left. That news crew arrived just in time to see all the action."

Pansy tapped her pen against the paper. "Yeah, the news crew is kind of what I was thinking about. You know, when I showed her that first clip from the local news—Dario's mom had taped it for me—Summer looked worried and asked if it was just on the local channels. Then, after we found that country music dude and I was up in her apartment crying about being on the news again, she was really jumpy. And you know, Summer was never jumpy. She was always so... calm. I mean, I was busy wallowing in self-pity and wasn't paying attention to anything but myself, but I think that clip they showed on Headline News of her at Chivington upset her. She left the next day and I can't help but blame myself for not paying more attention."

I rolled my eyes. If there was even a small crack where Pansy could blame herself for something she'd crawl in and set up camp.

"You can't blame yourself." Randy was frowning. "We all missed it. Migraine or not, we had proof, on camera, of a real haunting. Things were being thrown, lights exploding, and she chose that moment to leave? I swear to you, nothing short of losing a limb would have convinced me to leave the building that night."

"Maybe she was afraid that someone else would see her on the news and know where she was?" Chandra said. Pansy added that possibility to her list.

"Do you think she moved here to hide from someone?' Randy asked.

"Someone who would track her down and break into her house looking for her?" Greg added. "An ex, maybe?"

"It's a possibility," Chandra said. Shawn reached over and squeezed her hand.

"So, even if there was something here that might help us find Summer, whoever broke in might have taken it with them?" Pansy asked.

"Also possible." Chandra agreed.

Everyone seemed to be thinking about the what-ifs of the situation. The kind of person who had torn this place apart wasn't someone we wanted to catch up with Summer. But without knowing where she was, there was no way to warn her.

Sarah had her arms wrapped around herself as she stared at the pile of paperwork. "Do you think we should file a missing person's report for Summer?" she finally asked.

"Is she really missing?" Randy asked with a shrug. "I'm sure that wherever she's at, she knows exactly where she is and how to get back."

"Unless her body is in a morgue somewhere and there's no missing person's report to compare it to," Lee muttered. I did not pass that gruesome tidbit on to Pansy.

"Okay, but what if she's not," Chandra argued. "How would we know? She told Sarah she was going to visit family but how do we know that she ever got there? What if she like, I don't know, drove into a ditch, or an arroyo? What if she's two hundred miles away with amnesia and doesn't remember who she is?"

"Now who watches too many movies?" Shawn asked her.

"She's right, though," Greg said. "We know she left of her own volition but it's not like her to not send at least one of us some kind of postcard or letter or even a call from a pay phone to let us know that she arrived safe. She poured her heart and soul into this store, there is no situation that I can imagine where she'd just up and leave it like this and never check-in. Out of an abundance of caution, I think we should file a report at the police station. Maybe even get her face out on the news."

"I don't know about that. If this was just a random break-in, we don't want to advertise that she lives here in case she really was hiding from someone," Chandra said.

"Okay, we'll decide if that's needed later. I'll stop at the station and talk to Billings on the way back home. Maybe we'll find something here that will tell us where to find her family, assuming that was really where she was heading when she left. Either way, we're not going to know until you slackers start searching. Hop to it. Chandra, head upstairs with Pansy and start going through her things looking for clues. I mean, clean as you go, but let's look for anything that might tell us where she came from. Shawn, Greg, Dario, and I are going to take care of the heavy lifting down here. Sarah, you can tell us if there's anything you want to keep as we go by, but I want you to start on that pile of paperwork and look for anything that might be important."

For hours they cleaned, they sorted, and eventually, they filled Greg's trailer up with broken furniture and mangled merchandise stands. As the final task for the day, Pansy helped Chandra load all of Summer's surviving clothes into the back of her and Shawn's white Saturn. "If nothing else, I can make sure she has clean clothes when she gets back," Chandra said as she slammed the trunk closed.

Pansy sat a cardboard box full of houseplants into the back seat of the Tracker. "How did you manage to be put in charge of keeping plants alive?" I asked. Pansy had never been able to keep a plant alive in her life. I had lost count of how many of those cute little cacti with the brightly colored round tops that she'd over-watered in our lifetime.

I had concerns.

"What do you mean? I just need to get them into some pots before they die."

"It's them dying after you've put them into pots that I'm worried about. Like, what is that thing? It's massive." I pointed to a large plant with slim leaves that stood nearly as tall as Pansy. The leaves were bent, running about a foot across the vinyl roof of the Tracker just to fit.

"I have no idea what it is, but you're going to live for Auntie Pansy, aren't you?"

"Thank god Harvey has Sarah," I muttered under my breath.

"Are we ready to pack it up, people? I need to get home for Sunday dinner or Angie will send out the National Guard," Randy said as he tossed two more garbage bags into the over-flowing dumpster.

"Nah, she'd send her brothers before she'd send the guard,"

Greg laughed. "But yeah, I'm beat. We've made a good dent, though."

"I can't thank you guys enough," Sarah said. "This has been such a huge help. I'll keep working on cleaning the rest of it up, you guys just keep thinking of ways to find Summer. I'd hate for her to come back to this kind of mess but I just keep thinking, what if something happened? What if she never comes back?" The anxiety in her voice made my non-existent heart clench.

"Randy will file that missing person report," Chandra said, pausing to hug Sarah goodbye. "Maybe, together, we can annoy the police into actually helping us look for her."

"It's worth a shot," Greg said.

Lee and I looked at one another. It was good to have a team.

5

"Hey, when you get done there, can you run this basket downstairs and add it to the paper pile? I've filled it with all of the paperwork Summer had up here." Sarah set the basket on the kitchen counter next to where Pansy was finishing up the dishes. The woven reed basket had been filled with invoices, notebooks, scraps of paper, and what looked like a whole bunch of receipts.

"Yep, there's just one more mug left," Pansy said, pausing to rinse off the mug before setting it in the dish drainer with the handful of other dishes that hadn't been smashed. "And done."

Pansy took the basket downstairs and Sarah began placing the undamaged canned goods back into the cabinets despite all of the doors having been torn from their hinges. She'd already removed the twisted and broken metal hinges and was going through the remaining kitchen piles looking for salvageable food. The cans had fared way better than the boxes of pasta and the easily smashable tins of tea that Summer had collected. There had to have been twenty different blends that Sarah and Pansy had found strewn around the kitchen, most of the delicate bags ripped open and spilling their contents across the floor.

The bright yellow metal cafe table Summer used in the kitchen had been righted and the chairs placed across from one another. That had survived. The vase she had kept wildflowers in had been shattered, as well as the salt and pepper shakers and the colorful patterned napkin holder. The PPS had made a lot of headway the day before, removing the larger items and clearing most of the floors, but Pansy and Sarah had been working for several hours when I heard Bagel yelling from the front door.

"Bagel's out front with a pizza," I informed Pansy.

"I thought you had to work this morning," Pansy said to him as she unlocked the front door. The bell that normally hung over the door had been located in yesterday's cleanup but had been too damaged to save. Seeing the door open without the added tinkle of the bell hit me as really sad, for some reason.

"It was slow so the boss let me leave. He heard about what happened here and figured I'd want to come help. Here, take this before I drop it."

Pansy grabbed the two-liter of soda balanced on top of the box, as well as the unopened roll of paper towels. "Good, we've already filled up another five or six of the really big garbage bags since eight so we'll gladly accept all offers of food and assistance." Pansy led the way before yelling up the stairs. "Sarah, Dario has arrived bearing gifts of food, drink, and extra muscle."

Bagel set the box on the cafe table and lifted the cardboard lid, revealing a pepperoni special from Canyon Lanes. I sniffed the air, not that it did any good. No sense of smell was one of the cons of being dead. *But wow, I missed pizza.*

"Lunch break!" Pansy declared, setting the two-liter on the mostly clean counter. "Well, every glass was smashed, but these mugs were hardy enough to survive." She pulled three freshly washed mugs from the drainage rack.

"There's no ice though, I didn't think about filling up the trays yesterday."

"We'll survive," Pansy said, pouring out soda for everyone while Sarah ripped paper towels from the roll.

"Going with the fancy plates I see," Sarah said.

"It was cheaper and more... multipurpose," Bagel told her with a shrug.

"Here, a Snoopy mug for you, and Darth Vader for you," Pansy said, setting the drinks on the table in front of them. She leaned against the counter and crammed half a slice into her mouth, grease dripping down her chin. Did I mention how much I miss pizza?

"Dude, I didn't realize how hungry I was. Thank you," Pansy finally said around the mouthful of pizza. They were working on their second and third slices when the phone rang.

"Is that for the shop?" Bagel asked.

"No, the shop has a different number, that's Summer's personal line," Sarah said, walking over to the mint green phone mounted to the kitchen wall. "Maybe someone is just calling the wrong number. Hello? Wild Harmony, Sarah speaking."

I could hear a deep voice on the other end and she turned to hand the phone to Pansy. "It's Randy, he's asking for you."

"Randy?" Pansy asked, taking the receiver. She held it tilted just enough for me to listen to.

"Hey, I was hoping you'd still be there. I had another call today from a potential client and wanted to know if you and Gerri would be available to meet with her either tomorrow or Wednesday? This lady owns a bar where her husband was killed in some kind of shootout or something. She thinks his spirit is now haunting the bar and I swear to God she's called me at least fifteen times in the last month."

"And you're just now calling her back?"

"No," the duh was implied but silent. "I called her back after the first time and told her we were booked up, but she isn't taking no for an answer. We had a cancellation so I figured I'd call her again and get her on the schedule."

"So, she wore you down?" Pansy laughed. "Yeah, we can do it. Sarah and I might get done here today, but definitely by tomorrow morning at the latest. And I start my new job at the bowling alley on Wednesday, so that's out. What time were you thinking?"

"Evening."

"That works for me," she turned to raise an eyebrow in my direction.

"Oh yeah, my schedule is totally clear." Like, what else would I be doing?

"She's good, too," Pansy said, shooting a look towards Sarah. Sarah was busy talking to Bagel so there were no worries that our uninformed friend was wondering who the 'she' in that sentence pertained to.

"Great, Greg and I will pick you up from your house tomorrow around six."

"Do I need to bring all of the, uhh…" she glanced at Sarah again while searching for a not suspicious word. She finally settled on "Supplies?"

"No. If we do a seance I want lights and cameras, the whole shebang. We're just going to go get a feel for the place, see if Gerri spots any ghosts, and take some pictures for Blake to work up a report."

"Okay, works for me. See you then." They said their good-byes and Pansy hung the receiver back onto the hook.

"Randy has a new PPS client and wanted to know if I was available to go interview her tomorrow," she told the others.

"Oh, well I know you said you'd be available but if you have PPS work to do, don't worry about all this. I mean, I appreciate your help, but don't feel like you've got to stay until the last dust bunny is cleaned or anything," Sarah said.

"It's fine. We're not leaving until after dinner, anyway."

"Don't you have to start work Wednesday?" Bagel asked.

"Yeah, but not until noon. Even if we get in late there's plenty of time to sleep in."

"Oh, where are you working?" Sarah asked, wadding up her paper towel and tossing it into the open garbage bag next to her.

"Canyon Lanes," Pansy said, gesturing to the pizza box. "Your's truly will be running the concession stand and taking pizza orders."

"Oh, I worked there when I was in high school. I'd go home smelling like pizza sauce and popcorn butter every night," she laughed.

"Great," Pansy said. "But it's just for the summer, I'm sure it'll be fine. I figured that I should make some spending money before we leave for Greeley this fall."

"When are you leaving? You're both going to UNC, right?"

"Yeah. Classes start the day after Labor Day so we're moving down the thirtieth," Bagel answered.

"What are you guys going to major in?" Sarah asked.

"English for me. Photography for him. I want to be a writer but figure I can fall back on teaching as a real job. Dario's going to pay money to be unemployed," she said, jerking her thumb in Bagel's direction.

"Technically, with the scholarships, they're paying *me* to be unemployed, thank you very much."

Sarah set her mug in the sink and went back to sorting

canned goods as they talked. "Just leave your mugs here, I'll get to them later. Are you staying in dorms or off campus?"

Bagel crushed the pizza box and added it to the garbage bag. "I know a guy who lives in an apartment complex off campus and he helped me get approved for a two bedroom so we can be roommates," he nodded towards Pansy.

"Roommates?" Sarah asked, a sly smile began to form as she looked between Pansy and Bagel.

"*Just* roommates," Pansy said with some force. Her face was turning red and she was suddenly very interested in tracing the faded image of a feather that decorated her mug with one finger. Most of the words above and below it had worn off and I wondered who's yard sale Summer had found it in. Finishing off her soda, Pansy turned her back on the two of them, placed her mug in the sink, and washed the pizza grease off of her hands.

"Sure, I get it. Just roommates. Uh-huh."

I started to cackle as both Pansy and Bagel turned beet red. They really were just roommates, but reality had little influence on public opinion. Sarah, love her heart, was a wonderful woman but she gossiped like it was a part-time job. Half the town of Perth would know about this before Jeopardy came on tonight.

6

"Do you think it's really haunted?"

I stared at Lee for a full three seconds before answering. "How would I know? That's why we're going down there, to see if it's haunted or not."

"Well, Bias rented Scarface from Blockbuster and I'd rather hang around and watch a classic than go all the way down to some honkytonk in New Mexico."

"Where's your spirit of adventure?"

"It petered out in about 1976, actually. Besides, if you've seen one dive bar, you've seen them all. Bad lighting, loud music, and sticky floors."

He painted a lovely picture. "Fine, but if I find a ghost, I'm not going to tell you about it."

"Of course you will, who else can you tell about it? Now, you'd better get going, it's almost six."

I waited for him to turn back towards the break room where Officer Bias had set up the TV they kept on a rolling cart before I stuck my tongue out. I flounced out, not that anyone could see my theatrics, and flew across town, arriving at our house just as Pansy was getting into the back of Randy's king cab.

"Is Lee with you?" she asked as I joined her in the backseat.

"No, he's only interested if the place is actually haunted."

Pansy rolled her eyes and let the guys know that I'd joined the party. With a rumble of the diesel engine, Randy put the truck into drive and we were off. The weather was clear, the sun was bright, and the truck's AC was so loud they all had to speak loudly to be heard. I floated back so that just my head was in the cab so that I could hear their conversation, but stay out of Pansy's line of sight. Seeing me passing in and out of the back window as I tried to match my speed to the vehicle freaked her out.

"How's the cleanup going?" Greg asked as they rode past Wild Harmony. "Do you guys need any more help?"

Pansy let out a big sigh. She'd worked hard so I didn't tell her to stop being dramatic. "We got it to about ninety percent today and just have some final mopping and cleaning up to do tomorrow. I stopped by the Firefly for breakfast and Chandra said that a good amount of the clothes she took home were either okay or easily mended. She's going to store them for Summer at her and Shawn's house. Anything personal that was broken but maybe repairable we put into a box for Summer to look through when she gets back."

"A really small box," I said.

"Her cookware and silverware survived, of course. There were some mugs that only had a little chip out of them, and a macrame wall hanging that will need some new yarn strung through it if she can find the right colors. A metal lamp survived, it just needs a new bulb and shade."

We crossed the south bridge onto Sepulveda and Randy set the cruise control at seventy. "I talked to Crane yesterday," Randy said. "They subpoenaed the bank once there was officially a missing person's report. Except for the checks for the utilities that Sarah's been paying, the account hasn't been used.

It looks like Summer withdrew a thousand dollars in cash on the day she left and that's it. Not a peep out of her on that front."

After their poor display of detecting at the shop, I was, quite frankly, shocked that they'd even looked into her bank records.

"A thousand dollars will only get you so far. I mean, what's gas now, like eighty-nine cents a gallon? That adds up pretty quick," Greg added.

Pansy shook her head. "I know. What I can't get over is how secretive she was and no one noticed. I feel like the world's worst friend. She knew absolutely everything about me, and I don't even know if her parents are still alive or where they live."

"Well, to be fair, unless they're sick, most adults don't generally talk about their parents as much as teenagers do," Greg said with a shrug. "I mean, I know and love Randy's parents because we've been best friends since elementary school. Melissa's parents on the other hand? They could drop off the face of the earth tomorrow and we'd honestly both be okay with that."

Melissa, Greg's wife, had a mother who was known by the entire town as THAT WOMAN so that made perfect sense to everyone in the vehicle.

"We've all been like one big family for years and it's weird not having her around. But... I don't know. I wasn't worried about her until this break-in," Randy said. He tapped his fingers against the steering wheel in time with the seventies rock playing low on the stereo but seemed to be thinking hard. His dark brows drew closer together. "You know, I asked her what she thought about us setting up a website a few months ago. She cracked some joke about not putting her face on the internet or everyone's screens would crack, but now that I'm thinking about it, I feel like she was a little more serious than I thought she was at the time. We were going through some old photos, trying to decide which ones we should digitize and now that I think about it, she made sure that she wasn't in any of them."

"You know what it reminds me of? We watched an after-school special once about this Mom who had a son in elementary school and she didn't want anyone to take any photos of him. It turns out, it was because she'd kidnapped him and she didn't want his real parents to find out where he was."

"Are you suggesting that Summer kidnapped herself?" I asked.

"No, dummy. I'm saying I'm leaning more and more to the theory that she's running from someone."

"Dummy?" Randy asked, super confused because Pansy usually whispered to me instead of including her responses in the general conversation.

"Gerri was being a smart aleck. I was hoping that we'd find some kind of clue in all of her stuff while we were cleaning, but she didn't have any of the kinds of mementos that I keep. No old school awards, no graduation tassel, no diplomas, no photo albums."

"Maybe she took her photo albums with her? I mean, if I was leaving, that's a top priority to go with me," I suggested.

"Gerri said she may have taken photo albums with her."

"I don't know," Randy said, pausing as he passed a slow-moving old lady in a thirty-year-old pickup truck. "I've been in her apartment several times and I don't ever remember seeing photos. Not on the wall, no collages. If she kept them in albums, she must have kept them up in a closet somewhere, they weren't out where anyone could have casually flipped through them."

"Which doesn't mean they weren't there, it just means she didn't want you making fun of her with a bad eighties perm and giant glasses," Greg told him.

"True."

The trio were silent for a moment, the only sounds the rush of air from the AC, the tires on the pavement, and Robert Plant wailing about the evils of women on the radio.

"So, we have no clues, and no ideas of where to start looking for Summer," Pansy said, breaking the silence. "Next case. So how long has this chick's husband been dead?"

"Ah, questions that I can answer," Randy said with a soft chuckle. "He was shot, in the bar, by another guy about three months ago. Apparently, they shot each other, and they both died. The husband of the bar owner bled out within a few minutes of being shot, the other guy lingered for a few days in the hospital before giving up the ghost. Uh, sorry if that's, like, offensive, or something, Gerri," he said, glancing in the rearview mirror toward the empty backseat.

I shrugged. Was I now the PC police for the undead?

"Don't sweat it," Pansy told him. "So, there's a chance that one or both of them could be haunting the bar?"

"It's possible. Does the amount of violence involved in the death increase the odds of a ghost hanging around? We've always thought so, but you two have probably met more ghosts than we have."

Pansy considered the question. I could see the gerbil wheel in her brain spinning. "I don't know. Lee died in his sleep and he's still here. But Gerri's death was definitely violent, and Christopher had probably been drowned by his mother."

"Don't forget Thomas," I interjected.

"Yeah, and Thomas was murdered by his stepfather. In fact, that's another instance of two people trying to kill one another and both of them succeeding. So, I really think Christine is right and it's the individual guilt that keeps them here."

"Speaking of Thomas, did Gerri ever actually find him? I'd still like to interview him."

"Not yet. Lee says he only wanders into town once or twice a year when he gets really bored and Lee was never interested enough to follow him to see where he hangs out the rest of the time." We'd considered calling him forward in a seance but had decided that our first introduction should probably not be because we'd scared the bejeebus out of him. We'd wait for him to show up.

"Interesting, but, back to the case at hand. According to the half a million messages this woman has left on my answering machine begging us to come and investigate, she thinks her husband is haunting the bar and she says that she desperately needs to contact his spirit."

"Well, hopefully, his ghost really is haunting the bar and we can make that happen," she responded. Had Pansy told the 'rents where she was going tonight? Sure, she was helping out Randy and Greg with a preliminary investigation. Had she told them that she may eventually have to come back and conduct a seance to speak to the dead? Absolutely not. As far as Mom and Dad knew, Pansy was a perfectly well-adjusted teen who just so happened to be able to speak and see the ghost of her dead twin. No biggie. They had no idea that Christine, who had dropped by our house unexpectedly a few weeks ago, was one of the most famous paranormal mediums in the country. Because why would they know something like that?

In the last few weeks since discovering Pansy's newest skill, we'd abandoned our list of things that I could do and began testing out what *Pansy* could do. We knew she could open up a rift to the other side, but we'd tried twice to call Christopher back with no success. We'd performed these seances at Randy's house in one of his empty fields, which made Lee and my job of searching for the portal a lot easier when there was nothing but waist-high grass in all directions. Pansy had tried the second time with Christine in attendance before she'd left us to head to an investigation of her own up north, but neither of them had been able to call him through the portal. Pansy, insecure as always, had started to worry that her ability to call forth a spirit was a one-off fluke, so Lee had volunteered as a ghost guinea pig.

I'd been overly worried about this, but he had faith in Pansy's ability, more faith than Pansy had had, and I kept my concerns that she would accidentally poof him to myself. But she'd done it, and just like before, the candles had gutted as my sister said his full name, and the portal had opened about fifty yards away, a faint shimmer in the grass that Pansy couldn't see but had instantly caught mine and Lee's attention. Lee had begun to glow and was pulled like taffy. He'd later admitted it was a scary experience to have no control over your limbs and had wondered at the sheer power of Dr. Welling who had been able to fight against the restraint. Lee had been helpless. Pansy made him tell us his favorite color, midnight blue, and had then gone through the process of releasing him. Lee had been safe, the portal had closed, and she had the basics down. Christine had promised to stop by on her way back home in July and drop off some books for Pansy to read

"Maybe we'll get lucky and he'll be right there hanging out in the bar and I can just ask him whatever it is she wants to know," I said. That would be way easier than setting up a whole seance. Lighting all of those candles took forever.

"If we could only get that lucky," she muttered.

Greg started singing along to the radio and the three started talking about mundane things, so I floated up high above the road, taking in the rolling hills that were still green with grasses and scrub pine, broken up occasionally by a larger lump of rock here and there. Pieces of the former mountain range that hadn't received the memo about how erosion worked and refused to give up their place. The soil got sandier the farther south we went, and soon we'd transitioned from high plain to desert. I floated along, doing loop de loops and diving for the ground as we went, occasionally noticing the man-made entrances of mine shafts dotting the area. My first thought was to wonder how many dead bodies were at the bottom of these shafts. My second thought was that maybe this life of crime-solving was beginning to warp my perspective. I flew back into the air, careful to keep Randy's truck in view, and continued to do my loop-de-loops. There wasn't anything we could do about my warped psyche at this point.

7

We passed through a few small towns and after about forty-five minutes the sun was lower in the sky and I finally spotted a hand-painted sign at the side of the road that said Welcome to Berry. I would have flown down to check it out yesterday if I'd thought I'd be able to navigate here by myself, but Randy had taken several turns along the way and I probably should have taken note of the road numbers. I made a mental note to pay more attention on the way back.

"Go to the end and turn left onto Calle Chaparral, and it's on the right," Greg said, reading from the instructions Randy had taken down when he'd talked to the owner. I floated up out of the truck to take it all in. The town of Berry, New Mexico, was even smaller than Perth. From this angle, I could see that it was set up in a grid, if you can count being two blocks wide and four blocks long a grid. There wasn't a single street light, and the brick and adobe buildings were so close to the main street that there wasn't any room for cars to park. I wondered if Berry had started as, like, a mining town or something like that, but whatever had originally brought people here was long gone. A good quarter of the buildings were boarded up. After we checked out this bar, I decided I'd look through all of the other buildings for ghosts. A town this size should take me about twenty minutes, tops.

After crossing the entire four blocks of Main Street, Randy turned left down a side street and into a gravel lot on the undeveloped side of what, according to the wooden post that marked the road corners, was called Calle Chaparral. The weed-infested gravel parking lot contained about twenty vehicles, mostly trucks, of varying age and repair, which I thought was a lot for a Tuesday night, but maybe there just wasn't a whole lot else to do here.

"Do you think they can't spell or that someone rearranged the letters?" Pansy asked me as she climbed down out of the truck. She nodded toward the dimly lit marquee set by the roadside proclaiming this desert oasis to be The Wild Dawg, and 'Wendsday' to be 50 cent beer nite. One of the metal legs had been replaced with a stack of cinder blocks making the whole sign lean drunkenly to one side.

I shrugged, eager to see what the inside looked like. The building was an unpainted cinder block rectangle with no windows, no landscaping, and a heavy metal door that had been painted black at one time. I could hear the bass thumping from the parking lot, which didn't bode well for a meaningful conversation with the owner. Both Randy and Greg put one hand on their lower back and leaned backward as soon as they were out of the truck, groaning like old men. I mean, they were both in their forties, so I guess they were old and stuff, but good grief.

I circled the building once, but there was nothing unusual about the place. I don't know what I thought I would find but I wanted to be thorough. On the back side of the building sat a dumpster—partially hidden by some broken down fencing, a second steel door with a big white Cadillac parked in front of it, and a gas meter. Not a single window, but also no ghosts. Yet.

I shook my head at Pansy as I came back around to where the guys were still doing some kind of awkward calisthenics routine. "It looks...lovely," Pansy said, giving the front of the building a once over. Her nose was scrunched up and while I agreed, we maybe needed to work on her face not showing every single thing she was thinking.

Greg chuckled as he reached back into the truck to grab his wallet out of the cup holder. "Yeah, we make fun of how classy the Buffalo Chip is, but this place..." he shook his head.

Randy led the way across the gravel lot and as he pulled the front door open, we were assaulted by a bazillion decibels of live music. I realized two things at that moment. One, I was glad that I didn't need to worry about needing to hide my own facial expressions, and two, I didn't need to worry about losing my hearing. Holy earplugs, Batman. Judging from the Cowboys and Cowgirls signs on the doors, the restrooms were in one corner next to a U-shaped bar. The wooden bar had metal panels along the side that made me think of a watering trough for cattle. The floor was unfinished concrete, patched in places and stained all over, while the walls were unpainted cinder block decorated with neon signs advertising various beers. *High class, indeed.*

On the other side of the room, a crowded stage held four homeless looking cowboys playing—loudly—what must pass for music in some circles. The main part of the room was full of tables, most of them occupied, and there seemed to be a line at the bar. The ceiling was one of those drop ceiling affairs with the little foam squares that are supposed to absorb sound, but maybe the cigarette smoke had damaged that part because it certainly wasn't working. Randy walked to the bar and began shouting something to the bartender who waved him around to a door on the other side. Randy turned, motioning for Greg and Pansy to follow the bartender. The door led to a space that seemed to be part storage closet, part office space and under the sickly yellow glow of a Spuds McKenzie lamp sat a harried looking woman holding a cigarette in one hand and a stack of receipts in the other. Would setting all of your paperwork on fire with a cigarette be the adult equivalent of the dog eating your homework?

The bartender closed the door behind them and the decibel level dropped by half. Sweet relief.

"You must be the ghost guys," the blonde said, eyeing each of them up and down like she was examining some new fungus that had grown in her beer cooler. She took another drag from her cigarette and blew the smoke out one side of her mouth. The end of the cigarette was stained red from her lipstick, and from the looks of the ash tray in front of her, it wasn't going to be the last one for the night. Her brown leathery skin looked like she'd been in a tanning bed since the early seventies and had refused to leave except to come to work. It was impossible to tell her age or if she was naturally dark-skinned or not. The bleach blonde of her updo looked crispy like she went through a can of Aqua Net each week.

"Is that the kid?"

"Uh, yeah. This is Pansy Bellafini. I'm Randy. I'm the one you spoke to on the phone, and this is my partner, Greg Abernathy. We've been running the Perth Paranormal Society since 1986."

"Yeah, yeah. Fiona Dale. Nice to meet you and all that. So how does this work? I saw on the news that she sees ghosts. Has she seen Gene yet?"

"No, uh," Randy stuttered, clearly caught off guard. "No, she doesn't actually see ghosts. She performs a seance to speak to those spirits that are stuck here on this side with us. But that only works if the spirit of the person we're trying to communicate with is still here on this plane and hasn't moved on like they should."

"Okay, but like I said on the phone, I need to ask my husband some questions about the business, so is he here or not?"

"See if she has a picture of him," I said.

"Mrs. Dale, do you have a picture of your late husband? That way when we schedule your seance I can be sure that I'm talking to the right person. Or can you at least describe him?"

"Aren't you supposed to be the psychic? What do I look like, some kind of sucker? You need to tell ME what he looks like."

Noticing a photo frame on her desk, I floated around to get a better look. The picture in the frame was clearly a wedding photo from some time back in the sixties, with both the bride and groom wearing bell bottoms and flower crowns. They looked young and in love. Slid into the edge of the frame sat a Polaroid of what I assumed was a more recent version of Gene holding a bottle of liquor in each meaty fist. His dark shaggy hair looked like it had last been cut with a weed eater, and his unbuttoned shirt revealed a gold chain glistening in a nest of graying chest hair. A heavy gold watch decorated one wrist, there was at least one ring on each finger .Although he was smiling in the photo, I could make out a few missing teeth. His nose had a decided tilt to one side. This would be a hard dude to miss.

"There is not a single floating being out there and absolutely no one that looks like this," I told Pansy. If there was a ghost in town this place may provide the most entertainment, but they weren't here now.

"Well, first, I'm a medium, not a psychic. If I was psychic, I'd be playing the lottery and not working at the bowling alley. Second, I'm not, uh, sensing any ghosts here now. But ghosts aren't just stuck in the place where they die, they can go anywhere they want. So, if he is on this side, maybe he hangs out somewhere else. Maybe at home?"

"Home?" Mrs. Dale asked. "He hardly ever stayed there when he was alive, I can't imagine why he'd start now."

"Well, then he's probably moved on and I won't be able to talk to him."

"Okay, but according to the messages you left on my machine," was I imagining that Randy emphasized the plural there? "You said that the bar was where you were experiencing the haunting? So, is it here, where he died, or at your home?" Randy asked.

"Um, here, at the bar. There's some really warm spots and the bartenders think it's his ghost."

"I'm sorry, warm spots? Not cold spots?" Randy asked, confused.

"Yeah, well, maybe they said cold spots. I wasn't really listening."

"And are these spots of varying temperature the only paranormal events you're experiencing here, Miss Dale?"

"Paranormal events? Look, I just need to contact my husband."

"Mrs. Dale, it sounds to me like you're not experiencing any paranormal events."

She eyed Randy like she thought he'd lost his mind for even asking. "My daddy built this bar in 1964 and the only people that have ever died here are my husband and his former business partner. Who else would be haunting it?"

"Again, as Miss Bellafini just told you, ghosts can go wherever they want anytime they want," Randy said. He eyeballed her for a second, giving her what I called a *you'd better not be lying,* look. "I understand you think he wouldn't be at home, but if it's close by we could at least check it out, since we're already here, see if Pansy can sense his spirit there."

She eyeballed him right back as she sucked the cigarette down to the filter and stubbed it out in the overflowing ashtray. "My house is out of the question. I have a full bar tonight and don't trust these thieving bartenders as far as I can throw them. Besides, Gene spent more time at his girlfriend's than at home. Trust me, he won't be there."

"Fine. I'm going to take some photos of the bar for now, we'll get a layout and then do some research on the building. We'll schedule you for a full investigation and a seance." He pulled out his pocket calendar and flipped to August. "We had a cancellation for August 12th, if that will work for you?"

"August? Why can't you just do it right now? Like you said, you're already here."

I'm ashamed to admit that I watched in fascination as she pulled an entire pack of cigarettes out of her bra. I didn't know that was a thing people did in real life, which distracted me from the point. Was this woman on crack? She thought they could do a whole investigation right now while she had a band and what had to be half the town of Berry soaking up her AC while simultaneously losing their hearing?

Greg laughed, planting one giant hand on the edge of her desk before leaning forward. "That is absolutely out of the question."

Fiona sniffed and patted at her beehive, shifting the whole thing over by a good half inch. *Was she wearing a wig? I'd never met anyone in my life who wore a wig.* "I don't see why not. You're here, aren't you? Just do it now."

"Mrs. Dale, I don't know if you heard about the case we had south of Perth where Pansy here found the body of young Christopher Fairchild, but we got a lot of press out of that. As I explained over the phone, at least twice, right now we're booked out until next February. An investigation for paranormal activity is extremely labor intensive and would require more than just the three of us," Randy explained.

Four of us, thank you.

"We'd need to set up several video cameras which require a lot of cabling and monitors, we'd need people with audio recording devices to ask the ghost, uh, your husband questions just to see if he will respond. We take photos using both regular and infrared film. The whole building will need to be quiet and have all of the lights turned off, which doesn't seem to be possible right now, not that we have any of that equipment with us. As I told you on the phone, this is just a preliminary research journey."

"Okay, but how about we skip all of that and this one here just does the seance. You don't need a bunch of fancy equipment for that, do you?"

Pansy looked like a deer in the headlights.

"No," Greg said. "Again, we'd need quiet, dark, and a full crew."

Pansy snapped out of it. "Besides, we'd first need to confirm that the entity, um, your husband, Gene, is really here on this plane. And we'll want to film and make sound recordings of the entire event, so yes, we'll need all of the fancy equipment, as you called it." Pansy said. She was taking a *tone*, and I was proud of her for standing up for herself and not letting this woman tell her what she was going to do. Big Sis wasn't going to bend over backward to please someone. *Finally.*

With a sigh, Fiona consulted the calendar blotter on her desk, being overly dramatic about flipping June and July over to get to August and penciling it in. Ghost people, she wrote in green glitter pen. "Fine, I guess I'll have to take that, won't I?"

Randy scribbled on his calendar before placing it back into the breast pocket of his polo shirt and giving it a pat. The motion made me think of Lee. He was going to love coming down here and watching this woman with me. And she was for sure going on my watch list because there was something off with her.

Greg pushed his way back through the bar like a battering ram and Pansy followed in his wake. The crowd had increased while we'd been in Fiona's office and a different set of homeless cowboys had taken the stage. The music had not improved. Randy pulled a disposable camera out of one of the pockets of his cargo pants and stopped to take some pictures as the rest of us hurried outside to the peace and quiet of the night.

"I'm staying," I told Pansy, as soon as we were outside.

"Dear Lord, why?" Pansy asked, pulling her shirt out to sniff at the fabric before making a face. "I'm never going to get the cigarette smell out of my clothes and I just bought this freaking shirt."

"I should have worn my coveralls," Greg lamented, sniffing at his own shirt.

"I'm going to follow her home and see if the husband is hanging out there." For some reason we all just had this idea in our head that people haunted the buildings they died in but like, look at me. I was forty-five minutes from home. In fact, I was usually only home if Pansy was home.

"Gerri said she's staying," Pansy said as Randy joined them in the parking lot. Taking photos didn't take long when the whole place was one open room. "She's going to follow this wackadoodle home and see if the husband is there or not."

"Is she good to get back home? Places like this don't close until three in the morning. It'll be dark and I don't want her wandering around lost in the desert."

You could tell Randy had three kids of his own.

"I'll be fine. I'll camp out here, check out the town,

and come back home in the morning." I mean, I mostly remembered how we got here. I'd figure it out.

Pansy relayed my message and by the way Randy's lips
pursed I could tell he didn't like that idea.

Greg laughed and smacked him on the arm. "Come on,
don't look like that. She's a grown-up ghost now. She was a
smart girl when she was alive and it's not like she's going to get
ghost-napped or something. I have faith in you, Gerri."

No pressure. Don't get lost in a strange town in the dark.
Surely, I wasn't that incompetent.

8

I floated in the parking lot, watching as the three loaded into Randy's truck and pulled away in a cloud of dust. As their tail lights receded into the gathering darkness, I turned to float back inside and legit screamed out loud when a man I hadn't noticed before lit up his cigarette. The flame of his lighter drew my attention to where he stood in the shadow of the building, leaning against the tailgate of a dark truck. There was something familiar about it but then I realized it was because it looked like Dad's—a Silverado, with the two-toned paint and the squared-off wheel wells. I caught a brief glimpse of his face before he flicked the lighter closed, some sandy-haired scruffy looking dude. He seemed like he was waiting for someone and I figured it could be any of the number of half-dressed women inside the bar. Floozies, my mother would call them. Or maybe he'd just needed to escape the noise.

I floated back into the office and quickly regretted my decision. The music was still some insufferable country/rock mix with too much drumming and a guitar so loud that it completely overshadowed the lead singer's warbling voice. I should have insisted that Lee come along to keep me company, but honestly, I hadn't intended on staying. Fiona looked firmly ensconced at her desk. She was working her way through a whole stack of receipts on an adding machine, her long, red fingernails tapping the keys and the printer going off like gunfire as it spit out the tape. She'd pause long enough to scribble numbers into a ledger, paperclip the calculations to the stack of receipts, and start over. Judging from the piles of paper around her, she was going to be there for a while, so I decided to make a run through some of the buildings on Main Street. Maybe Gene haunted the local ice cream parlor or something.

"Don't leave without me," I told Fiona as I escaped into the night. The two lone security lights were on, although it wasn't completely dark yet. I decided to hurry before the sun completely disappeared. There was a whole lot of nothing outside the edges of town and I knew from my nocturnal wanderings that that meant it would get dark fast. Besides the lights at the bar, there was a light in the parking lot of the small general store and the weaker lighting of porch lights with the occasional dusk-to-dawn lights scattered about. Five feet outside of town was going to be like, dark-dark.

I started with the first business from the West. North West One, I thought to myself, deciding to think of this in quadrants to track my progress. First up was a clothing store specializing in farm chic, as far as I could tell. A lamp in the front window and one in the back hallway gave me enough illumination to determine that there was no one floating around. No ghosts here. The neighboring hardware store was also a bust.

To ensure she didn't leave without me, I floated back to the bar after every other store. On my first trip back, I noticed that the Marlboro Man had made it out of the parking lot and was at the bar showing something to the bartender. Something small. A photo, maybe? A postcard? Whatever it was, the bartender shook his head, and the Marlboro Man already had it back in his pocket by the time I'd made it over there. Maybe he had a blind date who'd stood him up.

Fiona was still clacking away on her adding machine, so I left to hit the next two businesses. Even after I'd investigated the beauty shop, the pawn shop, an accountant, and a butcher, the stack of receipts had only grown. I was turning to head back out to check on the general store when I heard her sigh. Like, a long, drawn-out death rattle. She started to cough halfway through and for a second there I was concerned that she was about to join her husband in the afterlife. After thumping her chest with her fist a few times and taking a drink from her nearby coffee cup, she moved the tassel of the ledger into the crack of the open page and shut the whole thing. Storing the ledger in one of the desk drawers, she reached into her purse and pulled out the biggest wad of keys and key chains I'd ever seen. It looked like there was a decorative keychain for each and every key, and there had to be at least fifteen keys. After shaking them for a second or two, she finally located a tiny one and used it to lock the desk drawer. Standing, she arched her back and made groaning noises that I wasn't quite comfortable witnessing, before shuffling around the corner of the desk and across the room. Reaching up under her hair, confirming for me that it was a wig, she gave her forehead a good scratch before opening the door that led behind the bar and leaned out to tell Tony— the bartender, I presumed—that she was calling it a night.

While she'd been hidden behind her desk, I hadn't noticed that she was wearing fuzzy pink house slippers and a red leather mini-skirt. She picked up her purse and a pair of red stilettos that she'd probably begun her day in, and turned off the desk lamp, giving Spuds a pat on the nose as she did so. Leaving out the back door, she only had to shuffle a few steps across the gravel before she was to the Cadillac. I guess being the owner had its privileges. With a practiced flick of the wrist, she tossed her oversized black leather bag into the passenger seat and slid behind the wheel. Her seat was pulled so close to the steering wheel that I hoped her car didn't come with those new airbag things. She was going to get smashed in the face if they ever deployed.

It wasn't even ten o'clock yet, so I was excited that I didn't have to wait until the wee hours of the morning to follow her home. And as a bonus, following Fiona's beast of a vehicle was a piece of cake. She went straight on Calle Chaparral, across Main Street, and followed it to the other side of town where it meandered out to a trailer park whose landscaped lighting proclaimed it to be called Golden Acres. There was another road that turned off before the trailer park, Dale Lane, which led to individual houses.

For the first quarter mile, the houses were all scrunched up together, but they eventually got further and further apart. The end of the dead-end road was revealed with brick columns flanking a concrete driveway that circled in front of a three-story brick house with an attached garage. Her headlights washed over the scene, revealing that, at one point this had been a really nice house. For some reason, there was a refrigerator next to the driveway beside a big pile of metal parts. Most were so rusted that I couldn't even begin to guess what they'd originally been attached to. The space between the front porch and the driveway as it made its loop, held the remains of what looked like a landscaping project that was never finished. Bags and bags of decorative gravel and plastic pots full of dirt and dead plants surrounded the front porch. A shovel and rake were still lying in the sandy soil, the plastic sale tags still zip-tied to the handles. The paint on the shutters was peeling and there was a general air of neglect about the place.

The garage door trundled open and I assumed Fiona was going to pull inside, but quickly realized that was impossible.

The garage was stacked with boxes and totes, tools, and all sorts of things that apparently didn't belong in the house but needed to be stored. She and the dead guy didn't have any kids, did they? Why on earth did they need this much stuff? Fiona parked her Caddy in the driveway and got out, slinging her leather purse over one shoulder. She shuffled sideways through the boxes to a table where a forty-pound bag of cat food sat next to several food bowls. A flap I hadn't noticed in the door leading into the house exploded with the entrance of at least five cats who came to beg at her feet. She sat her stilettos on the bench before reaching for the scoop, filling four large bowls. As she sat them on the floor, four more cats came trickling out the cat door. Apparently satisfied that everyone was eating, she grabbed her shoes and made her way up a short set of wooden steps, hitting the button that closed the garage door before entering the house. None of the cats looked up from their noshing as I floated over them.

My first thought as I entered the house was that someone needed to call Dr. Phil about this lunacy. Messy houses were one thing, but nothing in this house made sense. The light over the kitchen stove was on and Fiona didn't turn on any additional lights as she made a beeline towards the stairs. Even in that soft lighting, I could see that every flat surface in the kitchen held boxed foods and cans stacked at least two feet tall. Something told me she wasn't saving up items for a local food drive.

I floated through to the adjoining dining room where an eight-person table was set with a hunter-green Christmas tablecloth and gold jacquard table runner. Gold chargers displayed a set of Christmas Pfaltzgraff decorated with holly leaves and berries. Fancy cut-glass drink ware, the kind Mom kept in a cabinet and never let us use, sat next to each place setting. Two five-arm candelabras decorated with fake pine limbs and holly sat on either end of a Christmas-themed centerpiece that came complete with pine cones. Every inch of the table and its festive table settings were covered in a thick layer of dust and cat hair. It was June, so she either just really loved Christmas, or she'd decorated in 1991 and never bothered to put any of it back up. Feeling a furball of my own coming up, I looked around the room, noting every space between the table and the wall was stacked with Rubbermaid totes and cardboard boxes. Had they been preparing to move? Most of the boxes were printed with the letters QVC or HSN and as I floated closer, I could see the original shipping tape was undisturbed. She bought things through cable shopping networks and never opened them?

I was so distracted by the house that I'd forgotten I was here to search for a ghost, but quickly realized that no ghost would hang out here. No wonder Fiona hadn't wanted Pansy and the others to come to the house. I hadn't been the tidiest of teenagers, Pansy was the neat freak, but even I wouldn't have spent more time here than necessary. I floated into the living room, where boxes and totes also lined the walls, and the couches and chairs were all covered in layer after layer of shopping bags that looked like they were still full of clothes. The layer of dust and cat hair was thicker towards the bottom layers and I was at a total loss as to what was happening. Who bought clothes and didn't wear them?

While Fiona was in the shower upstairs, I flipped on lights in all of the overcrowded rooms of her house, including the attic after I realized she had one, but there was not a single ghost hanging out there. I mean, unless they just really liked cats and *stuff*, I couldn't blame them a bit.

"Gene Dale? Are you here?" I yelled, just in case. Silence.

I floated outside and tried again, maybe there was a shed or an underground bunker he stayed in to avoid being inside the house. I didn't see anything. The French doors off the dining room opened onto a wooden deck with stairs leading down to a gently sloping lawn area. Although *lawn* was generous as there was no grass. There was nothing beyond the boundary of the back fence. Just a drop into a ravine and then miles of empty land and darkness. The only sounds were the singing crickets and a neighbor's dog baying at the waning sliver of the moon. And... wait. There was something else. There was rustling coming from under the back deck. The space was hidden behind rotting pieces of wooden lattice and devoid of any light.

"Uh, hello? Are there any ghosts here?" I asked, feeling like a total dweeb. A weird, squeaky, chittering sound replied and I moved back a few feet. It could be rats, mice, opossums, or bats, none of which I wanted to play with this evening.

Satisfied that no ghosts were haunting the Dale home, I went back to town and finished checking out all of the businesses, which ended up being a waste of my time. It wasn't quite midnight and I'd looked through every public building. I'd found butkus. Floating down the road until I hit 72, I paused for a moment to think about which way would be east. With no street lights, traffic, or civilization of any kind for the most part, I navigated by the light of the waning moon and the stars, which were brilliant this far from any cities. As I was coming up Sepulveda, I decided to go ahead and make my daily check-in on Mrs. Garcia before updating Lee. Pansy wouldn't be awake yet and Lee would only be mildly interested, anyway.

It was the middle of the night and Mrs. Garcia was in her La-Z-Boy, snoring away with her teeth in a jar on the TV tray next to her.

Yep, no change there.

From here, I could fly home with my eyes closed.

9

I entered the Perth Police Station and found Lee floating behind the two officers on duty as they watched Christie Swanson kicking vampire butt on the small TV kept in the break room. They had a stack of Blockbuster cases on the counter so I figured it must have been a really slow night.

"What's up kiddo?" Lee asked when he saw me. "How'd your trip go yesterday evening?"

"Actually, I am way past curfew and just now getting home."

"You've been in Berry all this time?" His entire posture changed when he thought there was a chance that I had a good story. "Why? What happened?"

I filled him in on my adventures exploring the most boring little town in New Mexico and tried to convey just how deeply weird Fiona Dale was. I'm not sure I was successful, but I had every intention of dragging Lee back down there with me later in the week. He could judge her level of weirdness for himself.

"So, they're going to go ahead and book the investigation?" he asked as I completed my tale.

"Yeah, that guy in Orton canceled once he realized it was his dog leaving the refrigerator door open, so there was an opening."

I stayed to finish watching Buffy and even made it through most of Top Gun before I began feeling restless. There were so many questions running through my head and sitting here watching movies wasn't going to solve any of them. I needed action. I needed movement. I needed Pansy to be awake so I could tell her about Fiona's house.

I checked the break room clock. "I'm going to head home. Pansy starts her new job at the bowling alley today and I need to fill her in before she leaves to finish the cleanup at Summer's this morning." The bowling alley didn't even open until eleven, and she was scheduled to start work at noon. If she got up at a reasonable time she'd have plenty of time to help Sarah with the finishing touches.

"Well, I think we're watching When Harry Met Sally, next. So, I'll be here if you need me."

"Seriously?"

"What? It's a classic!"

"Whatever. Look, I'll check in with you later, let me know if anything exciting happens."

With that, I took off for my own house.

I entered through the kitchen and listened to see if anyone was up yet. The clock on the stove read a little after five and I could hear the shower running upstairs. That would be Dad, showering before work. I waited in the kitchen for him to come down, dressed in his go-to work uniform of dark blue jeans, work boots, and a tie with a short-sleeved dress shirt - white with thin blue stripes. The automatic coffee pot was ready by the time he came down and he poured his cup of bean juice, no milk no sugar, into a World's Best Dad mug before taking a sip. It must have been good because he did a little butt waggle, which was the same thing I did, or at least, used to do, whenever I ate or drank something that made me happy. He reached into the fridge for the sandwiches that Mom had made for him before bed, and then he paused, one ear cocked toward the stairs to listen for footsteps. Sneaking to the snack cabinet he pulled out a packet of Ding Dongs and I smiled as he slipped them into his lunch box. Mom must have put him on a diet again.

I watched as he drank the rest of his mug of coffee, emptied the pot into his green metal Thermos, and then set the machine up to come back on in an hour and a half for Mom. It all seemed normal, so very routine, and it made me happy to see him doing something so ordinary. It meant they were moving on with their lives. After my death, when Mom was so depressed and Dad had to cry alone in his truck, their grief had been a living thing. It grew and grew, sucking up all of the oxygen in the house. And now that Pansy was preparing to go to college? I was worried about what they were going to do on their own. Sure, Robbie and Pansy would come home every few weekends and on holidays, but I was afraid that the silence, not having someone's music blaring or teenage girls giggling and screaming on the weekends, would invite that grief back into the house. It made me want to hug him as he walked out to the garage, but he wouldn't be able to feel it.

I went outside and hovered in the power line to keep myself charged until the sun was fully up and it was time to wake my twin. Pansy was still buried under her comforter with one arm thrown up over her head. I pulled the cord on the window blinds, dumping a load of super cheerful sunshine right into her sleeping face.

"Good morning! It's time to get up."

"Oh my god," she said, raising one palm in my direction. "Talk to the hand 'cause the face ain't listening. Why can't you just let me sleep in for once?"

"Because I need to tell you about the whole lot of absolutely nothing that I found last night and you need to go help Sarah before work"

"Okay. Just close it, okay? It's too early for sunshine."

I reached over to tug at the string, but my session in the power lines must have supercharged me and I pulled the entire blind down. It slammed down on top of her desk, knocking over her lamp and desk phone, which narrowly avoided hitting Summer's giant plant that Pansy had sat next to her desk. Pansy sat up straight, her hair plastered to her head on one side and frizzy on the other, staring at the mess. The phone started to beep to announce that it was off the hook.

"Oops."

"Well, I'm awake now. Hang up the phone, at least. I'll get the rest later. Tell me about last night."

It was a struggle, but I finally pulled the phone receiver back onto the hook to shut it up. Then I launched into a much more detailed version of the story than I'd given Lee, including the state of the house and Fiona's weird obsession with buying things and then never using them.

"I read something in one of Mom's Good Housekeeping magazines about that kind of thing. They're called Hoarders. It's like people who just collect things with no rhyme or reason behind it."

"It seems like a huge waste of money to me."

"Well, she owns the bar. They had no kids, she's got to spend her money on something, I guess. Were there any ghosts at all in that town?"

"Nothing. I mean, I only checked the businesses, not the houses, but I went up and down the streets yelling if anyone could hear me and nothing came out."

"Did you learn nothing after Chivington? What if there was some other evil thing lurking out there."

"Dr. Welling was never a threat to me, he was strictly after the living."

"I remember him being a distinct threat to you when I had to block you with my whole body to not be dragged into some, I don't know, interdimensional portal thing, right along with him."

"Okay, but that was a really strange instance and there was no chance it was going to be duplicated on the absolutely quiet streets of Berry. I mean, Perth shuts down at nine, but I swear, nothing but the bar is open there after six."

"Whatever, but you didn't run into anything scary?"

"Other than some kind of varmint that scared the crap out of me? No."

"Well, Mrs. Dale is on the schedule now, and we've got that church investigation on Saturday. The First Lutheran in Wilcox. Is Lee going?"

"I don't think so. I told him about their candles moving and stuff but he thinks it's a mouse or something. He said no self-respecting ghost would hang out in a church all the time when there's a perfectly good police station and gas station right here." The Loaf N Jug was Lee's second favorite place to hang out because it was open twenty-four-seven and only the most interesting people came in after midnight. I had to agree with him, hanging out in a quiet church all the time would make eternity really boring.

"I might as well shower and head over to Wild Harmony. We needed more garbage bags so I'll stop at Foodarama first and get some, and some more mopping stuff."

We were almost out the front door when we encountered our first problem of the day.

"Pansy Rene Bellafini, I need to have a word with you before you walk out that door." Mom was in her bathrobe at the dining room table with the paper, and a cup of coffee. Her hair was wrapped in a towel on her head like a giant blue swirl of ice cream.

"Why, what's going on?" Pansy asked, stuffing the clean polo she'd grabbed out of the dryer into her book bag so she could change before work.

"It's about this Summer person that you're friends with. It's come to my attention that the Summer who owns Wild Harmony on Main Street is also the same Summer who is a member of the PPS."

Crap.

I saw the panic light up Pansy's face for half a millisecond before she decided to play it cool. "Yes, and..."

"And imagine my surprise when I was doing one of my client's nails yesterday at the salon and she mentioned how her niece, Sarah, was working so hard on cleaning up the store and apartment after some teenagers broke in and destroyed everything. And wasn't I Pansy's Mom? Because Sarah only had great things to say about how much Pansy had helped her clean up everything. I had to pretend that I of course knew where my teenage daughter had been spending her days, because what kind of mother wouldn't know that kind of thing?"

"Umm, I literally told you that Summer had a break-in Saturday night. You knew I was at the police station giving a statement."

"I knew that your friend Summer, who I assumed was a teenager living with her parents, had had a break-in. I find it interesting that at no point was I ever informed that Summer is a fully adult person who owns that occult shop downtown. The shop I specifically told you two to never go into."

Well, Mom was feeling her oats this morning.

"Mom, all of the members of the PPS, with the exception of me and Dario, are fully grown adults. We're not running around with a bunch of teenagers like an episode of Scooby Doo or something. And while I do vaguely remember you telling us to avoid that, as you called it, occult shop, five years ago when it was opened, since Summer is one of my very best friends and a member of the PPS who has taught me so much about investigating, and has a very cute store full of suncatchers, candles and a whole lot of books, oh, and because I am also now an adult, I assumed that I could choose who I hang out with all by myself."

My jaw was on the floor, and a quick glance confirmed that Mom's was too. Pansy wasn't done.

"Also, as most of the books in Summer's store are about the occult, and ghosts, and witchy things, and I can see and hear the ghost of my dead twin, I think her shop is the perfect place to hang out. Unfortunately, she's been missing for two months and no one has any clue where she went, and we can't even tell her that everything in that shop and most of the stuff in her apartment upstairs has been completely destroyed."

"See, who has someone break in and destroy all of their things? She sounds unstable," Mom began, but Pansy cut her off. Our mother. She talked over our mother. I was flabbergasted.

"She's not unstable, but she is missing and I am really worried about her. So, if you don't mind, I'm going to go help Sarah finish cleaning up the place, then start my first day at work at Canyon Lanes, and just continue hoping that she reaches out and lets someone know that she's safe." And with that, Pansy tossed her book bag up onto her right shoulder and walked out of the house. I lingered for a minute, stunned and extremely curious as to Mom's reaction to all of that. She just muttered, "Well then," and picked up the section of the paper she'd been reading.

"What on earth was all of that?" I asked, as I jumped back into Pansy's Tracker. She was halfway down the street, probably running on pure adrenaline.

"I'm tired of hiding who Summer is to protect Mom's weird views about what is and what isn't appropriate for her children. She's only got two left, maybe she should lighten up a little."

I fell behind as I thought about what Mom was going to tell Dad when he got home tonight, but then it occurred to me that Pansy was right. Maybe it was time to stop keeping so many secrets from them.

I followed Pansy through Foodarama as she gathered garbage bags, more mopping solution, and a dozen freshly made doughnuts. "Get some juice or milk, or you're going to have a mouth full of sugar and nothing to wash it down with," I told her.

She nodded her head, agreeing with me without having to actually speak, and headed for the juice aisle, where she ran into Chandra.

"What are you doing here so early?" Chandra asked, looking unashamedly into Pansy's basket to see what she was buying.

"We were planning to finish up at Summer's this morning, but we were out of garbage bags."

"And doughnuts, I see."

"Yeah, I start my new job at the bowling alley and have to be there at noon, so I figured I might as well eat something before I go."

"I'm not sure that counts as *something*, but stop by the cafe before you head over there and I'll have a sandwich for you to take for lunch. How's that?"

"I will not turn down free food."

"So, how did last night go? I haven't talked to Randy or Greg yet this morning."

"Mrs. Dale was a very strange person who seemed more

interested in talking to the husband than whether or not the bar was actually haunted, but Randy put her on the schedule."

"Well, I'm sure Blake will enjoy researching that one," Chandra chuckled. "Maybe we can hook him up with a nice bartender."

Blake, the historian of the group, was also her husband Shawn's best friend and Chandra had recently decided that Professor Casey needed a wife.

God help the poor man.

Sarah was already there with the glass dude when Pansy arrived, and the two finished cleanup while the window glass was replaced. Pansy and Sarah had taken out the final bits of garbage, mopped and vacuumed the whole place, and left the box of slightly dented and chipped things that could maybe be salvaged on the kitchen counter.

"I think that's as good as it's going to get," Sarah said while wrestling her carpet cleaner back into the back of her Durango. "I can't thank you enough for all of your help. And the rest of the PPS, too. Tell them how much I appreciate it."

"Well, I couldn't just let you do it all yourself. Summer is still my friend even though I'm beginning to really worry that she won't be back."

"Me too. I never thought that she'd be gone this long. And I never would have expected her to not call. I have no idea what to do now. I hate that I can't keep the business going without her, it makes me feel like a failure."

"You did the best you could for as long as you could. No one can say that you didn't try, but who could have predicted this?"

My mind went back to the first time we met for an investigation with the PPS and I'd noticed that the entire backseat of Summer's VW Bug was covered in clothes and what looked like toiletry bags. I'd thought she was just a slob like Bagel. Now, I saw the clothes as a sign that Summer had known it was a possibility, I just wished I knew what she was running from.

Sarah and Pansy were hugging in the parking lot when I took my last stroll through Wild Harmony. The yoga studio was lit by the clerestory windows along the top of the wall, but the light wouldn't come through directly until the afternoon when it would make the entire floor glow like molten honey. The small office space was dim, the beaded curtains gone. The desk was still in place but now there weren't thirty-odd boxes for the living to trip over. Everything had been cleaned out. The remaining displays were empty, the unbroken bits of inventory boxed up, and the wooden shelves—permanently bowed from the weight of the books over the years—sat empty and dust-free. Pansy had taken a few of the damaged books home with her. She didn't care if the covers were torn off or not, but they couldn't be resold in that condition.

Harvey was safely ensconced at Sarah's house. There would be no more wind chimes tinkling outside the door, no more suncatchers or prisms throwing rainbows across the sidewalks. The whole thing was pretty depressing. I was floating in the middle of Main Street being all tragic and sad when Pansy trotted past on her way to the Firefly to collect on that free lunch.

Another milestone I wouldn't be participating in. Baby's first job. I floated slowly behind, because I definitely didn't want to miss it, but still couldn't shake the feeling that I was missing out. Could ghosts get depressed? I felt like if you were a ghost for long enough, the amount of things that would make you feel like you were missing out could become a pretty long list. Was I going to be here, just hovering as Pansy found a boyfriend, got married, had kids? Was I going to be Auntie Gerri, the friendly ghost? A Jeep drove through me and made me look up. That's when I noticed him.

Well, I noticed the truck. And only because it looked just like Dad's, but in two-toned grey and black. There was some random dude I'd never seen before sitting in the truck parked right in front of the Elementary school, staring at Wild Harmony. He wasn't reading a book, looking at a newspaper, picking his nose, nothing, just staring at the building. *But you* have *seen him before*, the voice in my brain, the one that offered up dumb advice on the regular, said. *The Marlboro Man. At the Wild Dawg.* What were the odds that I'd see the same dude two days in a row in two different towns that were almost an hour apart? *Slim to none and Slim done left town.* As Sarah's Durango pulled out, the man started up his truck, flipped his cigarette out the open window, and pulled out behind her. Was he following Sarah? Who was this dude?

There was only one way to find out.

10

The truck was already passing Wild Harmony when my brain offered the helpful suggestion that maybe I had also seen that truck the night Summer's apartment was broken into. Before Pansy got there, before the police arrived. When it was just me being all worried about Harvey and hopeful that Summer had returned, had that been the truck that drove past while I waited at the curb to cross the street? It had been a dark color, but charcoal and black? I wasn't sure. My desire to watch Pansy learn how to run a concession stand at the bowling alley lost out to my desire to stalk the Marlboro Man and see what he could be up to. I wished for a ghost phone at that moment, to call Lee, but I was afraid that if I flew to the Police Station to get him, the stranger would turn off somewhere and I'd never find him again. Of course, if he really was following Sarah, then he'd be at her house, but what if she wasn't going straight home? Just because she'd turned in the direction of her house didn't mean that's where she was going. I couldn't risk it.

Sarah lived just north of town and I put on the speed to catch up, passing Pansy who was coming out of The Firefly with a white paper bag and a giant Styrofoam drink cup. The two vehicles had stopped up ahead as they waited for someone to make a left-hand turn into my neighborhood. The Marlboro Man was like, right behind her. Had this dude never watched a single buddy cop movie? Everyone knows you had to give some distance when you were tailing someone. Like, duh. I put myself in Sarah's Durango, where she was singing along to Love Shack and obviously had no clue that she was being followed by some creep. Well, probably a creep. I mean, I didn't know for sure, but I calculated an 87% chance that he was up to no good.

I fell back as they began to move forward again, floating into the passenger seat of his truck which was giving Bagel's Bronco a run for the filthiest vehicle I'd ever been in. If someone had actually opened the passenger side door thirty paper bags full of garbage and empty Styrofoam cups would have fallen out. I checked out the back seat, and it didn't look any better than the front, although there were a whole bunch of Gatorade bottles lying on the floorboard full of a yellowish liquid that did not have the fluorescent glow of lemon-lime. It took a minute for that to make sense.

"Gag a maggot," I finally said out loud. If you need a rest stop, Colorado has some very pretty ones, why on earth would anyone pee into a Gatorade bottle?

Unless he's been doing a whole lot of stalking lately. Spying from the truck, like he'd been on a stakeout. Except even the Perth PD treated the interior of their patrol cars better than this dude treated this truck. Sarah's turn signal was on and her brake lights flashed as she made a right onto Mariposa Lane.

It was now or never, what was he going to do?

He braked, didn't use his turn signal, of course, and followed her down the residential streeet. Sarah only lived a few houses down Mariposa, and when she turned into her driveway he continued past until he was around a curve in the road. As soon as he was out of sight, he pulled into someone else's drive-way, put the truck in reverse, and turned around, heading back towards 105. The speedometer was barely fluttering around the five-mile-per-hour mark as he crept past Sarah's house and an expression I can only describe as a leer crossed his face. I didn't like this at all.

Sarah had pulled into her garage and the door was almost closed, leaving only her legs visible, so she probably had no idea what this dude was doing. Even if she had noticed the truck following her, I figured that the average person wouldn't give it a second thought. I had never been an average person.

"I, myself, am strange and unusual," I muttered my favorite *Beetlejuice* quote under my breath as I continued to float along-side the truck. I wished for a way to warn Sarah, but I couldn't let this guy out of my sight.

He paused briefly before turning south onto 105, slamming the gas and chirping the tires as he pulled out, sending the stray gravel scattered across the intersection flying behind him. He covered the quarter mile back into town in record time, suddenly hanging a left into the Sycamore Plaza lot with no turn signal and barely any braking. He drove past Pansy's Tracker, making two full laps of the parking lot as he nodded and mumbled something to himself. I definitely didn't like where this was going. He parked in the back of the lot, close to the exit, and got out of the truck, striding in his bowlegged way towards the first business at the end, Spin Time Records.

He seemed annoyed when the scrawny dude behind the counter at Spin Time greeted him, and after pausing to look around the open space, walked back out the door and over to the Wash and Fold next door. This was followed by a trip inside Blockbuster where the shelves were taller and he had to actu-ally go in and walk around in his search for what I suspected was my sister. Blockbuster was also a bust.

I considered tripping him as he sauntered toward the front doors of Canyon Lanes in the very corner of the L-shaped shopping center, but decided weird was better than weird *and* angry. He entered through the plate glass doors, and sure enough, his eyes lit up when he spotted Pansy. He ignored the cheerful greeting from the front desk attendant who was in charge of the lanes and the racks of shoes and headed left towards the bar area. He took a seat at a table where he'd have a great view of Pansy over in the arcade section behind the concessions counter. I was not pleased with this turn of events.

I floated over to Pans who was being shown where all of the supplies and backup candy were kept.

"It's important that the counter display is always kept stocked," the middle aged woman with the long blonde ponytail was telling Pansy. "If you empty a case of any particular kind of candy, don't throw it away. Just lay the box on my desk back here so that I'll know what we need to order on the next restock. Got it?"

"Got it. Don't throw the box away." Pansy was wide-eyed like she was trying to memorize nuclear codes. She was literally only going to have this job for the next six weeks or so until she moved to Greeley—she was taking it way more seriously than I would have. Pansy kept shooting me dirty looks but I waited until the Manager Lady—Kim, according to her little gold name tag—finally stopped talking about the garbage rotation long enough for me to get a word in edgewise.

"When you get a second, don't be obvious about it, but I need you to look at the guy over at the bar. Not the old man, the one that kind of looks like Patrick Swayze on crack."

Her eyes widened even more as she glanced over to the bar area. She focused on me for a second and gave a little nod of her head which I translated to mean, *what about him?*

"So, I saw that dude last night at the Wild Dawg. He was

lurking out in the parking lot when you guys left the bar, and he pulled out right after you left. Then I just watched him follow Sarah home from Summer's. Now he's in here stalking you."

She was now so focused on Marlboro Man that she didn't follow the Manager chick as she walked around to the back storeroom to show Pansy something. We both jumped when we heard a very stern, "Miss Bellafini!"

"Keep an eye on him, I'm going for backup," I told her as I left. He'd just ordered a beer so that should keep him occupied for at least the three or four minutes that I needed to find Lee.

Pansy threw her hands up in the air in a how-is-this-my-problem gesture, and I took off for the police station. Lee was right where I'd left him a few hours earlier, but he was entertaining himself by messing with a drunk driver, making the pen on the desk roll back and forth when they weren't looking. Judging by how freaked out the dude was, he might never drink again.

"Quit teasing the dumb animals and come with me."

"I didn't expect to see you back so soon. I thought Pansy was starting her new job today?"

"She is, but I need you to come with me. I'll explain on the way." I gave him the Reader's Digest abbreviated version of events as he followed me back to the bowling alley. "This is his truck," I told Lee as we approached it.

"What a pigsty," Lee muttered as he floated in and pulled the glove box open. It fell open with a thump, revealing a pistol of some kind. I didn't know jack about guns but I knew it wasn't a revolver. It was the kind that you shoved the little case of bullets up into the butt of the handle—like they did in the movies.

"Interesting," Lee murmured. Reaching in, he pulled a small piece of paper forward where we could read it. "The truck is registered to Donald Chojakni. Looks like he's from somewhere in Kansas that I've never heard of. Why is he hanging around here?"

"My guess is that he came to break into Summer's place," I said, pointing towards the claw part of a crowbar just visible beneath the driver's side seat.

"This could explain why she took off and didn't tell anyone how to find her."

"If he's the one that broke everything in her place then I'd run from him too."

"Probably wise on her part. I've reported on a lot of domestic scenes and they rarely end well for the wives and girl-friends."

"Do you think he's an old ex?"

"Could be. For some men, once they think a woman is theirs, they think of her only as property to be owned. If the woman runs away it only makes these kinds of guys even more determined to teach them a lesson."

"Well, in that case, I hope she stays hidden until we can find out more about him. And then figure out how to get rid of him."

"And he's in the bowling alley now?" Lee asked, continuing to paw through the glove box in his search for more clues.

"Yeah, he picked a place at the bar where he'll be able to see Pansy while she's working."

"Nothing creepy about that," Lee muttered. "Let's see if I recognize him."

"Do you want me to close the glove box?" I asked. It was still hanging wide open with the gun visible from the passenger side window. I mean, we didn't have a lot of crime in Perth, but surely that was just asking for someone to break in.

"Nah. Let him worry about why it's open. It'll keep him on his toes."

Inside the bowling alley—where the twenty greatest rock hits of the seventies were always on repeat—Pansy was filling up the popcorn machine with a thick yellow liquid that was probably a butter-flavored something. I wasn't sure that I wanted to know what kind of chemical sludge created popcorn, but I guess we were both learning all kinds of things today.

Pansy saw me come in and I held up one finger to indicate that I'd be with her in a minute. Lee was already over by the bar and I pointed out the sandy-haired stranger. "I was calling him the Marlboro Man, but I guess Donald could work, too."

"Assuming that's his real name," Lee said, still giving the man an up-and-down assessment. "Cowboy boots look real but they're worn out. So, not a tourist but he can't afford new boots. Watch is cheap, but the Stetson is relatively new and of good quality." He floated all the way around the man who was reading the paper between sips of beer. It looked like he was trying to make it last as long as possible so he could stay here and stalk Pansy in the air conditioning instead of out in the truck in the sweltering heat.

"Jeans are Wrangler, tee looks like it came from K-Mart. It's either a carefully crafted persona to fit in or the man is just some regular Joe."

"Maybe he doesn't know Summer and was just looking for a place to rob."

"But was Summer actually robbed?" Lee asked, floating next to Donald with his hands on his hips. "There wasn't any money there because Sarah had already gone to the bank. She was keeping the checkbook at her house, and I didn't get the feeling that anything was actually stolen. It was all just broken."

"Maybe he broke in with the intention of stealing money, found out there wasn't any, and then got mad."

Lee watched the Marlboro Man as he kept sneaking glances at Pansy. "No. A robber gets in and gets out. Making a mess would just waste time. People who destroy everything are either stupid teens or people with some kind of hatred simmering in them. This guy looks like he's got all kinds of bad things bubbling on the back burner."

I couldn't disagree. Out of the corner of my eye, I saw Pansy leave the counter and make her way toward the restrooms, and she sent me a very pointed look that indicated I should follow her in so we could talk.

"Okay, I've got to go fill her in."

"Go, I'll keep an eye on Donnie boy."

I found Pansy in the first stall with her arms crossed and all but tapping her foot waiting for me.

"What is going on?" she hissed as soon as I poked my head through the stall door.

"I went and got Lee and we snooped through his truck. According to the registration in the glovebox, his name is Donald Chojackni, he's from Kansas, and he's got what Lee said is a 9mm in his glove box. He's also got a crowbar under his seat and little bits of broken glass on his floorboard. He drives a dark grey and black Silverado and I kind of remember seeing that truck out on the street on graduation night."

She slowly blinked three times while processing everything that I'd just thrown at her. "So, why is he following me?"

"I have no idea, but now that we know he's here, Lee and I are going to follow him. And we're like, way better at it than he is." *Score one for team ghost.*

"Good."

"He followed Sarah home. I think you should call her later this evening and tell her that you've noticed a guy lurking around and that you saw him following her as she left Wild Harmony. Just... make sure she locks her doors and keeps an eye out, you know?"

"Yeah, I can do that. Which reminds me, Sarah mentioned earlier that the only thing she couldn't find in the mess was Summer's address book. We never found it while we were cleaning and I just assumed that maybe someone had thrown it out accidentally when the PPS was helping, but now..."

"Yeah, if he's looking for Summer, her address book would be a good piece of information to have. It's even more suspicious since before yesterday I'd never laid eyes on this dude. If he was just coming through town he wouldn't know that Summer was gone to rob her, and if he did break in just to rob her, he would have been a hundred miles away by the time the sun came up. This guy wants something."

"Well, go do your thing and I'll be careful. Maybe I'll go flirt with him and see what kind of bullcrap story he makes up."

I snorted before falling into full-blown laughter as I thought of Pansy playing femme fatale. "Dude, I triple dog dare you," I said between cackles.

"I could flirt if I wanted to."

"I'd love to see it. Too bad Lee and I can't enjoy any of that popcorn you're out there making, it'd go great with the show."

"Oh, stuff it."

"Well, you're stuck with us here until he makes his next move. If you decide to flirt with him, make sure you tell him that you're here until midnight."

"I get off at six."

"Duh. I know that, but there's no way he's going to hang out here that long. If he knows where you're going to be and how long you'll be here, he may wander off somewhere else in the meantime."

She nodded her head and checked her Swatch. "I've got to get back, Kim is going to think I've fallen in."

"Yell if you need me."

11

Since it was a Wednesday afternoon in the middle of summer, there were plenty of kids in and out of the bowling alley and arcade, all wanting candy, soda, and to escape their parents for a few hours. The Chinese restaurant was next door, and the bowling alley concession stand was the only pizza place in town, so the lunch crowd hit hard. Pansy was kept too busy doing real work to play spy. Lee and I hovered for about an hour waiting for the dude to move or do something, but once he finally finished his beer, he just went back to the bar to order another one. Was he skipping lunch? Although, with all of the garbage in his truck, who knew, he could have been eating a burger while Pansy and Sarah were cleaning.

I was zoning out, watching some younger kids bowl, when loud voices pulled me back to the present. A floppy-haired boy who looked to be about eleven or twelve was yelling at three slightly older kids to stop laughing at him, but they continued to sling insults. I heard the smaller kid mention the word Mom and assumed that one of these delinquents was an older brother. My money was on the most overly dramatic of the bunch. A quick glance at the digital scoreboard told me the older boys were beating the younger kid pretty badly.

What the heck, I had time to kill.

"Where are you going?" Lee yelled to be heard over the Lynyrd Skynyrd track being blasted from the speakers as I floated down into the recessed bowling area and across the polished wood lanes.

"Just making a nuisance of myself," I yelled back. I saw his mouth moving as he muttered something but I was too far away to hear him.

Big brother was up to bat. Or up to…throw? Roll? I was never a fan of bowling so I wasn't sure of the terminology, but I knew the goal was to knock pins down. Not on my watch, buddy. The kid stepped up and did a fancy little step while drawing the bright orange ball behind him. He threw it smoothly down the lane and I lunged for it to knock it off into the gutter. Unfortunately, the ball was moving too fast and I went right through the floor about two seconds after the ball had already passed me. This whole haunting thing was always harder than I expected it to be.

Six of the pins fell but I was ready for him on the next throw. I hovered horizontally in the middle of the lane with my hands clasped in front of me. As the ball approached I concentrated on making contact with my whole arm, diverting the ball into the gutter. There was much screaming from the boys as they gathered around the scoring table.

"You look like you're swimming," Lee said as he floated over to either make fun of me or to participate. He probably hadn't decided which, either.

"Why haven't we done this before? Can you imagine on a league night?"

"Yes, disrupting the games that a bunch of drunk men have

placed bets on. Sounds like a brawl waiting to happen," he responded dryly.

The next kid was ready to bowl and I couldn't prevent the huge grin that split my face as I teed up to block the bowling ball. It came flying down the lane with a little bit of spin which made it easy for me to flick it into the gutter right before it hit the pins. It wasn't too obvious but still enough to send the boys into screams of despair.

"You're having entirely too much fun with this," Lee said.

"Just wait," I replied. I looked up to make sure Marlboro Man was still at his seat and prepared myself for the next roll. Delinquent number two was up for his second attempt and still visibly angry. After taking a lot of ripping from his friends he stalked out to throw another ball down the lane. I was ready for him. All I had to do was nudge it a little as it went down the lane, causing it to teeter on the edge of the wood and only knock down one pin. This was so much fun.

The smaller kid was up next. I watched him gather the ball in both hands and get into a kind of squat, swinging the ball between his knees before throwing it out onto the lane. The ball was moving in a relatively straight line but didn't have enough power behind it to knock down all of the pins. With my assistance, he scored a strike.

Screams erupted from the group.

"I'm sorry, were you or were you not just making fun of me for aggravating the drunks in the police station? What do you call this if not teasing the dumb animals?"

"Oh, come on, you have to admit that these punks deserve it. Besides, this has given me a great idea for how we can get this guy out of here so we can follow him back to his lair."

I floated back over to the Marlboro Man and took a look at the beer on the table in front of him. It looked like he still had two-thirds of a bottle left, which was more than enough for my purposes. I waited for a good opportunity—when he moved his arm close enough to the bottle to be believable that it could have been his fault—before I knocked the bottle over onto him. Beer spilled all over his arm and pants. He yelped, standing and flinging beer in all directions as he flopped around in surprise.

Mission accomplished.

Lee was laughing behind me as we watched him dance around, kicking his leg like that was going to make it dry faster. I hoped he decided to go home or wherever he was staying to clean up. He looked up, his expression hardening as he became acutely aware that every eye in the place was turned towards him. Being noticed was probably not high on his to-do list.

"Well, that was effective," Lee said as we followed the man out to his truck. "You realize that now Pansy can't tell him she's working until midnight."

"It got him moving, didn't it?"

Marlboro Man wrenched the driver's side door open and Lee and I both laughed when he saw that the glove box was open, his pistol on full display to anyone walking past his truck. I was pretty sure that this dude had never moved so fast in his life as he jumped across the seat of the truck, slamming the glove box closed. Nothing suspicious here.

The man was creative with his cuss words, I'd give him that. He cursed a blue streak even as he was putting the truck into reverse, narrowly avoiding the row of cars behind him.

His tires chirped once again as he pulled out on Main Street. Then he broke several speed limits as he headed north towards where 105 connected to County Rd 22. I suspected I knew where he was going.

"What do you want to bet that he's heading to The Cowboy Lodge?" I asked Lee.

"Well, it is the only motel within 20 miles of Perth," Lee

said. "That does kind of narrow down his options for a hideout."

We really needed to get another motel around here just to give our bad guys some options, I thought. Sure enough, ten minutes later the Silverado was pulling into the garbage-strewn and pothole-filled parking lot of the motel.

The Cowboy Lodge was situated on a lonely stretch of highway and had absolutely nothing going for it other than providing four walls, a roof, and questionable plumbing. The rumor was that it was always a big hit on prom night as the owner didn't ask a lot of questions if there was cash involved. There was a giant metal sign painted like a cowboy waving his hat in the air, with most of the neon lights blown out and rarely replaced. The Marlboro Man pulled into a space in front of room number eight and was trying to pull his room key out of his beer-soaked pocket as Lee and I floated into his room. It was a mess. I was not even remotely surprised.

"There are times that I'm glad I can't smell," Lee grumbled as he floated over the food wrappers lying on the floor. There weren't a lot of chain restaurants in the area because there just wasn't enough population out here to support one, so most of the wrappers were plain white wax paper, in plain white or brown paper bags. As far as clues went, they left a lot to be desired.

Donnie's open suitcase was sprawled on top of one of the matching twin beds in the room, and the clothes spilling out of it looked like they were sorted into piles of dirty or dirtier. I shuddered as a cockroach skittered across the lampshade on the nightstand between the beds.

"I wonder how long he's been here?"

Donnie started stripping before he'd even closed the door behind him and I quickly turned to avoid having to see anything that I most definitely didn't want to see. Lee started laughing behind me when he saw what I'd done.

"You know, if I'd been a ghost as a teenage boy, I would have been awful, I have to admit."

"Are you saying you would have haunted the girls' locker room?" Honestly, it was one of the first places I'd looked for other ghosts when I came back, but it was surprisingly empty of spirits.

Lee laughed again, "Absolutely. I would have never left. It's probably best for the modesty of the entire town that I was an old man who'd already seen it all by the time anyone had to worry about me lurking in the dark."

"Is he done yet?"

"You should be safe in about thirty seconds, looks like he's opting for a shower." I heard the shower curtain being pulled back, followed by a curse and some thudding sounds. I could only imagine what kind of creature he was beating into submission in there. Gag me with a spoon.

I finally heard the water come on and the shower curtain screech into place.

"Your modesty is safe, kiddo," Lee advised with a chuckle.

"My gag reflex, you mean," I mumbled. Lee was standing by the dresser hunched over something and I floated over to assist.

"He tossed his wallet onto the dresser," Lee explained, pointing to the license displayed in the plastic sleeve. "Look at the name. Same first name, different last name. Different state."

Sure enough, the name said Donald Sunderland, and listed his home as being in BFE Nebraska. "I mean, maybe he moved?"

"Geraldine, you can't just fill out a card at the post office to change your last name. This 'dude,' as you say, is a liar."

"Well, that's not shocking. So, how do we get him pulled over so the police can pick him up and start asking him some questions? Maybe we could jerk the wheel while he's driving down the road and run him into a tree or something?"

Lee frowned at what I thought was a really good suggestion. "And what if you take someone else out who's just standing on the street? Once you jerk the wheel you can't predict what will happen next. That's too risky."

"Well, what do you suggest then?" I asked.

"I don't know yet. I'm sure something brilliant will come to me. Or, worst case, we wait for him to break in somewhere else and have Pansy call 911 from her cell phone. They can't trace those, just tell her to make sure she doesn't have her name on the voicemail if they try to call her back."

Not quite a foolproof plan, and it would require Pansy to be somewhere in town where there was a signal and not out and about where she'd be 'roaming.' If it happened to pick up some other company's cell tower, the roaming charges for a phone call would absolutely get her grounded. Although, now that she was gainfully employed, I guess she could pay the charges herself. Could Mom even still ground her now that she was eighteen? It certainly wouldn't stop her from trying.

"Wait," I said, spotting something purple sticking out of the back pocket of Donnie's discarded Wranglers. I leaned down and pulled it out a little further, my suspicions confirmed as I spotted the Hamsa, which represented the hand in yoga, stamped in gold on the fake leather cover of what looked an awful lot like an address book. One of these things was not like the others.

"I think I just found Summer's missing address book."

"Good job, Nancy Drew."

"Hardy har har." I rolled my eyes and made a mental note to tell Pansy later that we'd found it. "I think this clenches the theory that he is the one who broke into Summer's."

"It solidifies my theory that he's probably the reason she ran in the first place."

"Well," I said, staring at the address book. "I guess that means we need to find her before he does."

12

Donald, if that really was his name, finished his shower and I fled the room entirely until Lee floated out the door to tell me our subject was redressed and pulling on a not-so-fresh pair of socks. It looked like he was heading back out and I was curious to see where he'd decide to go this time. I fully expected him to go back to the bowling alley, but he pulled up in front of the high school and made his way into The Firefly Cafe.

The little bell tinkled as he pushed his way through the door and into the nearly deserted cafe. It was almost four, and during the school year, the Firefly was always packed full of teenagers as soon as the three o'clock bell rang. In June, it was all but deserted. Donnie slid into a booth and Lee and I moved over to keep an eye on him. He'd dressed in an almost identical pair of Wranglers, these not covered in beer, and a ratty band tee shirt for Screeching Weasel. I'd had him pegged for a Garth Brooks man, but to each his own.

Donna was the waitress on duty this afternoon and she came immediately with a laminated menu and questions about what he'd like to drink.

"Uh, a Sprite would be fine. Hey, are you the one that does that ghost-hunting stuff?"

"Oh, Lord no, sweetie. That would be Chandra. She owns the place."

"Oh, is she here? I saw a bit about what they do on the news and I'd love to learn more about it." He had a surprisingly pleasant speaking voice and seemed to be able to turn on the charm at will. Although I'd referred to him as looking like Patrick Swayze, when he smiled, there really was a resemblance. Donna was not the least bit suspicious.

"Well, she's already left for the day but she'll be back tomorrow morning to open. We open at six if you're still going to be around."

"Oh, well maybe I'll do that. I planned to stay for a few more days. I was supposed to meet a friend but it seems like she's out of town. Maybe you know her? Summer Hopkins?

"Well of course. Everyone knows Summer. But she left, well, seems like it was almost two months back. Said she had a family emergency and took off up out of here real sudden like."

Oh. My. God. Donna. Shut up.

"Really? Well, she'd written to me earlier this spring and told me to stop by if I was out this way. I'm a salesman and my sales area covers a big chunk of Colorado and Wyoming," he offered with a thousand-watt smile. Even *I* almost believed him. "I would have called before I made the detour but I'd left my address book at home and forgot to bring it with me. Do you think I could maybe leave her a note to let her know I stopped? Or do you think she'll be back soon?"

"Well, as far as I know, no one has any idea when she's coming back. She didn't even leave a phone number where she could be reached. Why," Donna cast a glance toward the only other diners in the place, a couple on the other side of the room before she leaned forward and dropped her voice so as not to be overheard. "Summer's business, Wild Harmony just down the street, you know? Well, it was broken into Saturday night and I overheard the police talking about how they couldn't even call her to let her know about the damage."

He did an impressive job of acting surprised by this news. "Broken into? I hope nothing was damaged." He looked so sincere. I wanted to stab him with a fork.

"Oh goodness, the whole place was broken up as I heard it. Teenagers most likely. It was graduation night and some of these kids, I swear they're feral."

"Well, that sounds like a mess but you're sure no one has any way to contact her? I feel bad, what with her not even knowing about the situation."

"Absolutely not," Donna said. "I know that poor Sarah was just broken up about all of the damage and not knowing what to do next with it, but I heard her and Pansy got it all cleaned up. Hopefully, Summer will be back soon.'

"Pansy? Now, is that the girl with the long dark hair? I saw her coming out of the store earlier."

"Yes, that's Pansy Bellafini. She just graduated high school, but she's something of a local celebrity around here."

I started chanting "Quit talking, Donna," but my Jedi mind powers never quite kicked in and my suggestion had no effect on the waitress.

"That Pansy, she's been on the news a whole bunch of times with the PPS and them investigating. She uncovered a whole scheme about fake diamond mining a few months back and we had reporters from three states away showing up to interview her about it. And then she and that boyfriend of hers, Dario, well they found the body of Stuart Mayes just a month or two ago. You might have heard about that one, I heard Tom Brokaw himself reported on that story."

"You know, now that you mention that, I do seem to recall

seeing something about it. That's really impressive. I didn't quite catch her name though and I didn't realize that she lived here in Perth. And to think, she and Sarah went through all that trouble to clean up the damage. They must have been really good friends with Summer." Donnie said.

"Well, we here in Perth like to pride ourselves on how friendly and caring we are," Donna said.

"Friendly, caring, and with big mouths," I told Lee.

"Then I guess there's no point in leaving a letter if no one knows when she's going to be coming back," Donnie said.

"You know, if you really want to, you can just leave it here at the cafe. I'm sure Chandra would be more than happy to give it to her if she comes back."

"Subtle," Lee murmured as Donald finished pumping the waitress for information.

"It's not like she's the soul of discretion. He barely even had to work for all of that."

We hovered as he ordered a slice of pie and a burger, and Donna scuttled off to put his order in. He was quiet, eventually getting up to grab a discarded newspaper off a nearby table and sat down to read like he hadn't just read most of it at the bowling alley.

He ate quickly and didn't talk to anyone else as we stalked him in the diner. Barely twenty minutes had passed before he was finished and back on the street walking to the corner to the payphone. He entered the booth and pulled out the phone book. My heart sank as he started flipping through the pages and I stuck my head into the booth with him. Sure enough, he was searching under the Bs for Bellafini. There was our address in black and white. *Crap*.

He ripped out the page—*rude*—and folded it up, slipping it into his jeans pocket before walking across the street like he belonged there and getting back into his truck. I turned to look at Lee but he already knew what I was going to say.

"I'll follow him," Lee said. "You go tell Pansy."

I nodded. "If we don't cross paths again, meet me at the police station at nine o'clock if you can," I said. "We'll compare notes then."

I floated back to Canyon Lanes to let Pansy know what was going on. She looked worse for wear, a big ketchup stain smeared down the front of her white polo, and about a fifth of the hair that had started the day in her ponytail was now hanging down around her face. Appropriately, Lunatic Fringe was blasting over the speakers.

"Rough day?" I asked.

She growled in response.

"I'm about to make it worse. Lee and I followed Donald to the Cowboy Lodge. He's definitely been staying there and we're 99.9% sure he's the one that broke into Summer's apartment because he's carrying Summer's address book around in his back pocket. Then we followed him to the Firefly where he was pumping Donna for information, trying to find someone who might know how to contact Summer."

"What's the connection?" Pansy asked under her breath as she picked up a pizza from the kitchen pass-thru. "How does he know her and why is he trying to find her?"

"Lee is convinced that he's the reason she ran in the first place. He thinks that judging by the amount of anger displayed in the way he broke everything in the shop and apartment it fits with him being either an ex-husband or an ex-boyfriend. One Summer doesn't want to see."

"I can't blame her for that." She handed the pizza to an old dude standing by the counter. "Be careful, it's hot. Napkins and utensils are there at the end of the counter. Just let me know if you need anything else." She waited for him to move to the end of the counter before turning back to me. "I guess that makes the next question, how do we get rid of him?"

"I'm not sure yet, but he seems pretty fixated on you and Sarah. Which is, umm, slightly concerning."

"Fixated in what way?"

"Well, Donna told him everything but your shoe size, so as soon as he left the Firefly he went to the pay phone and ripped the page with our phone number and address out of the phone book. Lee is following him this evening and I'm watching you. I almost expected him to come back here, but, like, he doesn't need to stalk you at work if he already knows where you live. Either way, you need to call Sarah and warn her," I said.

"Okay, I get off in an hour," Pansy said, looking around the crowded bowling alley. It was starting to pick up with the dinner crowd. Even on a Wednesday night, pizza and beer were a big draw. "While I'm stuck here, you go find Bagel. I think he should be home from work by now. Let him know we need to have an emergency meeting."

"How am I supposed to tell him all of that?'

"You're resourceful, figure it out. Hi, welcome to Canyon Lanes, what can I get you today?" she asked the pimply teen behind me.

As much as I didn't want to leave her alone for even a minute, I figured if I could find a way to bring Bagel to her, she'd be safer in the long run. I took off, flying over the football field and the police station, crossing Main into the Foodarama parking lot to make sure Bagel hadn't decided to work overtime. No Bronco.

Back north I went, flying directly to his neighborhood and to the Ventura family split-level where Bagel's Bronco was sitting in the driveway. I found Bagel in the kitchen buttering French bread to be toasted while his mom made dinner. I smacked him 3 times on the arm to let him know I was there. He squealed and tossed the butter knife across the kitchen.

"Dario Allesandro," Mrs. Ventura yelled. "What on earth?"

While Bagel was fully aware of my current status, his mother was not. She would have called a priest for an exorcism if she had any inkling that I was lurking around, haunting her son.

"Sorry, I just remember that I have, umm, something I need to do really quick," he said, retrieving the knife that had slid halfway under the fridge. "Do you mind if I go finish that up?"

"What something?" his mother asked, one black brow arching. "You've graduated. It's not like you have homework anymore."

"Yeah, I know, but it's, umm, summer reading for one of our college classes this fall. I promised Pansy that I was going to have this chapter read by tonight so we could discuss it and I totally forgot to read it. So, while this bakes, do you mind if I run upstairs and get some speed reading done?"

"I can't believe they make you spend your summer reading things for these ridiculous classes, but yes, we don't want Pansy to think that you're a slacker now do we?"

"Yeah, I won't be long. Let me just look for the important words and skim them so I can pretend I know what I'm talking about, okay?" He didn't wait for a reply and I followed him up the stairs to his room. It was almost like old times—he just didn't have to keep the door open now.

Once we were safely away from prying eyes, Bagel pulled the Ouija board out from under his bed and I moved the planchette to the word "Pansy."

"Okay. What's going on?"

Next, I spelled out S U M M E R with the planchette.

"Okay, Summer..."

X

"Oh my God, is Summer dead?" he whispered.

Ugh.

I quickly moved through the letters for 'boyfriend' which seemed to confuse him even more.

"Pansy, Summer, x, boyfriend. Summer has a boyfriend? Ex...oh. Oh! Are you saying Pansy has a suspect?"

YES. He was on the right track, anyway.

"I'll just call her tonight. I don't remember, does she get off at 6 or 7?" he asked.

I moved the planchette to the 6 but what I really wanted him was for him to drive over there and pick her up. I didn't want her to be alone when she walked out to the parking lot tonight, but that was a lot to write out letter by letter.

A P T, I spelled out.

"Apt? Apt to do what?"

NO

"Umm...apt... abbreviation for apartment?"

YES.

I pointed to the word 'go' and then spelled out G E T, before moving the planchette back to 'Pansy.'

"Go get her? Why doesn't she just..." he trailed off as I moved the planchette to one of the skulls that decorated the corners of the board and circled it around for emphasis. "Oh." I could see the wheels turning in his brain as he tried to interpret this. I rattled the trash can next to his desk in the world's worst game of charades, but it seemed to click for him. "This is the guy who trashed the apartment. You think Pansy's in danger?"

YES

"Okay, like, I'm not sure how much of a bodyguard I'll make but I'll pick her up at six and take her home..."

I moved the planchette to the NO response. H E, pause, I S, and then circled the eye at the top of the board.

"He's watching her? And what? You want me to bring her

here?" his whisper was getting a little more panicked. He began pacing around the room, kicking dirty clothes out of the way to clear a path. After a minute he turned back to the Ouija board to address me. "Okay, new plan. Tell Pansy that I'll come pick her up, bring her here for dinner. We'll leave her Tracker at Sycamore to confuse him. Is he watching her right now?"

NO

"Okay, so just to be safe, tell her to leave by the back loading dock just in case he's watching the front. I'll pull around to the back and kidnap her. But warn her that my mother is going to think we're dating if I bring her home for dinner and there will be no talking her out of that idea."

I mean, Mrs. Ventura was kind of scary, but not in the same way as the creepy guy with a gun. At least she'd be safe and hopefully, the Marlboro Man won't know where she went for a few hours. And bonus points to Bagel, because leaving the bright yellow Tracker in the parking lot might confuse Donnie. Two taps for yes.

I flew off to let Pansy know about the change in dinner plans.

13

"I'll tell you all about my first day when I get home, Mom," Pansy said into her cell phone. She opened the back door to the bowling alley and looked both ways, even though I'd already told her that the coast was clear. She hustled the three steps to the Bronco and wrenched the passenger door open. I expected an avalanche of soda cups, but it looked like Bagel had actually made an effort to clean it out. I made a mental note to make sure Pansy told him about our suspect beating him out for the dirtiest vehicle in the tri-state area, but I'd save the teasing for later—we had bigger issues right now.

"No, I'm not avoiding you. I'm sorry about this morning. Yes, I'll be home before nine, I promise." Bagel didn't even wait for her to put her seatbelt on before taking off.

"Thank you," she said to him before turning back to the Mom problem. "I know, but we have some summer reading for one of our courses next semester. We were going to go over it earlier this week and get it over with, but you know, with everything happening with Summer we're really behind."

I heard sounds through the phone that reminded me of

Charlie Brown's teachers talking. Bagel stopped at the sign before making the right onto Main Street.

"Do we even know who this guy is or what he drives? I need details if I'm going to be helpful," Bagel said, looking both ways.

"Mom, I've got to go, I'll talk to you tonight. Okay, love you too." She tossed the cell into her purse with an audible thunk and joined him in scrutinizing the vehicles that lined both sides of Main. "He drives a black and dark grey Silverado and he's a dirty blond cowboy-looking dude."

Bagel made the turn. "Gerri said something about Summer's ex? And then she pointed to the skull on the Ouija board, and then the eyeball, and honestly, I've invented about thirty different scenarios since she left so if you could fill me in as to how you could be in like, mortal peril or whatever in the whole twenty-four hours since I last talked to you, that would be great."

Pansy gave him the quick and dirty version of everything that had gone on, starting with me seeing the Marlboro Man last night at a bar forty-five minutes away, then him following Sarah home, stalking Pansy at the bowling alley, and ending her story with him pulling our address out of the phonebook.

"He was carrying Summer's address book in his back pocket," she was saying as Bagel pulled into his driveway.

"Okay, so yeah, he seems to be the prime suspect. Do we know where he's at right now?"

"Gerri's sticking close to me, and Lee is following Donald, if that's even his real name. She's meeting him tonight at nine to compare notes," she said as they walked toward the front door. "Hey, can I bum a clean tee shirt before dinner?" she asked, eyeballing the ketchup stain on her shirt.

Once she'd switched out shirts and fixed her ponytail, Pansy had dinner with Bagel's mom and dad. It was a grueling forty minutes of our lives that none of us would ever get back. Mrs.

Ventura was now firmly under the impression that they were dating and seemed to be beside herself, offering Pansy the first choice of chicken and asking her at least three times if she wanted more food. Pansy and Bagel did not bother to correct her assumptions—sometimes it's just easier to lie.

"I triple dog dare you to call him Honey," I said at one point. She gave me a death glare which made me laugh even louder. The laughter didn't stop for me as Mrs. Ventura continued to tell Pansy story after story about Bagel as a child like Pansy hadn't known him since Kindergarten. Other than a random comment about Bagel certainly having a type, and a request to pass the salt, Mr. Ventura didn't contribute to the dinner conversation at all.

As soon as they could escape the dining room, Pansy followed Bagel upstairs to his room. "I think your mom is ready to propose for you. Good grief."

"Tell me about it, I have to live with the woman," he said, flinging himself onto his bed. Pansy dumped a stack of comic books out of his desk chair and settled in. "Anyway," he said, rolling over to face her. "Now that that's over, what's the next step? How do we catch this guy?"

"I was thinking about it while you guys were eating, and I think we need to bring Chandra in on it," I said. "He told Donna that he'd stop in at the Firefly and talk to her tomorrow morning so if we can get her to mention that she has something Summer sent her, a letter, a postcard, I don't know, then maybe we can get him to break in to steal it."

"You mean, set up a trap?" Pansy asked, nodding slowly as she thought about it. She relayed my idea to Bagel.

"She should say that she's not sure if there's a return address on it," he said. "Make it seem like she didn't think to look. Otherwise, he'll wonder why she doesn't just know this information."

"It should be a postcard," Pansy said. "Something short and vague that wouldn't give away any information. She could say she's lost it in her office and will have to look for it to see if it has a postmark on it."

"Definitely in her office at The Firefly, I don't want this dude following her home," I said.

"Or, and I know you're going to say no before I even say this out loud, but we could just call the police and let them deal with him," Bagel said.

"Oh yeah, because the police love me so much," Pansy said. "I had to practically beg them to come out to investigate the break-in Saturday night. Besides, we don't have any proof that he's done anything. The only thing we have tying him to Summer is her address book, but even if they tried to pull him over he could toss that right out the window. What if we happened to wander by while he was breaking in… like, Gerri could follow him and let us know when to let Chandra and Shawn catch him red-handed. They're adults, the Perth PD would actually believe *them*."

"What if it was on tape? I asked. "What if we set up video cameras inside the diner? I mean, it's not like we don't have access to the equipment."

"Gerri said we should catch him on video. Set up cameras to record."

Bagel nodded to himself and lifted his torso on one elbow. "That would work. Chandra could explain it by telling the police they were ghost hunting at the Firefly. We could set up like three or four camcorders to make sure we catch him no matter which way he breaks in."

"As long as Chandra can lie convincingly enough to get him to break in, I don't see any reason that we can't make this work," Pansy said. "I'll call Chandra when I get home."

"You two need to call everyone in the PPS and let them

know to be on the alert for this guy. He could break into anyone's house. And don't forget to tell them about the gun."

"Oh yeah," Pansy said, turning to Bagel. "Gerri and Lee also found a pistol in Marlboro Man's glovebox."

"So he's armed and crazy—this just keeps getting better and better."

"I know, but I feel better now that you know and we've got a workable plan to get him out of here. Maybe they'll take him to jail, throw away the key, and then we can track down Summer and let her know that it's safe to come home." She turned toward the desk and pulled open the top drawer. "Do you have a pen in here, I need...what's this?" she said, her voice suddenly turning playful as she became distracted by a stack of opened letters. I wasn't sure I'd ever seen Bagel move as quickly as he did at that moment, jumping off the bed and snatching the letters out of her hand. Pansy was still in the chair, mouth agape as he took three steps away from her and held the letters behind his back.

"Who are they from, Dario?" she asked, drawing out his name playfully.

"Nothing. No one."

"What? Did you fill out the form in the back of a magazine and get a pen pal or something?"

"No, it just isn't any of your business, Polly Prissy Pants."

I immediately floated behind him to read the return address. "Jason Nelson in Greeley," I said to Pansy.

"So who's this Jason Nelson in Greeley?" Pansy asked, her smile widening.

Bagel turned around, swatting the stack of letters at me like that was going to make me move or something. "Some kind of BFF you are," he muttered.

"You know we're really good at snooping. You might as well

just tell us," Pansy said, crossing her arms like she was prepared to wait there all night.

"I swear, it's like having two annoying sisters. Fine. I don't know if you remember him or not. He came down after we found Stuart Mayes in the woods and interviewed me. He's trying to get me a job as a photographer for the paper he works for."

"Really? And getting you a job requires, what? Fifty-six letters back and forth?

"Seven," I said. "And I remember him, he was super cute."

"Seven letters back and forth with a guy that Gerri calls super cute. Mmm hmm," Pansy said, batting her eyelashes at Bagel.

"Look, we have a lot of stuff in common and we've been talking."

"Wait, is this the 'friend' who helped you get our apartment?"

"Well, yeah, I mean, yeah." *Was Bagel Boy stuttering?* His whole face was flushed.

Pansy started laughing at his discomfort and held her hands up in surrender. "Okay," she said coyly, "that's fine, you keep your secrets. Just know that I'm really happy for you."

Bagel mumbled something under his breath and went back to the bed, stuffing the letters under his mattress.

"Now, before we leave here, what freaking book are we supposed to be reading?" Pansy asked as she gathered her purse and stained polo. "We need to have our stories straight because you know your mom's going to ask."

"Let's say *The Jungle*."

"We read that our junior year," Pansy said.

"Exactly. If they ask any questions at least we can answer them correctly."

Pansy snorted. "All I remember was that it made me vegetarian for three months."

"Okay, well, now the lie is sorted out, let's get you home. Do you want me to drop you at your Tracker or should we leave it there to confuse this Donald guy and I'll just take you home?"

"I need to work tomorrow so drop me off at Sycamore and I'll call you after I talk to Chandra."

"I'm going to go scout the parking lot at Sycamore Plaza and make sure he's not lurking anywhere," I told my sister.

The parking lot was clear and I wondered where Lee and Donald were as Pansy made the transfer back to her own vehicle. I had less than an hour before I was scheduled to meet Lee at the police station, but I wanted to see how Pansy handled the parents. "How much should we tell Mom and Dad?" I asked.

"How about nothing?" Pansy said as she made the turn onto Main Street.

"If we weren't sure this was the guy who broke into Summer's place and just thought he was some random weirdo, then yeah, I wouldn't bother worrying them. But like, we know better and they should, in fact, be worried."

"Okay, but there's a difference between being aware that there may be a situation, and blowing it all out of proportion and being afraid that I'm going to like, I don't know, be kidnapped or something."

"Okay, but we at least should tell them that a situation exists."

"Fine, I'll tell them that we think we've solved the case, that you spotted the guy and followed him and think he's who broke in. We leave out the parts where he's following Sarah and me."

"And that he has a gun," I said. I mean, it was Colorado, a lot of people carried guns around with them, there wasn't anything unusual about it so there was no need to add it to the list of things our parents would naturally worry about.

"Hang on, let me see what they're doing," I said as we pulled up in front of our house.

I fully expected Mom and Dad to be waiting to ambush Pansy in the kitchen, but they were watching TV in the living room just like any other evening. "They're watching TV. Good possibility that you can just sneak past them if you're quiet."

It was, however, not to be, as Dad happened to be walking into the kitchen as Pansy came in. "Hey kiddo," he said as he refilled his glass of wine. "How was the first day on the job?"

"Oh, it was fine. I just need a shower because my hair smells like popcorn."

Mom, hearing Pansy's voice, came into the kitchen but made no mention of this morning's argument. Apparently, they'd worked it out when Pansy had called her earlier. "So, are you going to like your new boss?" she asked.

"Yeah, she's okay I guess."

"And nothing exciting happened?"

"Well, nothing at work. But Gerri got bored and started following some random dude who was lurking outside of Summer's place and found out that he's the one who broke in and destroyed everything."

"Did you call the police?" Mom asked, clearly surprised at this turn in the conversation.

"And tell them what? That my dead sister told me this guy that no one has ever seen before is the culprit? They already think I'm crazy."

"Well, no, not that exactly, but we can't let him get away with it."

"Tell her you're going to have the other members of the PPS set a trap for him, that you won't be involved, and they're going to catch him."

Pansy filled them in on the plan to have Chandra lure him

into breaking into the Firefly to have the police catch him red-handed.

"That sounds like it would be a really iffy plan. It would only work if he's sticking around and falls for it. If you want, I can just go talk to the police," Dad offered.

"And tell them what, Dad? We have to catch him actually doing something. I promise, it's fine. I'm going to go take a shower and then I'm calling Chandra and emailing the rest of the group to set it all up."

"Okay, but if you need any help from us, just let us know, okay?"

"For the record, I'm not okay with any of this. There is no reason for either of my daughters to be involved with criminals," Mom said, crossing her arms as she alternated staring at Pansy and Dad. "But, I appreciate you actually telling us what's going on. I just want you to be safe."

"I understand, I do. And if you see anyone driving a truck that looks just like yours but in charcoal and black, who looks like Patrick Swayze in Road House, that's the bad guy. So, like, avoid him."

With the 'rents duly warned and Pansy showered and de-popcorned, she opened the top drawer of her desk and pulled out her sunflower-covered address book. She picked up her desk phone, the clear plastic case glinting in the lamplight as she punched in the numbers. Untangling the hot pink cord so that she could flop down on the end of her bed, she waited for someone to answer.

"Shawn? Hey, it's Pansy. Is Chandra there?"

There was a pause as she waited for Chandra to come to the phone and I checked the time on the alarm clock next to her bed.

"Hey, you got this? I'm going to go meet Lee and see what Donnie has been up to."

She shot me a thumbs up and I headed out.

14

Lee didn't keep me waiting, he was already at the police station reading the reports on Crane's desk when I floated in.

"Anything interesting happen after I left?" I asked as I came up behind him.

"Interesting? No. He drove past your parents' house about five times, making slow laps around the neighborhood to check it all out. I was sure that nosy old woman down the street would have called the cops on him, but her eyes must not be what they used to be. Then he headed back to the Cowboy Lodge and started doing some..." Lee shot me a look, "let's just call them recreational pharmaceuticals. From the looks of it, he's going to be down for the night."

"Good, maybe Sarah will be safe tonight."

"Well, he didn't look to be in any shape to go out and break into anyone's house tonight, that's for sure," Lee muttered.

I filled him in on Operation Firefly and he agreed to participate in lookout duties.

"Chandra doesn't strike me as being someone who lies

easily, so if there's any flaw in the plan, it may be her acting skills. Otherwise, I think it will work. It should get him off the street for a while, at least. I'm betting he can't afford bail, so if he gets locked up he should be out of our hair for a bit. I don't know if that will be enough time for us to find Summer, but it'll give us a head start." He flipped over the report he'd been reading on Crane's desk. "This crew sure isn't putting any effort into trying to solve the first break-in. Obviously catching them red-handed is the only way they won't chalk it up to 'kids being kids.'"

Hopkins was written at the top of the file, with a big CLOSED stamp across the cover. Figured.

"So since we know Donnie Boy is safely tucked away, what are your plans for the night, Kiddo?"

"Well, I was just planning on following him around, but since that's out, I guess I could head over to Wilcox and check out that church that the PPS is investigating Saturday. I went over there once already but didn't see anything. No ghosts that time, but maybe they were just out running around."

"That shouldn't take long."

"No. Afterward, I could fly back down to that bar we looked at Tuesday night and see if the husband's ghost decided to show up. You want to go?"

"Ehh, I might as well. Bias rented Weekend at Bernie's for tonight's entertainment and I've already seen that movie a hundred times. I'm ready when you are."

We floated north out of town, passing over the trailer park where some jerks had tried to fake out the PPS a few months back. They hadn't understood how infrared cameras worked and that the teenager they'd hired to move things around would absolutely still be visible. Flying, the investigation site was another five minutes northeast of there.

The security light nailed to a pole in the dusty gravel lot cast a yellow-orange glow across white clapboards that hadn't seen a paintbrush in a few years. I assumed that most of the congregation was too far past their prime to keep up with the maintenance.

"I remember this place," Lee said as we approached. "When you first mentioned it, I wasn't sure if you were talking about this one or the one that's about ten miles north of here. When Diana was alive she'd drag me out here a couple times a year. She used to attend when she was a kid."

"Did you ever see any ghosts when you were here?" I asked.

"If there were any lurking while I was alive I didn't notice them, and I've never seen one hanging out here since I've been dead. But I certainly don't come to hang out on the regular."

"So, this is probably just a waste of time." Since we were already here, I went ahead and floated inside.

A single light shone above the wooden cross displayed on the back wall of the church and I was surprised to see a boy standing by a grouping of unlit candles. There were no cars in the parking lot so I'd assumed the place would be deserted. Maybe he'd walked? I had just realized that the light cast a shadow for everything but the boy when Lee spoke up.

"Thomas?"

"Thomas? Thomas as in the Arapahoe kid we've been looking for for weeks?"

"Mister Bradley?" the boy asked, turning towards us. He was older than I'd first thought, but still young in that weird preadolescent way where his body was composed of gangly limbs and sharp angles. What a terrible age to be stuck in for eternity. He looked my way. "What do you mean Arapahoe? My mom was Apache."

I smacked at Lee's arm for not getting the details correct. I couldn't hurt him but it made me feel better.

"It's been a while, I was close." Lee shrugged.

I closed my eyes and bit my tongue. We had bigger fish to fry.

"Well, kid, Gerri and I were out investigating because there's been some talk about a ghost haunting the church." Lee waved his hand in Thomas's direction.

"Oh," he said. His dark eyebrows drew together. "I didn't mean to scare anyone. I don't think I moved anything too much," he said looking around. "I was just trying to straighten it up a little."

"It's okay, kiddo. Trust me, as far as supernatural things to find in a church go, you're the least scary thing we could have imagined."

"What do you mean?" he asked. "What kind of scary things? I've never seen any scary things out here."

"Oh, do I have some stories for you," Lee replied. "But nothing you need to worry about right now. What are you doing out here? How long have you been haunting this place and why a church in the middle of nowhere?"

"I don't know, I've been hanging out here for a few years, I guess. I stay out at a ranch nearby most of the time, I like the horses. But this church, they have pretty music sometimes and I like to sing.

My little dead heart grew three sizes.

"Hi," I said, moving forward a few steps and giving a little wave. "My name is Gerri and I'm, uh, well, recently deceased, I guess. Lee here has been showing me how this whole ghost thing works, but I understand you've got more practice at it than he does?"

"Yeah, I guess you could say that." It was hard to tell in the near darkness, but his voice sounded like he was smiling when he replied.

"Great, it's always good to have an expert ghost on the

team. I understand that you like to keep to yourself, and this is going to sound really weird, but Lee told me about you a few months ago and I've been searching for you ever since. My sister and I would like to track down your family but there's a lot we don't know and we've kind of hit a dead end, so to speak. It would be really helpful if we could ask you some questions about them. I mean," I added, "that's assuming that you actually want to find your mom and sister. Because if you don't, that's fine too. We weren't sure and I didn't know how to contact you." I was rambling but it had taken us so long to find him that I didn't want to scare him away.

"My mom?" he paused, seeming a little stunned. He quickly got over it. "You're looking for my mom? Is she alive? Do you know where she went? Are you a detective?"

"I mean, I'm not like a licensed PI or anything, but I think we can track her down if we knew more about her family. The real question is, is she still alive? It's been, what, twenty-two years since... she left." I'd almost said since you were murdered, but changed my mind at the last second. It was best not to dwell on the bad stuff. "I mean, I don't know for sure, but I figure there's a good chance they're still alive somewhere"

"I know you like your peace and quiet, and if you'd like to find them, you don't even have to come back into town with us if you don't want to. I'm sure Gerri can ask you questions here and then go back to her sister and have her type it all into their fancy little computer and see what they can find."

"A computer? I've seen them around, but aren't they just for typing and playing games? How can you find my mom with a computer?"

"Well, there's this new thing called the internet and there is like, so much information on it, and more and more gets added every day. We'd just need some basic stuff from you like maybe your grandparents' names or if you can remember what town they lived in. Any old memories about them or where they lived would help. We can even have Pansy—that's my sister—set the Atlas out and we can work out how to get there and back so we can go look for them."

"I never thought I'd be able to find them," he said, his voice almost a whisper. "I didn't know how to get to my grandma's house. I knew it was south, and I tried a few times to go there, but could never see anything that looked familiar. I was really little the last time we'd gone down to the reservation. Once, I got lost and it took me two weeks to find Perth again. I was... honestly, I was too scared to leave again, after that."

"There's never a road map with a big You Are Here arrow on it when you need it, is there?" I said, but I totally understood. When I first came back, I'd been terrified that I'd float out too far and then not be able to figure out how to get back home. It made me wonder how many ghosts were out there, miles from home without access to a map.

"But what if Bobby already found them? He wouldn't need a computer, he always found her when she'd ran away, before. When I came back, I didn't know what had happened. I watched the house but no one ever came home. I didn't know if they'd been safe or not. When I met Mr. Bradley, he was the one who told me Mom and Bethy had packed up and moved. What if Bobby found them again?"

"Did you not tell him that Bobby was dead?" I yelled at Lee, waving my hands for emphasis.

Lee tilted his head to one side, his thinking pose. "I'm not sure. It was about twelve years after the murder when I first met young Thomas here, I think I just assumed that he already knew." I could barely make out Lee's shrug in the darkness.

"Bobby's dead?"

"Yeah, you two kind of killed each other." I watched him closely to make sure that this tidbit of info wasn't going to poof him, but he seemed stable. "So, they were safe. From him at least." I mean, they could have been hit by a bus the next day, but now was not the time for existential doom and gloom. "Again, if you want, we'd be happy to help you look for them."

"But we've got that thing at the Firefly tomorrow morning," Lee said.

"Yeah, assuming Pansy talked Chandra into it, I want to be there to see if he falls for it." I turned back to Thomas. "Okay, so we've got to go follow a guy in Perth in the morning and, well, we're trying to set a trap for him."

"Is he a bad guy?"

"Ninety-nine percent chance, yes. So, we're going to follow him in the morning to make sure he falls for it, and that he doesn't hurt anyone else. If the trap works, he'll be in jail by tomorrow night. I can get Pansy to search online for your family then."

"I don't understand, how will your sister be able to help us? Is she a ghost too?"

"No," Lee said. "Gerri's twin, Pansy, has just enough paranormal *oomph* that she can still see and talk to Gerri. It comes in really handy when you're trying to get things done, I promise."

"Speaking of Pansy, she's part of a group of people who investigate paranormal events, which is why we're here tonight. Like, scoping it out. The entire group is going to be here Saturday night with a bunch of cameras and stuff, and it's up to you. If you want to make it haunted, we could, like, put on a whole show for them. Or, if you don't want anyone to know that you're here, that's fine too. We'll just keep it quiet and pretend you're not here. But just so you know, if we go the haunted route, then there might be a whole bunch of weirdos who show up to try to get you on film themselves. Which could be fun, but also annoying after a while."

There was a long pause as the kid processed this. "A few

weeks ago, one of the church ladies came in one evening and was waving a bunch of sticks around. They were smoking really bad, and I thought she was going to set the church on fire. She kept mumbling about cleaning stuff the whole time. Is that the kind of weirdo you mean?"

"Yeah," I said, nodding. "That's exactly the kind of weirdo." I almost asked him if the smoke smelled like sage, but luckily as I opened my mouth, I remembered that we couldn't smell. I was proud that I hadn't said the words out loud.

Thomas was silent, which I figured meant his brain was stuck on a loading screen—it was hard to tell in the near darkness.

"You know what, maybe, we'll worry about all of that later. Our plan this evening was just to swing by really quick and see if we found any ghosts, and hey, what do you know, we found you. Then we were going to go look for a different ghost in this bar down in New Mexico. Do you want to go with us?" I doubted he had more important ghost business scheduled for the evening.

"How far away is that?"

"Well, it's about forty-five minutes if you're driving but probably twenty, twenty-five minutes flying now that I know where I'm going."

"That's a great idea," Lee added. "It'll be easier to split the search up three ways. We'd appreciate the help."

I was glad that my facial expression was hidden by the darkness. Lee Bradley being all kind and stuff?

"And you know how to get back home?" Thomas asked, still unsure.

"Absolutely," I assured him. "We have to be back by, what do you think Lee? Five?"

"Yeah, I wouldn't give him any longer than that in case he's an early riser. We'll tail him all day and then make sure we're in position to send the calvary when he breaks into the diner tonight."

"Wow," Thomas said, his head swiveling between Lee and I. "You guys are awfully busy for ghosts."

You're telling me, kid.

15

Our trio of not-so-scary ghosts flew south, crossing Perth and San Isidro Creek, following Sepulveda towards New Mexico. "Have you met Christopher?" Thomas asked me as we passed Mrs. Garcia's house.

"Oh, yeah. You could say that." Ignoring Lee's chuckle, I filled Thomas in on our adventures with Christopher and his final moments on this plane.

"What do you mean he went poof?" That slightly panicked tone was back.

"I mean, like, poof. Gone. Now you see him, now you don't." I moved closer to the ground to get a better view. It was pitch black with only the barest sliver of moon and the two-lane was deserted.

"Do you think he went to heaven?" Thomas asked.

"I would hope so," Lee answered. "Or at least somewhere safe where he can enjoy himself. Poor kid was dead longer than he lived, and from what I saw, he didn't have a lot of fun in either state."

"I didn't realize that we could change. I thought we just... were."

We finally popped out on a road labeled NM 72, and as we moved closer to town, I explained our friend Christine's theory about guilt holding us here, and how relieving that guilt could make us move on, wherever that may be. Thomas was quiet, obviously thinking it over as we approached town.

"We'll start at the bar," I said, leading the way. We were still floating over a few of the outlying houses that surrounded the town, rundown ranches and one old farm house that I'd assumed was abandoned, but tonight the light of a television set flickered through the curtains.

We entered The Wild Dawg and I was relieved to see that there wasn't a live band. At least we wouldn't be assaulted with bad country music the entire time we were here. I waved my hand, indicating that they should follow me, and made my way behind the bar to the small office storeroom. "Here," I said, pointing to the photo of Gene on Fiona's desk. "This is the guy we're looking for. Or, the ghost of the guy we're looking for. You know what I mean."

"He looks like a criminal," Lee observed.

I couldn't disagree. "Well, he owned a bar in the middle of nowhere. What better place for illegal things to go down, right?" I mean, I watched movies. I could instantly imagine three or four other things they could be selling out here besides beer and tequila.

"Who's she?" Thomas asked, pointing at Fiona.

"This is the wife of the man who may be a ghost. She wants to ask him some questions and she told Randy that she thinks he's haunting the place, but I think she's lying. I think she just wants Pansy to do the seance."

"Seance? Isn't that," he leaned closer to whisper the words. "Devil worshiping stuff?"

"Umm, no. No, we accidentally found out that Pansy has a

real knack for talking to spirits, she just needs a little bit more help if it's anyone but me."

"What does she want to ask him?"

"I have absolutely no idea. She was kind of vague about what it was she needed to know, just that she had some questions for him." If she got too pushy I guess we could always borrow Bagel's Ouija board and I could pretend to be him and we could make some stuff up. Was it dishonest? Yes. But as I watched Fiona chain smoke her way through her next Virginia Slim, I thought it may be an option if we couldn't get her to give up on this idea. I mean, Pansy could push the planchette around herself and Lee and I could move stuff around the room to make it look authentic. If Pansy flunked out of college, we could always join the circus and take our show on the road.

"So, where do you want to start?" Lee asked.

"How about we just split it all into three. It's late enough that there shouldn't be a whole lot of living people up and about. I'm sure these people need to get up and go to work in the morning so they'll be in bed."

"Thomas, do you understand what we're trying to do?"

"Yeah, I think I understand. Look for the guy in the picture, right? Or his ghost at least?"

"Yeah, there's no question about him being dead, we just don't know if his ghost came back or not. If you see his ghost, you don't need to talk to him or anything. We just need to know that he exists in, like, a spectral kind of way."

We split up, Lee taking the houses to the north of town, me to the east including the trailer park, and Thomas took the south. Unsurprisingly, we found nothing.

"I had a bunch of people sleeping, one guy that I thought was going to die because he stopped breathing every third breath, and a few people who watched TV in their underwear that I absolutely did not need to see," I reported back.

"I didn't see anything that looked like a ghost," Thomas said.

"In all honesty," Lee muttered, "would you want to haunt this town?"

"There is less to do here than in Perth," I agreed. "There's not even a gas station to break up the monotony."

"What are we going to do next?" Thomas asked, seemingly eager to continue the search.

"Well, now that that's marked off the list, let me show you Fiona and Gene's house." A few moments later we arrived at Casa Dale and unsurprisingly, the yard was still a mess and the inside was untouched. Nothing had changed except maybe there was an extra bag on top of the pile on the couch? Honestly, I couldn't tell.

"Wow, this place is a mess," Thomas said looking around at the piles and piles of bags.

"Hey now, kiddo, the lady has been through some stuff. She just lost her husband and she's trying to run a business on her own. She probably has more important things to do than clean her house." Lee said.

"My mom used to clean people's houses. I remember her talking about how dirty some people could be. She said they were lazy."

"Well, there's lazy and then there's overwhelmed, but we're not here to judge her. We're looking for the husband. Gerri, where do you want us to start?"

I pointed towards the master bedroom and the pair followed me. "Now, Fiona said he had a girlfriend two towns over. I haven't had time to get Pansy to look in the atlas yet. I was kind of busy today, but if you see anything that looks like something he may have hidden, something with an address on it, or a phone number scribbled down, that may be a clue." I mean, it was too much to hope that we'd find a pink envelope with a lipstick imprint and a return address on it, but maybe we'd find something interesting.

The only light in the room was the red glow of the alarm clock, so I flipped the light switch. The light on the overhead ceiling fan casting a dull yellow glow over the contents of the room. Thomas floated in the middle of the room, staring up at the inch and a half of dust gathered on the fan blades. Cleaning ceiling fans had been one of my chores at home and I briefly wondered if anyone had done it in the months since I'd been dead. *Ours may look just as bad,* I thought, making a mental note to check them when I got home.

We searched the bedroom and Lee began opening drawers while I did my best to search under the bed without a flashlight. There was nothing but a cat and some dust bunnies as far as I could tell, so I quickly moved on to the adjoining bathroom. The counter there was also piled high with random stuff, but it looked like that tub was cleaned and the toilet didn't look like a hazmat area. I guess she had that going for her.

I knew from the first trip that the room on the other side of the bathroom was what I assumed had been Gene's office. A giant maple desk and leather chairs took up the center of the room, and the walls were lined with shelves stuffed with books and various odds and ends. It was a clutter free zone. A giant Navajo rug covered the hardwood floors and even the mantel held only a deer skull and a pair of candlesticks that looked like birch logs.

I started looking through the shelves examining each book to see if there was anything stuffed between the pages; a piece of paper, an envelope, anything like that. Lee came in and started going through the desk drawers. The three of us searched the room for a good ten minutes before finally calling it quits. We hadn't found anything unusual, just some old ledgers from the bar, business paperwork, and old tax forms—

stuff that you would expect a business owner to have. Nothing jumped out at us as being unusual or related to an affair.

We searched the rest of the house, not quite as thoroughly as the bedroom or the office, but poked and prodded for other clues that might help us find this guy's ghost. Based solely on the photo Fiona kept on her desk, I couldn't imagine he was the type to feel guilty enough over anything that his spirit would hang around for eternity. But again, I needed to work on being so judgmental, I reminded myself.

We reconvened in the backyard and I was eyeballing the shed, wondering if it was worth my time and effort to come back in the daytime to see what was inside, when one of my furry little friends came rolling out from under the back deck.

"Oh look, a raccoon." Thomas immediately floated over to get a better look.

"Oh!" So, not rats, thank goodness. "Aww, he's a round little thing, isn't he?"

"It's probably a momma," Thomas said, floating over to the hole in the lattice work under the deck. "She probably has babies around somewhere that she's going out to feed."

The thought of seeing baby raccoons made me squeal a little bit, and I floated through the lattice to see if I could hear anything. Bingo, there they were, multiple purring chirps coming from somewhere against the foundation. I was definitely coming back in the daylight. Too bad Pansy was going to miss out on this.

"If you two are done harassing the wildlife, I think it's time to go back home. Even if this guy did end up a ghost, he's not going to hang around here."

"Well, worst case scenario, when Pansy does the seance nothing will happen." I turned to Thomas to explain. "Every time we've done it before, the candles do this weird thing where they almost go out when she calls their name. So, if they stay lit then we can be fairly certain that he's not on this side. Pansy just wanted to know so she could prepare herself."

"And while I'd love to see the woman who would agree to be Gene's girlfriend," Lee said, "without an address or even knowing which town she lives in, we're just going to have to let that drop. Going into a seance blind won't kill her. I suggest we head home to keep an eye on Donnie."

I had to agree, snooping through Fiona and Gene's lives was entertaining, but we had more pressing matters at the moment. Besides, we wouldn't have to deal with the Dales until August. We had plenty of time.

16

"Hold up, you two." We weren't more than five minutes out of Berry when Lee stopped, hovering over the highway in front of a reflective green road sign advising that the town of Raton was fifteen miles west.

"What's up?" I asked, floating back towards where he was framed in the lighting of the sign, Thomas right on my heels.

"Thomas, do you ever remember your mother mentioning which reservation she grew up on? Jacarillo, Mescalero, Fort Sill, White Mountain? Do any of those sound familiar?"

Thomas thought for a moment before shaking his head. "No, I remember Bobby would call her an Apache, he... he said it like it was a bad word. But Mom never talked about her family. None of those sound familiar."

"What are you plotting?" I asked Lee.

"Well, I did a story out on the Jicarilla Apache Reservation once, it was, I don't know, '68 or '69. But they were right off of Highway 64." He gestured towards the sign and I could see that he expected me to put some part of a puzzle together but I had no idea where he was going with this. He must have realized I was clueless, so he continued with a sigh. "US-64 meets up with I-25 in Raton, follows it south for a bit, and then breaks off going west toward the reservation. What if I escort Thomas over to the rez and we have a look around, see if he sees anything that looks familiar?"

"You mean like, right now?"

"No time like the present. We're already halfway there. It's what, three? Three-thirty in the morning? Donnie isn't going to do anything but wait at the Firefly to talk to your friend Chandra. Besides, I can't imagine that this will take too long, either the boy will recognize things or he won't. Unless you want to go with him and I'll go back to watch Donald?"

And miss watching Chandra lure him into a trap? Was he on crack? The half smile he was trying to hide told me that he knew exactly how nosy I was and which option I would choose.

"You're right. Splitting up makes sense, but you guys need to be back before tomorrow night. Assuming this all works, I'll need your help catching Donnie."

"Oh, you know I wouldn't miss that. What do you think, Thomas?"

"Are you sure that you can follow the bad guy by yourself?" he asked me. "We can wait if you need help."

"No, no, you guys go ahead. Maybe you'll get lucky. Pansy goes into work at eleven, so when you get back, go watch over her and I'll keep checking in so that we can meet back up."

"Works for me, let's go see what we can see, kid." We all stayed together for another few miles until we reached the road that would eventually run into Sepulveda. I paused to watch the two of them float away into the darkness before turning north and decided to swing by Mrs. Garcia's along the way. I could knock her off the day's to-do list before I stopped to talk to Pansy.

For the second day in a row, I was visiting too early, even for Mrs. Garcia, and she was snoring in her recliner exactly where I expected her to be. She'd made some nice progress on her latest blanket, another five rows as far as I could tell, and as I watched her snore I thought about her day to day existence. It was almost as lonely as Thomas'. Maybe Thomas would be open to haunting Mrs. Garcia instead of the church? But we hadn't even explained the situation to the pastor yet, so we should probably wait to see if they actually wanted their resident ghost evicted or not.

Pansy was also snoring when I floated into our bedroom, and as much as I hated to wake her up at the butt crack of down, I wanted to get back to Donnie before he woke up. "Hey, wake up real quick. I need to give you the rundown."

"Hmmmph?" came the grumble from under the covers.

"We found Thomas last night."

She bolted upright and turned on the bedside lamp before shoving her hair out of her face. "Oh my god, where?"

"Well, funny story, he's the ghost haunting the church you guys are going to investigate Saturday. So, you can tell Randy and Greg that it's haunted but it's up to them if they really want to drag out all of the bells and whistles." There was no point in setting up cameras and recorders when the ghost in question could be interviewed directly. Or, close to directly, anyway.

Pansy grunted as she rubbed the sleep out of her eyes. She was also nodding her head, so I knew she was processing what I was telling her even if she was still mostly nonverbal.

"So, Lee and I ghostnapped him and took him with us to go look for Gene down in Berry."

She rolled her eyes as she processed that one. "Any luck?"

"No, there's no sign of ghost Gene anywhere."

"Okay."

"Lee took Thomas to go look over the Jicarilla reservation in New Mexico to see if anything looks familiar and I'm on my way to the Cowboy Lodge to watch Donnie. Did Chandra agree to set him up?"

"Yeah, she was in. She was excited to put on a show this morning."

"Good. Then I'll come back to fill you in on how she did once that whole shebang is over."

Pansy grunted again, still squinting, but maybe she'd remember most of this conversation in a few hours when her alarm went off. I reached over to turn the light back off. "Go back to sleep, I'll talk to you in a few hours."

She snuggled back into her pillow. "Okay, be careful. Love you."

She was definitely not fully awake. "Love you too, dork," I whispered as she resumed her snoring.

Donnie was also snoring, but he made sounds like a diesel engine that was about to break down, not the cute little snorts that Pansy made. He also slept with the bathroom light on, and I could make out Summer's address book laying on the nightstand like it was bedtime reading.

According to the LCD display of the alarm clock, I managed to hang out in his disgusting motel room for a grand total of three minutes. Since the noises he was making made me slightly insane, I moved to the parking lot to camp out in the electric lines. I could watch the door to his motel room from there and get some peace and quiet.

I was still vegging out, watching a robin work on its nest that was tucked into the giant metal sign that held the waving neon cowboy, when I saw the overhead light come on in his room. After a few more minutes, Donnie finally made an appearance, carrying his battered suitcase out to the truck and shoving it into the backseat before meandering toward the front office. This got my attention. Was he leaving? Settling up his bill? Why now?

I flew down to check out his room, and while it was still mostly trashed—garbage everywhere and the bed still unmade —all of Donnie's personal things had been removed. I made it to the office just as Donnie was handing over a wad of cash. What was his plan? Had he found some clue in Summer's address book? Was he heading straight for some other town? Was he going to stop and question Chandra first? If Chandra didn't tempt him to break in tonight, would he give up and move on? Would that be good? He'd get away with the break-in, but he'd be gone and everyone else would be safe. Unless he came back. Should we call it off? Catching him red-handed might make him even more determined to harass the PPS members once he was out again. But letting him get away with destroying everything Summer owned wouldn't be right, either.

He turned the ignition key and revved the engine a few times before roaring out of the parking lot. His rear tires flung dirt and gravel everywhere, including directly into the other two cars sitting in the lot.

What a jerk.

Our luck held and I followed Donnie to the Firefly where the early morning crowd was beginning to clear out. Donnie slid into a booth. His patchy facial hair hadn't been shaved in a day or two and his hair looked even greasier than it had yesterday, like he'd sweat all night. Maybe the air conditioning in his room hadn't been working.

He pulled a car magazine from his back pocket and ordered an omelet and a cup of coffee. The waitress was working her way around the room refilling coffee cups and the bus boy was clearing plates when I saw the white Saturn pull up at the curb. Chandra worked such long hours that Shawn normally dropped her off and picked her up when she finished up at night. Chandra was still tying her apron as she came through the door, and she stopped to greet some regulars, eyeballing Donnie all the while. After making sure that everyone was happy and well-fed, she moved on to her primary objective.

"Hi," she said, approaching Donnie's booth. "I'm Chandra, how was everything this morning? Can I get you anything else? More coffee?" she waved her hand in the general direction of his almost empty cup.

"No. I mean, no more coffee, food was fine. But you're Chandra? Hey, let me ask you a question real quick—you're part of that group of people who hunt ghosts, aren't you?"

"I sure am," Chandra told him. "It's called the Perth Paranormal Society. How did you hear about us?"

"Well, I saw something in the paper last time I came through here. I'm a traveling salesman, the name's Don Bisbee."

Dude, what was this, like your fourth last name? I doubted he was smart enough to keep track of which last name he'd told people so I wasn't sure why he thought using so many was a good plan.

"There was a picture in the article that I was reading, and what I noticed first off was that and one of the women in it, well, it looked like a girl that I went to high school with. I thought I'd stop by and see if I could reconnect with her."

"Really?" Chandra asked. "The only other woman in the group is Summer, but I'm not really sure where she went to high school."

"Well, her name wasn't Summer back then, but maybe she changed it along the way. She was always kind of hippie dippy, if you know what I mean."

"Well, that sounds about right," Chandra said with a laugh.

"So, I was actually talking to your waitress yesterday, and understand that, uh, Summer, she's been out of town. I was wondering if I could leave a letter with you, you being friends with her and all. That way you could get it to her, if you don't mind."

"Oh, I wouldn't mind at all. In fact, you know, I got a postcard from her the other day. I think I left it somewhere on the desk back in my office." She jerked a thumb back towards the kitchen. "I'll have to see if there is a return address on it and then maybe I can just forward that letter for you."

Chandra was winning awards for best actress, in my opinion. I was impressed.

"Oh yeah that would be great," Donnie said. "I'd really appreciate it if you could get that to her. She was always a super sweet girl and I'd love to reconnect. I'll be sure to get that letter to you tomorrow."

"Well, in that case, I'll look for that postcard tonight."

"I surely do appreciate it. And this omelet was fantastic by the way. Thought you should know."

"Well, thank you. If you need anything else you just let me know."

As Chandra turned toward the kitchen I kept an eye on Donnie. Had he fallen for it?

His smile had fallen away as he twisted in his booth to look at each corner of the restaurant. I realized that he was looking for security cameras and the cold look on his face told me that he was already plotting.

Yep, she had him, hook, line, and sinker.

17

Pansy was eating a bowl of cereal in front of the TV when I got home. Donnie had set up shop in the corner phone booth and was busy running up the balance on his long-distance phone card as he placed calls to everyone in Summer's address book. He'd bummed a pen from Chandra before he'd left the restaurant and was checking off names like it was his job. It seemed like he'd be there for a while, so I'd floated over the ravine and through our neighborhood to home, where Pansy was chowing down on Captain Crunch.

"What are you watching?"

"Infomercials. I thought you were following Donnie this morning?"

"He's going through Summer's address book right now, so I popped over to give you an update. He's packed up his bags and has checked out of the motel. I think he was planning on leaving, but Chandra put on quite the show this morning so I think he's going to stick around."

"Did I hear you right this morning? You found Thomas and Lee took him to a reservation to see if it looked familiar?"

"Yep, you heard that right. Maybe we'll get lucky and he'll find his family and then we can mark that off our list."

"But what if he poofs?" Pansy asked around a mouthful of cereal. "What if guilt about not knowing where they are or if they're okay is what's holding him here. What if he poofs as soon as he sees them?"

I hadn't thought about the poofing issue, and I liked the kid. Would wanting him to stick around for a little longer be considered selfish? He'd been lingering here all by himself for so many years, maybe he'd be happy to move on. Had I explained the poofing to him well enough that he understood that the end of this quest may result in his no longer being here? I'd have to make sure he understood, unless he was already gone.

"I don't know and there's nothing I can do about it at this moment, so I'll worry about it later. Right now, I'm going to go back and keep an eye on our suspect for the rest of the day. If we're lucky, he'll be in jail by midnight."

"You're putting an awful lot of faith in our luck."

"Luck is what you make it. Besides, we have three ghosts helping out, it's not like we're going to lose him."

"Pansy, what time do you need to be at work?" Mom came downstairs and immediately to the kitchen where she began to pack her lunch for work.

"Eleven."

"Shouldn't you be dressed then? And don't you dare leave that bowl in this sink. I already started the dishwasher this morning."

"Yes, ma'am."

"You have...two...messages," the electronic voice on the answering machine announced as Mom hit the play button. The first was a hang up, the second however, was a very familiar voice.

"Miss Bellafini, this is Fiona Dale. I've thought about the time frame that man with the PPS gave me and that is just not going to work for me. If you can call me back, I'd like to offer you a considerable sum of money to move our appointment to this weekend. I don't even need all of the cameras and whatever else it is that you people do, I just need for you to perform a seance so I can ask my husband a few questions. It won't take long at all and waiting until August is absolutely ridiculous. I will not take no for an answer, young lady. I always get my way so I need you to return my call."

She was giving her phone number when Mom stormed into the living room. "I'm sorry, this strange woman on our answering machine wants you to do what? Did I hear her use the word seance in a sentence?"

Crap.

Pansy just stared at her, her spoon halfway to her mouth and her Crunch Berries falling one-by-one back into the bowl. Her eyes had the look of a deer right before a sixteen-wheeler barreled down on it.

"I'm not leaving until you give me an answer. What is this woman talking about? Why does she think you can do a seance?"

"Well," Pansy said, drawing the word out to stall while she set her bowl on the end table. "Do you remember when that lady showed up here, the one that could see Gerri?"

"I'm not likely to forget it."

"She is, like, one of the most well-known psychic mediums in the country. She communicates with ghosts who don't want to talk to her by doing a seance. It pulls them out and makes them, I don't know. It, like... freezes them. It forces them to tell the truth even if they don't want to."

"And this woman wants you to contact Mrs. Hermance?"

"Oh. No. See, it turns out that I also have this, ability I guess you'd call it. She taught me how to perform one safely."

"Perform one? Perform a seance?" Mom's voice went up with every word and was quickly approaching tones that only dogs could hear. "You've been hanging out with that yoga witch, and now you're performing seances. Next, you're going to tell me that you've been messing around with a Ouija board."

Pansy shot a dirty look at me when I started cackling. "Well not me. You'll actually want to talk to your other daughter about those."

Mom mouthed the word 'what' and clutched one hand over her heart. I could see that she was wondering where she'd gone wrong.

"Look, you have to admit that we are in a very unique situation here. Gerri is a ghost. I can see and hear her. We've kind of moved beyond regular means of communication, wouldn't you agree."

Look at Pansy over there being all commonsensical and stuff. I could see Mom wavering. Obviously, so could Pansy, because she kept talking.

"We're adults, mom. It's not like we're little kids messing around with stuff that we don't understand."

I mean, speak for yourself, but okay.

"We're always careful and besides, we have full grown adults that know how to do all of this helping us. Was it scary the first time? Yes, absolutely. But not everyone can do this and I can, so that has to mean that it's something that I'm supposed to be doing, right?"

Mom deflated into Dad's recliner. "I just worry about you. Both of you. My world had a lot less unknowns a year ago. And this guy being in town, and now this woman, who, quite frankly, sounds like a lunatic. I just... I feel like there's so much I don't know and I don't understand and I don't know how to keep you safe."

Pansy left the couch to go wrap Mom in a hug. "I know. I love you, too. But you have to trust us."

"At least you still have one another. I don't understand the how and why of it all, but it gives me comfort."

"Gerri loves you too. We'll be okay. We're together."

Hopefully for a while yet.

I went back to hover over Donnie, flying around in circles until he ran out of money on his long-distance card. He'd only made it to the M's in Summer's address book. I looked down the block to the bank sign at the corner and realized that I'd been watching him try to sweet talk information out of people for the better part of two hours. He had some colorful curses as he slid the card back in his wallet, slipping it and the address book into the worn back pocket of his dirty jeans.

I hovered over the street as he got into his truck, but we didn't go very far. Just up to Sycamore Plaza where he made a loop, hesitating as he passed Pansy's Tracker, before finding himself a little spot at the end of the lot by the exit. As far as plans went, I was okay with this one as it allowed me to watch both Donnie and Pansy at the same time.

Pansy was less thrilled to see Donnie walk through the front doors of Canyon Lanes, and he seemed startled when he noticed that she was staring him down. He quickly made his way to the other end of the building, sitting at the end of the empty bar. As a place to hide, it didn't offer much cover unless he created a wall of drink menus.

"He called a bazillion people and no one had heard from Summer since she left."

"So why is he back here?" Pansy muttered under her breath as she filled someone's drink order from the soda fountain.

"I don't know. Since he checked out of the motel, maybe he just needs a place to hang out until tonight. More importantly, I don't care because this means I get to hang out with yooouuu." I batted my eyelashes at her, just to annoy her. It worked.

"Here you go, sir. Have a nice day." Pansy handed the paper cup of soda over to the waiting customer and came back to where I was floating next to the soda machine, her back to the counter so no one could see her talking to me. "Has Lee made it back yet?"

"Not yet. I hope that means that they've found something and not that they're lost."

"I can't imagine Lee getting lost," she whispered.

I started to make a comment about the old man's knowledge of the tri-state area when I noticed someone coming up to the counter.

Well, well, well. This should be interesting.

"Customer coming," I said to my sister.

She turned, her smile faltering for only a second when she saw who it was. "Hello, what can I get for you?" To a stranger she would have sounded perfectly pleasant, but there was an edge to her voice that I knew meant she was nervous.

"Hi, yeah. Sorry to bother you but didn't I see you on the news? Aren't you a part of that ghost hunting group?"

"Yep, sure am."

"Oh, I think that sounds so cool." He pushed the fall of stringy blond hair out of his face and gave her what I imagined he thought of as his most disarming grin. Maybe he'd been good looking once, but the bags under his eyes and lack of dental hygiene weren't working in his favor.

"Do you know a woman named Summer? I think she's a part of that group."

"Sure do."

I guess he expected her to say something else because there was an awkward silence while they both stared at one another.

"Yeah, so I was hoping to see her while I was here but it seems like she's out of town. Would you know where I might be able to reach her?"

"Nope, no idea. Can I get you anything?" She gestured towards the menu on the wall behind her.

"Oh, oh yeah. Sure, can I get a Sprite and some cheese fries?"

Pansy keyed the order into the cash register and was straightening the wad of bills Donnie had pulled from his pocket when we noticed a commotion at the front desk.

"Never mind, I see her." The rasp of Fiona's voice carried even over the canned music and the clatter of pins bouncing off the hardwood. *What on earth?*

"There you are," she said, tossing her purse up onto the glass concession counter with a thunk. She was wearing head to toe leopard print today, skin tight hot pants and a flowing blouse with peasant sleeves. She was perfectly camouflage for a zoo exhibit. "I need you to do this seance for me," she said, pausing to rummage around in her red patent leather bag. "How much?" She slammed a checkbook covered in matching red leather onto the countertop and clicked her ink pen a few times, long red talons shining.

"How much what?" Pansy and I said at the same time.

"How much for you to do the seance tonight. I really need this to be done and over with."

"Seance?" Donnie asked, looking back and forth between Fiona and Pansy. He looked as confused as I felt.

"Hang on, Mrs. Dale, let me get his order in." Pansy walked

the ticket over to the kitchen pass through and then pulled a paper cup from the stack.

"Is this woman crazy?" I asked.

Pansy just snorted as she filled the cup with ice and Sprite. "Here you go, sir. Your fries will be out in just a minute." She turned to address Fiona. "Look, I don't have time to go all the way down to Berry right now. And it's not just me. If you recall, the PPS will need to film everything with different cameras and different kinds of film to see if they can find a way to detect spirits."

Donnie's eyes were open wider than I would have thought possible at this point.

"See, I was thinking about this. You said ghosts don't have to stay in one spot, so what difference does it make where we do it? I don't even need you to come down to the Wild Dawg—I'm here, you're here. How much do you make here? What, like five dollars an hour? I'll tell you what, I'll write you a check for a hundred dollars to just leave right now and we can go do this seance and get it over with."

I mean, I would have left. Pansy was a better person, though.

"Mrs. Dale, no one else is coming in to help at the counter until about six, so I can't leave. I wouldn't feel right taking your money anyway."

"Order up!"

All four of us turned to stare at the dude in the hairnet and the basket of cheese fries he'd placed in the window.

"One-hundred and fifty," Fiona said, tapping her pen against the counter.

"Take. The. Money," I said.

Pansy took the opportunity to retrieve the fries and slid them across the counter to Donnie. "There you go, sir. Napkins and utensils are at the end of the counter."

Donnie made his way to the end of the counter, gathering his plasticware and napkins while still shooting glances between Fiona and Pansy. To be fair, this was not a standard conversation one overheard at the bowling alley. After soaking his cheese fries in Tabasco, he ripped open the plastic fork with his teeth and dug in. Apparently, he had no intentions of moving out of ear shot.

"Mrs. Dale, I appreciate the faith you seem to have in my ability, but I really have something to do this evening and I don't have the things I'd need to perform a seance with me right now."

"Young lady, I don't think you understand who I am. I do not take no for an answer."

"And I don't think that you understand that I don't have time or enough people available to pull this off right now."

Both of their voices had raised in decibels and even the dude in the kitchen was looking out the window to see what was going on. The manager chick, Kim, was hustling over from the bar area.

"Hey, isn't that the lady from last night?" Thomas spoke about six inches behind me, scaring the crap out of me. I'd been so enthralled with the scene before me that I hadn't even noticed Lee and Thomas floating in.

"What's she doing here?" Lee asked. I knew when he finally noticed Donnie at the end of the counter shoving fries into his face because Lee's furry caterpillar eyebrows shot up another inch.

"She just showed up demanding that Pansy leave right now and go do the seance for her. She seriously thinks that she's all that and a bag of chips."

"How'd she even know where to find her? And is Donnie with her?"

"I don't know, and no, that's a coincidence. I kind of vaguely remember that she mentioned something about working at the bowling alley while we were at the bar, but who knows? Maybe Fiona stopped at the Firefly and Donna told her exactly how to get here. Either way, Donnie was already here trying to get info out of Pansy about Summer when she showed up. Chandra did great this morning, by the way. I'm a hundred percent sure that he's going to try to break in tonight. How did your adventure go last night?"

"Total bust. But he was really small when he was last at his grandmother's house. We covered every inch of the place but nothing stood out."

"Well, when we get Pansy home tonight maybe we'll have her get the atlas out and see how to get to the other reservations. Maybe we can get on the computer and see if we can find anything that way before we go stake out the Firefly."

"Looks like she might be busy," Thomas said.

I tuned back into the conversation between Pansy and Fiona in time to hear Pansy giving Fiona our home address.

What the what?

"I should be home a little after eight, meet me there and we'll do it. But I'm telling you, if he's moved on, nothing is going to happen."

"Well, I need you to make it happen. I'll see you at eight." Fiona tossed her pen and checkbook back into the bottomless purse and slung it over her shoulder.

Donnie had finished his fries and gave Pansy a quick glance, probably deciding that he knew how to find her if he wanted to, and followed Fiona out the door.

"Lee and Thomas are back," I told her. "We're going to follow Donnie and I'll meet you back at the house tonight for this seance, I guess. What are you thinking?"

"I might as well get it over with. Besides, I got her up to two-fifty."

Throwing my hands up into the air, I turned back to Lee. "Whatever. Come on, let's go keep an eye on Donnie and I'll tell you all about Chandra's great performance this morning."

I left Pansy talking to her boss about appropriate attitudes when speaking with customers, and followed the guys out to the parking lot. This was going to be a long day.

18

Donnie hadn't struck me as particularly shy, so I kind of assumed that he'd stop Fiona in the parking lot and strike up a conversation, but instead he slunk around the covered awning of the Sycamore Plaza shops and watched her get into her monster Caddy that she'd parked right up front in the handicap parking.

Jangling the change in his pocket, he waited for her to pull out before walking to his truck and following her out onto Main Street.

"Do you think he plans on following her?" Lee asked.

I shrugged, because at this point, I had no idea what was going on anymore. We followed Donnie and passed the Caddy that had illegally parked in front of The Firefly Cafe. Fiona was walking in the door, her purse bouncing off her right flank with each step. Donnie continued past Wild Harmony, the bank—where the sign told me that it was one forty-two in the afternoon and eighty-two degrees—and finally turned into the parking lot for the row of businesses in front of the Foodarama.

"What's he up to now?"

"Presumably," Lee said, nodding across the street to the police station. "He hasn't decided to turn himself in."

The three of us followed on his heels as he made his way to the front door of Konnect and pushed his way inside. A quarter til two on a Thursday wasn't exactly a busy time for the Internet cafe, and Donnie was the only person in the room. Donnie rang the bell by the register. The kid who ran the place, the twenty-something-year-old son of the guy who owned it, came out of the back room with a slice of pepperoni pizza in his hands.

"How long?" he asked Donnie, the slice held in his left hand while the right hand poised above the cash register.

"I figure half an hour should do it," Donnie replied.

"What is this place?" Thomas asked, looking around at the room full of computers. There were spaces set up on three walls and a row down the center where the spaces faced one another. A two-foot divider between each space broke up the individual spots and provided some measure of privacy. Framed sci-fi movie posters decorated the walls and a dusty blind covered the front window.

"It's called an internet cafe. People who don't have a computer at home, or who don't have access to the internet at home, can come here and use theirs for a price." I gave him a brief rundown on how computers worked and how it was connected through the phone lines to this magical thing called the World Wide Web. "So imagine all of these lines of information running from one spot to another, all around the world, and you can kind of picture it as a spider web."

Donnie pulled out another wad of crumpled bills and was rewarded with a scrap of paper with the password token to get online. We followed Donnie to an empty seat and watched as he logged in. The default homepage was now Yahoo, and Donnie immediately typed 'Wild Dawg Berry' into the search bar. I didn't think anything would come up as most of the internet was made up of college papers and research projects, but the local newspaper down there was now adding digital copies of their articles online. The top result was an article about a gunfight at the Wild Dawg Saloon in Berry, NM. This must be the fight Fiona had talked about, the one where her husband Gene had died.

Thomas was hovering over Donnie's other shoulder but Lee had disappeared into the back somewhere. "He's pulling up a newspaper article about the shooting that killed Gene," I announced, loudly enough for Lee to hear me, wherever he was.

"What happened to the guy he fought with?" came Lee's response from the back.

I looked the article over, waiting for Donnie to scroll down to the pertinent bits. Dude was a slow reader. "His name was Roger. Looks like he went to the hospital with a gunshot wound and died a few days later. I don't see anything about what started the fight. The final line of the piece says that county police have declined to comment at this time."

"Of course they did." Lee re-entered the main room to come and float behind Donnie with us. "We can have Pansy ask Fiona tonight. She can tell that old bat that it's necessary for her to know everything about how he died in order to call him forward."

"Because you're nosy?"

"Um, pot," he pointed toward me and then himself. "Kettle."

I shrugged.

"There's more," Thomas said, his nose a few inches from the screen now.

Donnie had scrolled down into the comment section where several people had left messages about how sad they were to hear about Gene's passing, how he was such a big part of the bar's personality, and finally one comment about how everyone knew that Gene and Roger had knocked over that bank down in Maxwell and that he was positive that their fight had been over the money.

"Bingo," Lee said.

Donnie immediately searched for 'bank robbery in Maxwell, NM' and was rewarded with an article written back in March about a bank robbery that had occurred during the early hours, before any customers were present. The suspects had managed to get away with almost five hundred thousand dollars. We were all silent as we waited for Donnie to catch up and scroll down to the comments, and sure enough, we weren't disappointed.

Once we were passed all of the comments offering thoughts and prayers for the souls of the criminals, we hit paydirt with the same commenter, Breadman63, saying again that everyone knew it was Roger and Gene up in Berry, going as far as to give the name of the bar in the comments. I had to wonder if the police ever read the comments on the newspaper articles, but then I thought about the police across the street with their IBM Selectric word processors and Smith-Corona electric typewriters. The Perth police station held one computer that I vaguely recall reading in the paper had been paid for with a grant. I'd never seen anyone use it. No, I decided. They had no idea what was on the internet.

"So, Gene and his good buddy Roger robbed a bank and then got into a fight at the bar, where they shot one another." Lee started to pace behind us. "So, what happened? They split the money but Roger spent his share?"

"Interesting," Donnie muttered to himself. He searched for Summer's name but came back with an article from the AP about Pansy and Bagel finding the body of Stuart Mayes. Summer had been mentioned in the article as owning the store and being a member of the ghost-hunting group. We already knew all of that.

"We'll see if Pansy can get anything out of Fiona tonight," I said. "What were you looking at in the back?"

"The kid who runs this place always looks stoned, and there's hardly ever anyone in here. I've suspected he had something illegal going on but hadn't actually bothered to float over here. So, I did a little investigating. He's turned one of the back rooms into a grow room for marijuana."

"He's growing pot directly across from the police station?" There was a thin line between bravery and stupidity.

"And selling it out the back door, if my hunch is right. I'd have seen if people were going in and out the front all day."

I was still processing that when Donnie logged off and left the building. After pausing on the sidewalk, he turned left and made his way back up the street to the Firefly. I could see that Officer Bias was out in the street arguing with Fiona about her parking job, and while Donnie did a full walk around the back of the buildings, Bias must have convinced her to park on the other side of the road.

"You guys got him? I'm going to go fill Pansy in on the bank robbery bit."

The two nodded, fascinated as Fiona stomped back across the street, cussing Bias the entire way. It was like dinner and a show for everyone inside The Firefly.

I floated back up to Sycamore Plaza but noticed Pansy's Tracker was no longer in the parking lot. I went inside the bowling alley, just in case she'd moved it, but the manager, Kim, was working the concession area and Pansy was nowhere to be seen. I did a quick sweep of Main St and the lot at Foodarama before crossing the east bridge and checking over at the Buffalo Chip. Food options were limited in Perth, we had to drive thirty miles just to get to a McDonalds, so it wasn't like there were a lot of places to check. As a last resort, I checked our house, and there was her Tracker parked at the curb.

I found her in the kitchen eating ice cream out of the container.

"What are you doing? I thought you had to work?"

"Well, that was the plan, but then I got fired."

"Fired? They fired you? For what?"

"Fiona. I wasn't professional enough with the customer."

"But she wasn't even a customer!"

Pansy slammed the spoon back down into the container of Rocky Road. "That's exactly what I said. Did Kim care? No, absolutely not."

"Oh. Well, since you're not at work, how about I go get Thomas and you can spend some time grilling him? He can be like, practice for your journalism career."

Pansy shoveled another lump of ice cream into her mouth while she thought it over. "Sure. Fine. Why not?"

"Great. I'll go get him and leave Lee to watch Donnie. Also, when I get back, remind me to tell you about the bank robbery."

I must have turned to leave before my words fully sank in, because I was already outside when I heard her yell, "Wait, what bank robbery?"

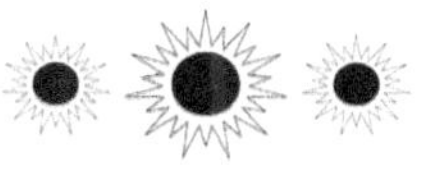

Pansy had the internet booted up and was sending out an email to Shawn, Randy, Greg, and Blake when we got back.

"What are you telling them?" I asked.

"Everything I know," she said, never taking her eyes off the screen as she typed. "Which, I have to tell you, is a great feeling. I didn't realize how stressful it was trying to solve things on our own. I am all for letting the adults pull their weight."

"Great, before you hit send, did you tell them about Thomas? We can save them a whole lot of time and effort on the church investigation. Thomas said he's never seen another ghost there. He is the sole haunter."

"I did mention that you'd found him but hang on, let me ask if they just want us to go talk to the pastor. You're right, there's no need to drag out cameras and monitors if we can avoid it."

"I'm imagining that conversation," I snorted. "Congratulations, it's a fourteen-year-old boy! Now, would you like to keep him? If not, he can go hang out somewhere else. He's open to other options."

Pansy snorted as she finished her email and hit send. "Okay, so is Thomas here?"

"Yep. We're ready when you are."

"Okay," Pansy pushed the keyboard away from her and picked up a notebook. Flipping to a fresh page, she pulled out a purple ink pen and scrawled her first question in her big loopy handwriting. Parent's full names. "We know this from the news article, Annamarie and Bobby Grayson. Thomas, do you know what your mom's maiden name was?"

"Her what?"

"What was her last name before she got married?"

He shrugged. I translated.

"Okay, how about your grandparents? Do you know what their names were?"

"I've been thinking about that since last night. I remember Granny Kay - she lived in South Dakota. She was Bobby's mom. She would come to see us at Christmas and he would pretend to be nice while she was there."

"Okay, so was Kay her first name or last name?" I asked.

He shrugged. Why was this never as easy as I thought it should be? "His dad's mom's name was Granny Kay, but he doesn't know if that was first or last name," I told Pansy. She wrote it down with a question mark in her notebook.

"No. Bobby wasn't my dad. He was Bethy's daddy. My dad died in the war."

"The war?" I thought being dead would exempt me from doing math, but here we were. "You would have been born in 1960, what war would that have been?"

He shrugged. "I don't know. Mom just told everyone that he died in a war. I never met him."

"Mmm-kay. Well, did she ever mention his name?"

He just shook his head and I decided that this line of questioning obviously wasn't going to find his mom.

"Okay, so Bobby isn't your Daddy and we can reasonably infer that your Mom would not have run to *his* mother after... the incident. Do you know what your mom's mother's name was? Did your mom have any brothers or sisters?"

"We called her Grandma Sarah but I'm not sure what her full name was. She lived on a reservation in New Mexico, I remember that. Mom met Bobby there and they moved to Perth when I was," he scrunched his nose up to think, "four of five, I think. He wasn't so bad then. He got a lot worse after Bethy was born."

"What about Aunts? Uncles?"

"She talked about her sister, Lulu, every once in a while. Usually when Bobby made her really sad."

I wanted to stab the guy myself for putting that look on this kid's face. I translated for Pansy and she continued taking notes.

Opening up WebCrawler, she typed Apache reservations in New Mexico into the search bar and we waited for the little hourglass to stop spinning in circles. The only result was someone's college paper on the indigenous tribes of New Mexico. "Oh, okay, this is doable," she said, skimming the paper.

"Do you think we should write to the councils and ask if they have any residents there by the name of Sarah who had daughters named Annamarie and Lulu?" I asked. I looked over at Thomas to see if he was excited by this prospect but he was staring at all of the posters on my side of the room. This was probably his first time in a teenage girl's bedroom.

"No, I think we should just show up and start asking around town. What exactly would I put into a letter? Hey, I have the ghost of Annamarie's son here and he'd love to know what happened to his mom and sister? They'd have me locked up for being crazy."

The idea had merit. "Do you happen to remember any really big landmarks?" I asked, giving it one last shot to narrow it down.

"There was sand and rocks."

"No, I mean, like roadside attractions. The world's biggest ball of yarn, the world's largest pat of butter, I don't know. Somewhere you'd stop every time you went to visit?"

"I think the biggest ball of yarn is actually in Kansas," Pansy supplied.

"Okay, but you know what I mean."

"I don't remember anything like that. We usually left in the morning and were there by afternoon."

"Okay, well, that's helpful." Sort of. "And we've already taken one place off the list. Tomorrow we'll check out one of the others." I sent Pansy downstairs to go get the Rand McNally atlas and together, the three of us worked out where the other reservations were and how to get there.

"That's a really far way to go," Thomas said quietly beside me as we watched Pansy scribble out the directions.

"Yeah, but Lee was a reporter. He drove all over the place when he was alive so it'll be a lot harder for him to get lost. He's got a pretty good mental map and I trust him. It'll be okay."

"Okay," he said, more to himself than me, as if he was trying to mentally psych himself up to travel out into the great big world.

Pansy stood and walked over to the telephone on her own desk.

"What kind of phone is that?" Thomas asked, the clear casing and brightly colored components seemed to catch his eye.

"It's just a regular phone, but instead of dialing, you push the buttons for each number you want to dial."

"I've seen that," he said, "but never one you could see through. Why is it like that?"

"Umm, duh. Because it's cool, dude." I used my very best Valley Girl accent and he looked even more confused. "Never mind, you'll get used to it. It's the 90s, we're trying to combat the absolute brownness that was the eighties. More color, more... pop, I guess you could say."

He blinked, twice. "Is that why there's poop on your shirt?"

"Poop? What? Oh," I started to laugh, the Green Day shirt I wore did indeed have a gigantic turd across the front. Most adults never gave it a second look or put it together that it was supposed to be poop. Kudos to this kid.

"Yeah, uh, Green Day is a band and the name of the album was Dookie, so, yeah, I thought it was really funny when I bought it," I explained. There were absolutely worse things to be wearing in the afterlife.

"Dario, yeah, hey, what are you doing tonight? Well, that lady I was telling you about, the one down in Berry, she showed up here and wants me to perform a seance for her. I need living people to make this happen and I'd rather not involve the parents if I can avoid it. Oh, also, Gerri and Lee found the ghost of that little boy we've been trying to find out more about. Yeah, they're going to go down to the Mescalero reservation in New

Mexico and see if they can find his family. Maybe they'll see something that will spark a memory and narrow it down."

"Dario is on his way over." Pansy hung up the phone and looked over at her computer which had just dinged. "Angie just replied to the email, she said she'll send Randy over at seven so he can at least set up one or two cameras."

"Well good, that's enough living beings. Tell Angie to have him meet us at the playground. We can set it all up at one of the picnic tables and then Mom and Dad don't even have to know what's going on."

"Mom might burn the house down if she found out."

Pansy replied to the email and hit send with a flourish. "Done. And now we wait."

"And now we wait."

19

"Did you bring extra batteries?" Bagel asked as he set up a JVC Camcorder. The tripod was positioned next to the swing set in our tiny neighborhood playground. The area was mostly dirt, with two swings, two horse-looking things on springs, and one metal slide. All of it was made for very small children to keep the teenagers from loitering.

"Yeah. I don't know how long we'll need to film tonight at The Firefly so I packed all of the batteries and some extra cassettes, just in case," Randy replied. The group usually switched out both batteries and cassette tapes at around the three-hour mark while on investigations, but since we didn't know when, exactly, Donnie would try to break in, tonight would be tricky.

"Is the picnic table in focus?" Randy asked, waving his arms over the table while Bagel squinted through the viewfinder.

"Yep, looks good. That's the last of them, then."

I'd left Pansy sitting on our front stoop waiting for Fiona to show up, and Lee was watching Donnie, who'd parked under the revolving BlockBuster sign in the Sycamore Plaza lot and had settled down to take a nap. This gave us hope that our plan was working and that maybe Donnie was resting up for a long night of breaking and entering.

Bagel checked his watch. "A quarter till eight. They'll be here soon. Is there anything else that you can think of?"

The candles were set up in a circle around the picnic table and Randy made a final inspection of all three cameras before giving Bagel a thumbs up. "Nothing left to do but wait for them to..." the white Cadillac pulled into one of the three parking spaces in front of the playground area. *Of course, she's early.*

Pansy exited the passenger door and wasted no time. "Mrs. Dale, you remember Randy. This is my friend, Dario. He's also a member of the PPS and has done a few of these seances with me before."

Like she'd put in a hundred hours of pulling spirits forth or something. But we'd discussed it earlier and the more she pretended to be a professional, the better her chance that Fiona would believe her if she couldn't actually bring Gene to the table. Fingers crossed that he would show up.

I'd already filled Pansy in on the bank robbery and the how Gene had died details, and she'd passed those onto Randy and Bagel so there'd be no surprises.

"Mrs. Dale, if you can sit here next to Pansy," he gestured to the bench seat of the table as Bagel scrambled to light all of the candles. Randy sat across from Fiona and Bagel tossed the lighter onto the table before crawling over the seat. Fiona stared at the table, finally reaching into her gigantic purse and pulling out a scarf, leopard print, of course, and laying it over the wooden seat before lifting one red leather high heel after another over the seat to sit down.

"Okay, before we begin, what is it, exactly, that you want me to ask your husband?"

"Why can't I just ask him? I mean, if you can even make him appear."

"It doesn't work like that. You won't be able to see him, either way. I'm the only one who can see him and I'm the only one that can talk to him."

Was that true? We actually hadn't tried to have anyone else ask questions when we'd had Lee trapped. And when we'd had Doctor Welling? We'd been a little busy trying to keep me from being pulled into the portal to test out any experiments. But Pansy said it confidently, and Fiona would never know if it was the truth or not.

"Well," I could see the hamster wheel in Fiona's brain rolling furiously. "My husband, Gene, he... he didn't trust banks. So, he paid cash for everything for the bar. But he also didn't trust our neighbors, so, all of the money we had saved for the bar? He hid it. Somewhere."

Randy's eyebrows shot up. "He hid all of the money he'd set aside for the bar expenses? Like, for payroll and taxes and stuff?"

Fiona snorted at the word taxes. "Well, yeah. So, I've got some money in the safe, but there's more, a lot more. Somewhere."

"And he never told you where?" Pansy asked.

"No. It's not in the house or at the bar."

I snorted at that. It could literally be anywhere in the house and she'd never know. "What do you want to bet that this mysterious amount of money came from a bank robbery and not just extra bar income?"

Pansy grimaced. "It's unfortunate that he died when he did then, isn't it?"

Fiona shot her a look. "Yes. Unfortunate."

"Okay, let's get this party started and see if he's still lingering on this plane." Pansy started with her incantation.

"Everyone, hold hands and close your eyes." She rang the bell she'd brought with her before grasping Fiona and Bagel's hands. "Spirits, we call upon you and ask that you lift the veil between worlds to speak with us. Our circle is protected by goodness and light. We ask that no harm should fall upon those within the protection of the circle."

"Wait, what do you mean harm?" Fiona snatched her hand out of Pansy's. "Harm from what?"

"Lay it on thick. She deserves it," I advised.

"I'm sorry Mrs. Dale, you were so keen to have a seance that I thought you understood the risks. There are a lot of spirits lingering on this side of the veil and not all of them are what you might call *nice*. There's always a risk when you pull back the veil that something evil might slip through."

"Evil? Are you trying to tell me that you expect me to believe in things like demons?"

"Not demons, exactly. Just spirits that aren't friendly and have no intentions of being helpful. Some can be downright malicious. Now, if you'll take my hand, I'll finish this and keep any of them from following us home tonight."

I was laughing as Fiona stared at Pansy's hand like she'd asked her to hold a poisonous viper. Finally, she gingerly placed her talons in Pansy's palm.

"Tonight, we call upon the spirit of Gene Dale of Berry, New Mexico," I was watching the candles, which fluttered in the breeze, but never guttered the way they did when a spirit showed up. But maybe he was really far away. Did a spirit have to fly from wherever they were to here or did they just apparate within the circle in an instant? We'd have to ask Christine or do some experiments later.

"I ask that the spirit of Gene Dale shows himself to those gathered here within the protective circle." I caught Fiona cracking one eye open, squinting at the circle of candles. They were still lit and nothing strange was happening. I floated around the open space to verify, but there was no shimmering portal, no door to the other side, and no strange ghosts appeared on the playground.

"Gene Dale, your wife, Fiona, would like to speak to you this evening. I demand you come forward."

There was a moment of silence and even Bagel opened his eyes to see if anything was happening. Nothing. Zilch. Nada.

"Dude, nothing is happening because he's not on this side."

"Mmm," Pansy said. "I'm sorry to say, Mrs. Dale, that it appears that your husband is no longer of this world. We won't be able to ask him any questions." Fiona tried to pull her hand away from Pansy's grasp but she held tight until she'd recited the words to close the circle, upping the drama to put on a good show. She was getting pretty good at this.

Finally, she released Fiona's age-spotted claw. "I'm so sorry that you weren't able to talk to him one last time. I'm sure you must have loved him very much." She even sounded sincere. To my surprise, Fiona teared up a little, her mascara snaking down one powdered cheek in a gray dribble.

"I mean, we had our problems, like any marriage does, but I really do miss him." She pulled her giant purse closer and dug around, finally pulling out a previously used tissue and dabbing under her eyes. Gross.

"That's perfectly understandable," Pansy said, standing and stepping away from the picnic table to stretch. Bagel began snuffing out candles, and Fiona also weeble-wobbled her way to standing on the other side of the bench.

"So, when are you available to try this again? I think we should do this in the bar, that's where he died, after all. My friend Tina has assured me that his spirit will be closer there."

"What?" Pansy asked mid-stretch. "No, this is it, Mrs. Dale.

If Gene didn't answer, he isn't on this side. Location won't change that."

"I think you just don't want me to talk to him. I think you're just trying to scam me out of my money. You hardly even tried. What did you do, ring a bell and say some words? Anyone can do that. This other side stuff is just hooey. You could call him if you really wanted to. Obviously, you have some prejudice against me. What, are we not classy enough for you in your little middle-class neighborhood." She said *neighborhood* like it was a swear word. "You rich people up here think that we're just beneath you or something?"

"Rich people?" I exclaimed. "Lady, we don't even have a McDonalds in this town." *Was she on crack?*

"Mrs. Dale," Randy interjected, leaning on both hands across the table. "I assure you, we aren't out to trick you or scam you out of anything. There are at least three planes that we know of, the one of the living, the one used by ghosts that only some people of a particular talent, like Pansy here, can see, and the one that exists for those who've moved on. Unfortunately, once they've moved on, we haven't found a way to call them back." He straightened up as he spoke, stepping over the bench seat, and coming around to stand closer to Pansy. "I'm not saying that it's impossible, but we haven't found anyone who can do it."

"Well, if you think I'm going to pay you people for this sham performance, you've got another thing coming."

Pansy stood with Bagel and Randy on either side of her, all three of them staring, flabbergasted, as Fiona wobbled across the grass on her tippy toes to avoid sinking her heels into the ground.

"Well, that was entertaining," Bagel mumbled as her Caddy roared to life and she sped down the street at at least twice the posted limit.

"Well, I wanted her to stop calling me," Randy said with a shrug. "Guess she'll want nothing to do with us now."

"You should send her a bill for the two-fifty," Bagel suggested as he gathered up the candles into a Foodarama paper bag.

"Oh, I never actually expected that she would pay me. Even if I'd been able to call him forward, she'd have found a way to stiff me."

Yeah, she was definitely the type.

I watched the living clean up all signs of the seance so the old busy-bodies in the neighborhood wouldn't be gossiping about devil worshippers or some ridiculous thing when Lee came floating up at a good rate.

"Oh good, they're still here," he nodded toward Randy who was just closing the doors of the van. "Stop him, before he heads to the Firefly."

"Pansy, tell Randy to hold up."

She yelled for him to hang on while Lee updated me on what was going on.

"Okay, so Donnie is parked directly across the street from the diner. Lee left Thomas there to watch him," I told her. This presented a problem in that from the front windows, you could see straight across the dining room, over the counter, and all the way to the back door through the large open pass-thru. There was no way to sneak the cameras in without a chance that Donnie would see them.

"We'll need to distract him," Pansy explained the issue to Bagel and Randy.

"Bagel could run his Bronco into Donnie's truck. Take out a mirror or something. That would distract him," I offered.

"Because we want the police taking notice of Donnie and his truck right before he breaks into the diner? It could scare him off, which defeats the purpose. Besides, Dario doesn't need a ticket."

"Wait, why would I be getting a ticket?"

"Never mind. Your BFF over here wants to use you as a decoy."

"Actually," Randy said, pulling the back van door open again. "A decoy is kind of what I was thinking. Dario, help me load these cameras into your Bronco and you take them around the back to sneak them inside. I'll block the front with the van, it's big enough that he shouldn't be able to see around it."

They had the cameras and the tote with extra cassettes and batteries loaded into Bagel's backseat in just a few minutes. Randy called ahead to the Firefly from the bag phone in his van to let Chandra know to meet Bagel at the backdoor. Lee, Pansy and I watched as Bagel followed Randy out of the neighborhood, their taillights fading away as they made the turn onto Vargas that led out to Main Street. Pansy was left holding her ceramic bell and a paper bag full of half-melted candles.

"I'm feeling pretty useless here," she said, looking around the empty playground.

I knew that Pansy was used to being right in the thick of everything and that all of this relying on the adults to catch the bad guy, even relying on the ghosts to track down Thomas's family, was probably giving her a complex. Regardless, keeping her safe was the top priority for me. This is why we'd decided to rely on the real adults.

"I know, but Bagel won't be in any danger, and I dare this dude to mess with Randy. They can take care of it. Go home, watch some TV, read a book, pretend to be normal."

"Easier said than done," she mumbled before beginning her walk back home.

"Sitting this out is going to be hard on her," Lee observed as we watched her walk away.

"I know. But there is no plausible way she could be involved in this if we want the police to take it seriously."

Lee and I floated across the ravine, just barely beating Randy and Bagel. We'd met up with Thomas who was floating in the middle of Main Street, when I saw Bagel's Bronco turn right onto the gravel roadway that led around behind the block of businesses to the lot where the employees parked and deliveries were made.

Randy continued south down Main, stopping directly in front of The Firefly Cafe and effectively blocking both the practically non-existent traffic and Donnie's view through the front windows. I flew through the diner, Lee and Thomas right on my heels. Chandra had the back door wedged open with a cinderblock and was already pulling the tote out of the backseat while Bagel carried the bag of cameras to her office. Once the tripods were also in the office, Bagel gave her a quick hug and headed back out the door, kicking the cinderblock away on his way through. He'd already jumped into the still running Bronco before the heavy metal door slammed shut. I watched as he drove through the lot and then the next. He'd come out onto Main right before Sepulveda, well behind Donnie.

"Here," Chandra said, handing Randy a white plastic bag with a to-go box in it. "We've got to make it look real, right?" she said.

"Good idea, but I don't have any cash on me. I'll pay you back later."

"Don't worry about it," Chandra said with a laugh. "The entertainment value alone is worth it. I'll get these cameras set up tonight before I leave and this doofus won't know what hit him."

Randy was almost to the door when I heard a weird whoop-whoop noise out front that could only mean Perth PD.

Oh no.

Lee and I exchanged a look before booking it back out to the street. Thomas was delayed by a second, but quickly caught on that this was bad news. The Keystone Cops were going to ruin the whole thing.

"Randy, what the heck are you doin' man? Why does everyone think this is a parking spot?" Bias had pulled behind Randy and was standing behind the open driver's door of his Yukon, hands flailing towards the illegally parked van.

I floated to the Silverado where Donnie had his hand on the key but hadn't turned the ignition over yet. He was watching Bias intently, ready to bolt if the Perth police officer showed him any undue attention. I held my hand over the shifter, ready to knock him back to neutral if needed to keep him in place, but Bias was focused on Randy and never looked over. Randy waved the white bag of food around as part of his explanation, and I could see Bias roll his eyes from here. The two men got into their respective vehicles and drove away without further incident. Donnie watched them in the rearview, not releasing his grip on the key until they were both around the bend.

He released his pent up breath and relaxed into the seat before checking his watch. Ten minutes until closing time for the Firefly and the last customers were gathering their leftovers. Chandra had disappeared from sight. I left Donnie flipping through an issue of Great Outdoors, clearly looking at the pictures because even with the street light overhead, it was too dark inside the cab of the truck to read the small print on the pages.

Lee was telling Thomas all of the latest gossip about the people still inside the diner when I floated in. Chandra was in her office, simultaneously changing the battery in a camcorder while holding the receiver from her desk phone between her ear and shoulder, and fighting the cord that insisted on wrapping around her arm as she worked.

"Yeah, babe. Give me another thirty minutes. Once I get everyone out of here I'll shut off the lights and get the cameras rolling. This creep is sitting out front right now, so at least I know where he is." The battery changed out, she screwed in the mounting plate and snapped it into the swivel head of the tripod. "Yeah, that works. Okay, love you. See you in a bit." Setting the receiver in the cradle, she gently leaned the camera/tripod setup into the space between the cluttered desk and the set of filing cabinets, next to the one she'd already set up.

As she pulled the final camcorder from the bag, she began humming "Another One Bites the Dust." Giving her a nod of approval that she couldn't see, I left her there.

Phase One of Operation Firefly was in effect.

20

Summer on the high plains meant that darkness didn't settle in until about nine-thirty as we crept up to the longest day of the year. The street lights came on at eight-thirty, but Donnie was parked in the middle of the block in relative darkness when Shawn pulled up to the front door in the white Saturn. Donnie slid down into his seat like he was trying to hide, the steering wheel digging into his gut preventing him from getting anywhere close to being below the window and out of view. Shawn did his best to pretend to ignore the Silverado, and Chandra locked the front door behind her as she left the building.

After pointing out the locations of the cameras to Thomas, we warned him to not float through one. Ghosts did terrible things to film. That took approximately thirty whole seconds, after which we left to float out in the street with Donnie because we were all nosy and wanted to see what happened next.

"This would be easier if Chandra just had an alarm system," I said.

"He may have decided not to break in if she did. He may not be the brightest Crayon in the box, but isn't the dullest, either," Lee replied.

Most businesses in Perth didn't have an alarm, because honestly, there wasn't a whole lot of crime in Perth. If anything was stolen it could generally be narrowed down to the three or four known criminals in the area. For the most part, everyone else worked hard for what they had and it would never occur to them to steal something that didn't belong to them. Also, most of them had multiple guns at home, so who was going to break in? At no point in my life did I ever remember locking our front door and I knew for a fact that Bagel's parents never locked theirs. I always just walked in whenever I'd wanted. I'd yell "hello" to let his parents know I was there, but I never even knocked.

"I wonder how he's going to do it?" Thomas whispered like he was afraid Donnie would hear us.

"My money is on breaking something," Lee said. "I doubt this guy would know what to do with a set of lockpicks if they landed in his lap."

I snorted. "Well, there aren't any windows in the back and the fire escape leads to apartments on the second and third floors that don't connect to the restaurant. If he breaks one of the big windows on Main Street, surely someone will hear it."

Lee just laughed. "I doubt he'll be that bad at it, but I certainly wouldn't take any tips or tricks on burglary from this guy. I'll tell you what, when we get all of this settled, I'll take you to the big city and we can hang out with real criminals. You can watch professionals at work."

"You'd go hang out with bad guys?" Thomas looked shocked that we were joking about criminals. I figured this was why he hung out in a church by himself all the time.

"We're just kidding," I told him. I mean, I thought it sounded like a good time, but didn't want to scare the kid off before we could help him. "Don't worry, I don't actually have any plans to become a professional ghost burglar or anything."

While we were waiting on Donnie to make his move, Lee recounted the story of his first attempt as a ghost to help the police catch a group of burglars, apparently assisted by Thomas. I was caught up in the story, and startled when the engine turned over. As predicted, Donnie wasn't a particularly patient man, and a mere fifteen minutes after Chandra and Shawn had gone "home," he'd started up the truck.

"Is he leaving?" I asked, confused. We followed him in an arc as he turned left into the alley and made his way around to the back lot, stopping in the spot by the back door where Bagel had parked not an hour before. As we watched, he reached underneath the seat, pulling out his crowbar.

"You were right, Lee, we are going low-tech."

Donnie stepped up to the door, looking both ways like he thought someone else might be lurking. I mean, there were actually three of us lurking, but looking both ways wasn't going to help him spot us. It took him three or four tries with the crowbar to finally break the deadbolt on the back door, but as soon as he was in, I was off. Crossing directly through the diner, across the street, through the high school, and out to the student parking lot where the white Saturn was waiting alongside Randy's Econoline, and an ancient, mostly rusted-out Buick Lebaron that I hadn't even realized still ran. Greg must not have wanted to use his fairly new truck for any potential demolition derby games that may go down this evening.

I gave Chandra three taps on the arm to let her know it was time. "Are you kidding me? It's not even fully dark yet," she grumbled as she dialed 911 from her cell phone. Shawn started the ignition and pulled out of the lot, Randy and Greg right behind him. There was no way for me to tell them that Donnie wasn't in front of the building anymore, but they were grown adults, surely one of them could figure it out.

"Yeah, this is Chandra over here at the Firefly. I just realized I left something at work and when we went back, someone was breaking into the restaurant." I heard the voice of a dispatcher talking, and Shawn was already at the intersection with Main.

"Where'd he go?" Shawn asked.

"Did he already leave?" Chandra asked.

One tap for no.

"No. Around back maybe?"

Two taps for yes.

"He's around back," she relayed to her husband. Shawn pulled the emergency brake and left the car sitting at the stop sign, running back to relay the information to Randy and Greg behind him.

"Yes, he's behind the restaurant. Can you tell the police to not use lights and sirens? I know, I know, but we don't want him to run before they actually get here." Randy's headlights turned off behind us and I turned to see Shawn jogging back up to the car. I ducked out to see why they were turning their vehicles off, registering that the van's engine was still running just as Greg turned off his lights too. *Ahh, stealth mode, engaged.*

When Shawn opened his door, I could hear Chandra sounding frustrated. "Look, this is probably the same guy that broke into Summer's place. Do you want to catch him or not? Good. Send somebody over here." She tossed the cell phone into the cup holder like she wished she could chuck it at the dispatcher's head.

Greg and Randy backed up until they could turn down the access road behind the high school. Shawn pulled forward, the nose of the Saturn barely out into the street, and waited until he saw Randy's van creep across Main at the intersection between the elementary and high school buildings. Randy cut the power halfway across Main, rolling to a stop in the center alley. Greg drove another block south to park in the southernmost alley, and Shawn pulled forward to block off the northernmost alley. Unless Donnie grew wings or wanted to take his chances in the ravine, easily a twenty-foot drop straight down, he wasn't getting away.

I went inside to see if Donnie had noticed the cavalry pulling in, but he was knee-deep in Chandra's office. Chandra's typically neat desk looked like it had been hit by a tornado.

"As you can see, he's showing the same care and attention here that he showed your friend Summer." Lee gestured to the piles of paperwork on the floor. Donnie seemed to be picking up handfuls of paper out of the filing cabinet drawers and throwing them behind him. At least he was wearing gloves.

Not that the gloves were going to save him, being on candid camera and all. He'd turned the office light on and I could see that Chandra had left the third camera on a shelf full of cookbooks with only the lens pointing out. Donnie, intent on searching the desk and now the filing cabinets for the non-existent postcard, hadn't made it to the bookshelves yet.

I moved carefully through the kitchen space, mindful of the cameras so that I didn't float through one and erase the film. Typically, the red light that indicated that the camera was recording could be seen on the front of the camera body, but Chandra had draped a dish towel over it to keep the red glow down to a minimum. You could tell that she was a professional with these things.

I heard the whoop of a siren and Lee and I exchanged a look.

"She specifically told them not to use the sirens or lights. I heard her say it."

"Well, some cowboy got excited out there. And... there he goes."

Donnie didn't even bother turning the light off before bolting from the office. He sprinted across the kitchen, the light spilling from the office illuminating just enough for him to see the way. I don't know if it glinted off the lens or what tipped him off, but he seemed to pause mid-stride, doing a double take as he stared at the camera that pointed directly at the back door. The pause was unfortunate, especially that close to the exit. We all heard the word 'Clear' and Donnie turned to face the door just as Stevens kicked it in, slamming the heavy slab of metal directly into Donnie's face and knocking him out cold. His knees went limp first, but the rest of his body caught up with the nighty-night plan before he'd even hit the floor. Stevens stepped into the room to see what he'd hit, his flashlight illuminating the pool of blood forming under Donnie's nose.

"That's going to hurt in the morning," Lee said, fists on his hips and bathrobe flung back as he stared down at the unconscious form.

Multiple people were all talking at once, but while Donnie was cuffed and pulled into a squad car, Stephens was making notes about the scene and Bias was talking to Chandra and Shawn.

"Everything should be on film," Chandra was telling him. When he questioned why, she launched into her prepared script about the PPS searching the diner for ghosts. She kept impressing me with her acting ability. In a few sentences, she had Bias convinced that the cameras were a coincidence and that she had no idea who this guy was or why he would possibly be digging around in her office.

"Was he looking for money?" she asked, looking very innocent. Shawn was holding her hand and was pulling off the concerned husband look really well.

"I doubt we'll figure out what he was looking for tonight.

We'll take him down to the station and lock him up for the night. It's late, you, all of you, should just go home and you can come by in the morning and see if anything was stolen or broken. You can stop by and give a statement or we can send someone over to do it, whichever works best for you. Do you, uh, mind if we take those tapes, though?"

"Be my guest," Chandra told him with a smile. I looked over to see Donnie sitting in the back of a cruiser, his head tilted back to stop the blood that was still oozing from his nostrils. No one had offered him a tissue.

"We'll also leave someone here overnight to look after the place since your door isn't usable."

"Oh, wait," Shawn said. "I've actually got something in my kit that we can use to secure it for the night." He'd pulled the Saturn into the back lot, probably to allow the police entry, and we all watched as he pulled out a cordless drill, a padlock, and some hardware from the tool bag in his trunk. He gave the drill two quick zip-zips to test the battery as he made his way over to the door.

"Hang on, hang on, we need to take pictures of that first." Stevens scrambled to get the camera out of his vehicle.

While all of the men were hopping around, loaded with adrenaline, I laid one hand on Chandra's shoulder. She seemed to understand and laid her hand over mine. "Good job, Gerri," I heard her whisper.

I wished that I had a better way to communicate with her. I wished that I could apologize for the giant mess that had been made in her office, and I wished that I could offer to help her clean it all up in the morning, but I couldn't do any of those things. I tried to put off my pity party by reminding myself that we had just done a really good thing and that it wouldn't have been possible if I was also able to pick up a broom, but sometimes it was hard to keep a positive attitude.

But, maybe now that they caught this guy they would figure out why he broke into Summer's place. Maybe we'll learn who he really is and what it is exactly that he wants with Summer.

Lee, Thomas, and I followed the procession of police cars back down the street to the station where they threw Donnie into one of the two cells there. He demanded an attorney but Bias informed him that his public defender would be contacted in the morning. When he insisted that he needed to talk to someone immediately they'd all just laughed at him and closed the cell door. Apparently, we weren't going to find anything out tonight.

I felt... let down, I guess. We'd been waiting to get this guy captured and now that it was done and over with, I felt like I had a whole lot of energy and no way to expend it.

"So, what do we do now?" Thomas asked.

"I don't know, but I need a night at home watching trash TV and not problem-solving."

"Sounds like a plan to me. Meet us in the morning when you're ready to go check out that reservation down south. Don't sleep in."

"Ha ha, aren't you funny." I waved goodbye to the pair and floated home.

Pansy and Robbie were playing poker at the dining room table, betting with Oreos and Chips Ahoys. "You know, you guys could bet with real money if you got jobs," I commented.

"Gerri finds our unemployed status entertaining," Pansy relayed to our brother. "Now," she set her card face down on the table and turned to me. "Tell me everything."

As there really wasn't a lot to tell, it didn't take me long to catch her up.

"So, they're not going to question him tonight?"

"You know neither Crane nor Billings is coming back in

tonight unless someone is straight-up murdered. They'll get to him in the morning."

"What are you going to do now?" Pansy asked, echoing Thomas's earlier question.

"I'm going to go watch late-night television and rot my brain out for a few hours, that's what."

And that's exactly what I did.

21

The theme song to Gilligan's Island snapped me out of my trance and I realized that I'd been watching nonsense for several hours without really seeing what was in front of me. Could ghosts meditate? I didn't know, but apparently, I'd needed time to chill and recharge. Pansy was sound asleep when I left and the sun was barely flirting with the horizon. I made my morning pilgrimage to go check on Mrs. Garcia, fully expecting her to be sitting in her recliner, or making her coffee, or even picking at a box of doughnuts that she probably should not be eating. But who was going to tell a little old lady that she couldn't have her fried sugar? Either way, I was really surprised when I floated into the house to find her sprawled face down on the floor, half in the den, half in the kitchen.

I panicked and flew to her, momentarily forgetting that I was dead and couldn't check for a pulse. My hands pushed right through her but this close I noticed that her back was moving up and down. She was still breathing. I flew across to where her phone hung on the wall next to the refrigerator. I took a calming breath that I absolutely didn't need, and concentrated. I managed to pull the phone receiver up off of the hook on my second attempt. It fell, hitting the top of the garbage can, bouncing off the side of the fridge, and then landing with a thud on the tile floor. For a moment, I was concerned that if I'd broken the receiver the call wouldn't go through. But, no, wait, I could still hear a dial tone. Her phone wasn't a rotary, it had been updated with oversized push buttons for a shaky old lady to use, which was good when you were a shaky young ghost. I dialed 911 and could hear the ringing sound coming from the receiver on the floor because the volume was up so high.

"911 what's your emergency?" came the voice on the other end.

Since I wasn't able to answer, I left the phone off the hook and hoped the dispatcher would send someone out to do a check on Mrs. Garcia. I flew back to her to make sure that she was still breathing and then flew to the front door which I saw still had the dead bolt thrown. *Crap.*

If they knocked and she didn't answer, would someone break into the house or would they turn around and leave? I wasn't sure, but if the door was open surely, they would come in, right?

I was suddenly grateful for the extra time I'd spent in the power line, and with some effort, I managed to get the thumb switch for the deadbolt flipped the other way. Now, I just needed to work on the doorknob.

It was a slippery little sucker but luckily the house was old and once I had the knob turned just enough, the weight of the door and the imbalance of the foundation meant the door swung open on its own. There, now when the cops arrived the front door would be open and they'd have to come inside to check on her.

"Hang on, Mrs. Garcia," I said more to myself than to her. "Just hang on."

I tried to give her hands a squeeze in reassurance before going back outside to float high above the main road. It's not like I could direct the ambulance, but it made me feel like I was doing something useful.

It seemed to take forever before I heard the first siren, although there was no such thing as a ghost watch. I spotted the red and blue flashing lights of a Las Animas County Sheriff's cruiser busting down Sepulveda and was relieved that my call had been taken seriously. When I came back in to check on the old woman, the clock on the VCR registered only ten minutes between my call and the sheriff's department showing up. My panic had only made it seem four times that long. I heard car doors slam and I floated to the door.

"Come on, walk faster," I muttered to myself.

The two officers approached the house, still laughing about some joke they'd obviously been in the process of telling, but both fell silent as they noticed the open door.

"Mrs. Garcia?" the older one yelled into the house.

"Ma'am?"

The pair were much more serious now and they entered the house slowly, each with one hand on the weapons at their side. I watched the older one use his thumb to flick the strap of his holster open.

I don't need you to shoot anyone, I thought. *Just get your butts in here and call an ambulance already.* I willed them down the hall, and the younger one went straight back through to the kitchen. I heard his yelp of surprise when he spotted Mrs. Garcia.

"Found her," he yelled before clicking the radio on his shoulder and requesting an ambulance. Immediately. The older officer came through the kitchen doorway and noticed the phone lying on the floor behind the garbage can

"Hello?" he said, picking up the receiver and checking to see if the line was still open.

"We're here Joe. Do you have everything under control there?"

"Yeah, the old woman had fallen and was unconscious but Bob already called in an ambulance. I'm going to go ahead and hang up the phone."

Joe placed the receiver on the hook, staring at it for a moment before turning to look back at Mrs. Garcia who was at least six or seven steps away. The cop named Bob, the younger one, had rolled Mrs. Garcia over. Her eyelids were fluttering and a dark purple bruise was spreading across her cheek where she'd hit the ground.

"It looks like she's been here a while," he said looking her over.

"Okay, but the call just came through, what, fifteen minutes ago? Who called? It certainly wasn't her."

"I don't know. And why was the front door open? Do you think someone snuck in here trying to break in and found her?"

"They broke in by walking in the front door and then called 911 and didn't steal anything? Doesn't make any sense to me."

Mrs. Garcia had her eyes open now and was starting to mumble. "Are you okay, sweetheart? Was someone here? Did they push you? Is anything broken?" Bob asked.

"I just fell," she got out before mumbling some more and smacking her lips together. I'd noticed that her dentures were still in the glass by her table so she must have fallen in the night.

"It's okay, ma'am. We've got you now. Hey Joe, can you go get her glass of water?"

"I just fell, my hip, it doesn't work like it used to." She

rubbed her right wrist with her left hand. "My wrist doesn't feel right."

"The ambulance will be here shortly. Mrs. Garcia, did you call 911?"

I had to admit that confusing people gave me a certain pleasure.

"It was probably just the ghost," Mrs. Garcia said, waving him away and accepting the glass of water that Joe brought her. She was sitting upright on the floor now, but still made no efforts to stand, yet.

"You think ghosts called 911?" Bob asked, giving Joe a look like maybe he thought she'd done more damage to her head than they'd first thought.

"Well I didn't do it," she said. "I've been here on the ground since I fell. I keep telling people that my house is haunted, and no one believes me. It wouldn't surprise me one bit if the ghost called you."

"Now, you know your house wasn't really haunted, Mrs. Garcia," Joe said. "It was just those real estate con men who were breaking in before."

"And I'm telling you, Sonny, my house has been haunted since the day I moved in here and my ghosts take care of me."

He threw his hands up in frustration and went out front to meet the ambulance.

Joe gave the ambulance crew a quick explanation of what they'd found. "I think this is a case of either sundowners or maybe you want'a check'er for a UTI. She's talking out of her head about ghosts and none of it makes any sense."

"Okay, we'll get her to the hospital and get her tested and x-rayed." One of the workers said as he pulled a gurney from the back of the ambulance. "Point the way."

Mrs. Garcia was upset to have so many people fussing over her all at once, but I was happy to see that they treated her with respect, except for the part where they didn't believe in ghosts. But really, I was only slightly miffed about that. A year ago I also would never have believed something like that.

I followed the ambulance all the way to the closest hospital in Trinidad, a 35 minute drive from Mrs. Garcia's house.

I noticed some ghosts lingering by the front desk and I tried my best to avoid them because I didn't want to miss the results of Mrs. Garcia's x-rays. The final diagnosis was a broken rib, a broken wrist, a broken cheekbone, and a lot of additional bruising. I overheard Mrs. Garcia on the phone with her daughter Delores, and despite the old woman's protests that she was going to be just fine, I could hear Delores telling her she was on her way. The nurses had her sedated to make her comfortable and after an hour of hanging around at the hospital, I felt good enough about her outcome to float home and let Pansy know what was going on.

"Where have you been?" Pansy asked, cracking one eye open as I floated into the bedroom.

"Well, you know Dolores isn't going to let her stay there by herself anymore," Pansy said after I'd explained. "She's been trying to get her mom out of that old house and to move in with her for the last three years."

"Good. There are too many things for her to trip on and she's too far out for anyone to get to her if something really bad happened." I looked at the clock and jumped up when I realized how late I was. Lee was going to be tapping his foot at this rate. "I've got to go."

"Good luck, today!" Pansy yelled after me.

I'd take it, we needed all the luck we could get.

22

I floated through the Loaf N Jug on my search for Lee and Thomas and found them making the bottles in the refrigerated section clink together. This sent the teenager behind the cash register running to the back to investigate the source of the sound. I began to admonish them until I got a good look at the clerk. It was Dean, Danielle Newhouse's boyfriend. Danielle had made herself Pansy's arch-nemesis over the last few months, starting several rumors about her and Bagel. As far as I was concerned, Dean was guilty by association.

"What are you doing?" I asked Lee. "Besides teaching the kid bad habits?"

"Lee said this guy is dating a mean girl that made your sister cry. We're trying to make him crazy."

I mean, I couldn't really work up any indignation over this childishness. Instead, I joined in, waiting for Dean to return to his place behind the register before rattling the wax paper wrappers of the Hostess Fruit Pies nearby.

Dean, who was trying to read some kind of outdoor magazine, darted over and began flinging pies onto the counter.

"I've got you now, you little twerp. I know you're in there somewhere." He'd obviously mistaken our noises for mice. This could be a new source of entertainment, but we had real work to do.

"So, have they interviewed Donnie yet?" I asked Lee.

"Well, they tried. He immediately asked for an attorney and refused to answer any of their questions, so it was a pretty short interview. It obviously wasn't this boy's first rodeo. I was surprised that you weren't there for it."

I quickly explained about Mrs. Garcia, assuring him that she was stable but was going to be in the hospital for a few days until they found her a bed in rehab. "So, what are they going to do?"

"Since it's Friday, and they arrested him last night, I'd say they're going to wait until five to actually charge him. Then he'll have to sit in jail until Monday morning."

"That means that either way, he's not going anywhere this weekend." I wasn't upset about it.

The sun was already well above the horizon, although it was partially obscured by the smoky haze that drifted down from the mountain wildfires. We took off, flying south at a break-neck speed. My joy at going really fast was enhanced by my relief that our scheme to get Donnie off the streets had worked. Hopefully, we could find something today that would look familiar to Thomas.

I recited the directions I'd memorized to myself. I-25 to Las Vegas, the New Mexico version, which was nowhere near as exciting as what Nevada had to offer. Then south on US-84 for what we'd calculated to be about fifty-ish miles until we hit US-54, turn right, and keep going south until we hit a town called Carrizozo. At that point, in theory, if we went diagonally at the junction of 54 and 380, we could pop over the Sierra Blanco Mountains and directly into the heart of the Mescalero Reservation. Or, if we wanted to play it safe, we could follow the roads and go around the mountains.

We'd already made the turn onto 54 and the sky had turned a lovely shade of cerulean dotted with fluffy little clouds. With the multicolored rolling hills, everything looked like a picture-perfect postcard. We came up to a little town along the railroad track that was full of brightly colored buildings. It was the first sign of civilization we'd seen in the last fifteen minutes. We whizzed past several of the stores until a flash of baby blue stopped me in my tracks.

"Hold up," I yelled to the others. I floated down a side street, stopping in front of a baby blue Slug Bug parked next to the General Store. "Does that look like Summer's car to you?" I asked Lee.

"It was a popular color back then," he said with a shrug. "Don't get your hopes up, kiddo."

The interior was clean, which was not a state that Summer had ever left it in, but as I floated around to the back the daisy sticker in the back window confirmed it. I'd just found Summer's car. Was Summer somewhere nearby?

"Well, okay," Lee said as he finished circling the car. "Maybe it really is her car. The scratch on the front bumper is in the right place, this piece of rust over here on the rear quarter panel is correct, and well... let's be real, this bumper sticker that says Honk If You Love Yoga can only belong to Summer."

"Do you think she's in the store?" I asked.

"Go look. We'll wait here in case she comes out of one of these other buildings while you're in there."

I passed through the side of the building, and into the freezer section, which was miniscule. The whole store would have fit inside the Loaf 'N Jug back home and was maybe a tenth the size of Foodarama. The building was one open room full of shelves holding dry goods and cookware, dishes, and laundry detergent—a little bit of everything crammed into every available space. The shelves were only shoulder height, so it took me approximately five seconds to realize there were no brunettes with dreadlocks or brightly colored scarves that would indicate that I'd found Summer. There were only two shoppers, neither of them under the age of fifty.

"She's not in there," I told Lee.

He looked up at the sun like he was gauging the time. "We can wait here for a little bit and see if she comes out. Maybe she's in one of these other shops or parked the car here and left with someone else."

"If we find her, at least we can tell Pansy where to look when we get home."

I took a peek at the sun myself and figured that it wasn't quite noon yet. The buildings still cast shadows across the blacktop, but I could see black pools of heat mirages shimmering in the distance. Chalk one up for team ghost, we weren't affected by the heat or cold. If I'd really had to be on a stakeout in what was probably a hundred-degree heat, I would have already quit and got a new job. There's no reason to not know these things about yourself.

Luckily, we didn't have to wait long before a gray-haired old lady came bustling toward the car with a paper grocery bag in each arm. She loaded them into the passenger seat but Summer was nowhere to be seen.

"Do you think that she's like, one of Summer's relatives or something?" I asked Lee.

"Could be," he said. "Or, maybe Summer sold the car when she ran. It does stand out in a crowd. If I was trying to hide, ditching the car would be the first order of business."

I spotted a half gallon of Mint Chocolate Chip in one of the grocery bags, giving me hope that she was going to drive straight home and we wouldn't have to follow her through three or four more errands. She drove west, away from the highway, turning onto a side street and finally into a dirt driveway. The houses were all on large lots, and between the three of us we investigated the house, the garage, and the back shed in a matter of minutes. There were no signs that anyone else had been living there.

"I'd say you're right," I said when we all met back in the kitchen where the woman was pulling groceries out of the bags. "Summer must have sold it. There's a handful of family photos lining the hallway, but none of them look like Summer."

"Well at least we know that she came this direction," Lee said before wandering over to the counter where there was a stack of mail. "1401 Pinon Street. Remember that. Maybe we'll have Pansy write her a letter asking about the car."

"I can't even imagine what kind of story she'd have to concoct for that, but that's why she's the writer, right? Are you guys ready to keep moving south?"

I left without them, busy mulling over my anxiety about where Summer could be in silence when Lee interrupted my train of thought. "Technically, since 54 ends with an even number, it's west."

"What? We are clearly moving south." Could ghosts get heat stroke? I turned back to look at him. Nope, looked the same as always. His swoopy hair didn't even get ruffled in the breeze even though we were going way faster than the cars on the highway below us.

"Highways that end in even numbers go west to east; odd numbers go south to north."

I blinked a few times, mostly to hide my eye twitching. I'd seen the map; we were moving south. Slightly west. South-southwest, if you will.

"I didn't know that," I heard Thomas saying behind me. I started to comment but became distracted when I noticed there was something wrong with the ground in the distance. Floating away from the highway to get a better look, I slowed to a stop when I saw how dark the rocks were here. They looked... burned.

"Oh, I remember reading about this," Lee said. "It's a lava flow that covers the floor of this valley for miles. Called, with the creativity that most things are named, Valley of Fires. Which means," he paused to orient himself, "that the Jornada del Muerto desert and the Trinity test site should be over there somewhere." He pointed over the range of mountains on the other side of the valley and I paused to rack my brain. Trinity. Why did that name sound familiar?

"Trinity, as in, like, the atomic bomb kaboom zone?"

"That's the one."

"And the reservation is over here, due east, where the wind would carry the fallout?"

"You act surprised."

I looked at Thomas, expecting him to have some comment, but he had a look on his face like he was doing advanced calculus. "I remember this," he muttered before floating closer to the ground where a road cut, literally, through the field of volcanic rock, leaving a ten-foot wall of lava on either side. "I mean, I don't really remember being here, but there was a photo of me and Mom standing next to the rocks that looked just like these. It was in one of those frames with lots of other photos, but I remember this one because she looked so happy."

"Whoomp!" I yelled. "There it is!" I proceeded to do a little dance to celebrate while Lee and Thomas looked at me like I'd lost my ever-loving mind. "Dude, it's a clue. Quit looking so sour. We're on the right track." Had we found Summer? No, but we had more information. Had we found Thomas's family? Also no, but again, we had more information. There was no such thing as too much information.

"If you're done, doing," Lee waved his hand in my direction, "whatever that was, we're almost to our turn-off. Let's go check out the reservation and see if there's anything there that looks familiar to our young friend."

Our young friend was still like two decades older than me, but sure, whatever.

We made it to the intersection we needed and then took off at roughly a forty-five-degree angle towards the south, heading toward what Lee insisted was a range of mountains. My years in Colorado had left me unimpressed with what looked like an oversized pile of rocks.

About two-thirds of the way over the Sierra Blanco range, however, I began to worry. I hadn't realized how much I relied on the roads to lead me somewhere, and that floating without that guide would give me anxiety. There was nothing out here. At the height we were flying, I couldn't see hiking trails or deer paths, and only occasionally did something that resembled a fire road appear. "Are you sure we're going in the right direction?"

"The town shouldn't be much further," Lee assured me, and what do you know, at the bottom of a green valley, which definitely stood out in New Mexico, I could finally make out the little rectangles of roofs down below. We floated closer, down towards the houses that dotted the landscape. The houses weren't clumped together like my neighborhood, where everything looked like it had been stamped with the Sim City neighborhood generator, but scattered around with plenty of room in between homes. The roads followed the creeks and washes, not a grid pattern, and I hoped this would make it easier for Thomas to recognize something.

"Does anything look familiar, kid?" Lee asked him.

Lee and I hovered well above the town while Thomas floated around in circles, occasionally diving down for a closer look. He finally returned to us, his shoulders drooped in defeat, and if we'd been able to, I would have offered him a hug.

"I don't know. It was so long ago. Nothing stands out, and I can't picture her house at all."

"It's okay. I think the picture with the lava flow is a pretty good indicator that we're close. We can get Pansy to call or maybe email the Tribal Council and see if they can give us any information about your relatives. We can tell them that we're doing a school project and hope they spill everything they know."

"Okay," he said, his voice barely a whisper.

I shot Lee a look. Thomas seemed to have shrunk three sizes and I wasn't going to contribute to the depression of a ghost if I could help it. We were on the right track; I could feel it. "I'm going to start with that big building down there. Maybe it's like a headquarters or something, and we can find a phone number for them. Come on and I'll let you pick what word we make out of the phone number to remember it."

I could hear him asking what I was talking about as I flew down to a large building set on the southern side of the highway. It had the largest parking lot, so I figured that was our best bet. Sure enough, the front reception area held a desk where a gray-haired old lady was pounding on a typewriter and smacking the return carriage like she wished it harm. A small radio beside her was set to a local country station and the low-volume music accompanied her symphony of clacking.

The place reminded me of City Hall in Perth, with the brown tile floors and the cement block walls painted an exciting shade of beige. There were display cases filled with photos and various trophies, and a large notice board hanging on one wall. There were two stacks of flyers on the desk, one advertising Ski Apache and the other a rodeo, but nothing for the place we were literally standing in.

I needed some letterhead. Moving around behind the woman, I tried to search the top of her desk without moving anything, finally locating a stack of letterhead next to the typewriter. I leaned closer, through the older woman's elbow. Her screech sent both of us flying backward, me floating, her rolling as she shoved off from the desk and started batting at her elbow. Oh, she was one of the sensitive ones. While she looked around trying to figure out what had touched her arm, I went back to my snooping, reading the number off to Lee and then we both recited it three times. I moved to the phone, instantly translating the prefix to the word HOG, but the number one in the last part of the phone number was really throwing off my wordplay. I was still puzzling over a solution when Thomas spoke up from over by the wall of photos and handmade fliers.

"Hey, you guys? I think..." Squinting, he reached out to place a finger on the board. "I think this could be my aunt. Mom's sister." Lee and I immediately came to stare at the Polaroid pinned to the board that showed a round-cheeked, dark-haired woman in her late forties/early fifties, holding a giant wicker basket. It was wrapped in blue cellophane, so I couldn't tell what was in it, but the caption written on the white portion of the Polaroid said "March '93 Raffle Winner Lulu Roane."

"Lulu. I think this is my mother's younger sister," he said quietly. "She reminds me a lot of my mom, and that's not a common name, right?"

I broke into another dance and noticed that even Lee couldn't suppress a smile.

"Do you see it?" he asked me.

"See what?" I replied, leaning closer to the photo. I saw a parking lot with some cars and a woman about a decade older than my mom. What was I supposed to be looking for?

"Her name tag," Lee pointed out. "She was either at work

when they took the picture or just hadn't taken her badge off yet."

Thomas and I both leaned closer, confirming that yes, she was wearing a name tag over her left breast pocket with a big red 6 on a blue background next to her name.

"Well, I guess that's why you got paid the big bucks. Did you see a Motel Six anywhere around here?"

"Not yet, but there was a bigger town northeast of here. I bet it won't take long to find if we follow the highway."

We left the receptionist slamming keys on the typewriter and flew down 70 into the town of Ruidoso. We almost immediately spotted the Motel 6.

"I guess I thought this was going to be harder to locate," I said.

"Motel owners generally prefer them easy for people to find," Lee said, looking at me like I was flunking his class on spycraft. I repeated the phone number for the Community Center to myself three more times.

We searched the motel but didn't see anyone that looked like Thomas's aunt. I mean, I saw three women who sort of looked like the woman in the grainy Polaroid picture, with short dark curls and the same basic body shape, but Thomas shot each one down. We were gathered in the parking lot discussing the Polaroid—it was three years old and she could work anywhere now, and what would our next steps be, when a hot pink Geo Metro pulled into the lot. Aunt Lulu stepped out and we watched as she walked into a back entryway of the motel. The three of us took a moment to stare at one another. This was going to work. We were actually going to make progress on this case. I couldn't stop grinning.

Nine hours later the grin had definitely worn off, and we'd all taken turns exploring the town while the other two watched the Aunt. She worked the front desk and by the time her replacement came for the night shift, I figured Pansy would think we'd all been lost forever and she was never going to see me again. Thank goodness Donnie was locked up and the only thing she needed to worry about was finding another job for the summer.

I had reached a level of boredom that had me singing show tunes by the time Aunt Lulu got back into her little pink jelly bean of a car, and the three of us followed her home from there, heading not back into the heart of the reservation, but just a short ways further east into Ruidoso and then up several back roads that crisscrossed the mountain side. There were no street lights here, but her headlights lit up the word Roane spelled out in gold foil sticky letters on the side of her mailbox when she pulled in.

The urge to take my shoes off was strong as I crossed the threshold into the white tile entryway and wasn't reduced at all when Lulu kicked hers off at the door before heading back toward the kitchen. The three of us looked around, floating as a group into the living room like we were invited company having a seat.

There had to be fifty or sixty framed photos covering the wall, some older, some newer. Thomas seemed stuck on one, and because I will always be nosy, I floated over to see what was keeping his attention. "This is my mom in the yellow dress," Thomas said, pointing to a photo of two girls, both about my age or a little older, with long dark hair. They looked enough alike that you could see the family resemblance. The one in the yellow minidress had her arm around the other and was throwing up a peace sign. They were both laughing, the girl in the green minidress pointing towards the camera, or more likely, the person who'd been holding the camera. The photo was yellowed with age and had been placed in a heavy black frame near the center of the wall. Next to it hung another photo, clearly of the same two women but twenty years later, plus a much older woman who was lying in what appeared to be a hospital bed. All three were smiling for the camera, the older woman's gnarled hands held by each of her daughters.

"Granny," Thomas whispered.

"Look at this one," I said, pointing toward one of the newer photos on the outside edge of the wall. The photo showed a blond-haired young lady in a cap and gown with one arm around the much shorter Aunt Lulu, the other arm holding a scroll over her head in a pose that proclaimed her victory.

"Is that Bethany?" I asked.

"I don't know. Her hair was brown as a kid, and she was so little when I saw her last time. But I think so. She looks really happy here, so I... I hope so."

"Side note, my friend, hair color means nothing. A good stylist can make your hair any color you want. The frame looks new, the photo isn't faded, and Aunt Lulu looks the same age as she is now. I think Bethany is a good guess."

Lee was looking at the kid like he wanted to give him a hug too, so I knew we needed to get out of here before we were all ready to eat a quart of Rocky Road.

"So, we're going to head back to Perth and fill Pansy in so she can start to make contact. Do you want to come with us or do you want to stay here?"

Thomas pulled his attention from the photo, flipping around, wide-eyed. "Alone?"

"Well yeah, that's why I figured you'd want to come back with us. I mean I wouldn't want to stay here all by myself. And we'll come back with Pansy and Bagel, now that we know where to go."

"Besides, kiddo, you've got a church to haunt," Lee said, straightening his robe and avoiding eye contact. The television clicked on, making us all jump. Aunt Lulu had snuck in with a bowl of popcorn and a glass of soda and was settling herself onto the couch amidst a pile of blankets and pillows as a tape began to whir in the VCR. I missed nesting on the couch.

"You don't mind if I come back with you?" The words came slowly as if he was afraid that we'd tell him he wasn't invited.

"I'd prefer it, actually. I'll worry about you if you don't," I told him.

The faintest hint of a smile crossed his angular mouth, and he nodded a few times before finally pushing the words out. "Yeah, I'd like to go with you guys."

He gave the photo of his sister a final brush of his fingers, the hope evident on his face. The theme song to Days of Our Lives began to play as we left Aunt Lulu behind and headed home.

23

We flew home at top speed, high above the desert and cutting corners as needed since we knew where we were going. Thomas was quieter than normal and I figured that the day had brought back a whole lot of memories about what his life had been like as a kid living with Annamarie and Bobby. Surely there could have been some good times in there too—they couldn't have all been terrible, right?

I don't know what kept Lee occupied, but he was also quiet. My thoughts returned to Donnie and what he wanted with Summer. He seemed to be the right age to have maybe been an old boyfriend, possibly a husband if they'd been married young, but I wondered what would happen if he continued to refuse to answer questions. How were we going to track her down if we didn't even know her real name?

It was a little after midnight by the time we crossed the south bridge.

I heard Lee asking Thomas if he was going to go spend the evening at the church or if he was gonna hang out with him at the police station and I thought for a moment what a difference these last six months had made for Lee. He was much more sociable than the cranky old fart that he'd been when I'd first ran into him. I guess you could socialize an old dog after all.

After arranging to meet them at the Police Station after I checked in with Pansy, I went home where Robbie and Pansy were watching the movie *Carrie* in the living room.

"Pause it! I've got real, actual, factual, information."

"I can't pause it, it's HBO. What information? What took you so long? Was it the right place?"

"So right. We found his aunt. And it took so long because she was at work and we had to wait for her shift to end so we could follow her back home."

"That's fantastic."

"Did they find the kid's family?" Robbie asked, turning the volume down.

"Yep. Sounds like they found an aunt."

"Oh, get a pen, write this number down before I forget it." I was proud that I'd remembered it but if we didn't write it down soon, who knows how much longer I would retain it. I told Pansy my adventures and she relayed them to Robbie while Carrie wrecked shop on her high school class in the background.

"I'll call Dario in the morning and see when he can go back down there with me."

"Are you guys still investigating the church tomorrow night?" I asked.

"Oh, no. I called Randy earlier to see if he needed a secretary for the summer, and he said he'd already explained the situation to the pastor at First Lutheran. They're canceling the investigation. Randy said the dude was really cool with the whole thing and said Thomas was welcome to stay if he wants."

"Good. Well, hopefully, Thomas will be back with his family soon, and it will be a non-issue."

When we had first joined the Perth Paranormal Society, the idea of having either an investigation or a meeting every single Saturday evening had not really been that big of a deal. After months of doing this, though, we realized that it would be nice to actually have a Saturday off. Now that we'd uncovered Pansy's superpower to the adults, we were freeing up a lot more Saturday evenings by not having to drag out all of the ghost-hunting equipment for every single investigation.

"So, did he need a secretary?" I asked, wondering if there was hope for more than a week of employment in her future.

"Uh, no," she said.

I didn't bother to repress my snort. "Okay, well I'm going to go see what's going on with Donnie. I'll see you in the morning. Tell Robbie I said goodnight."

I heard Robbie yelling out, "Goodnight, Geraldine," as I floated back out the front door. The streets were quiet as I crossed into downtown, and I paused before taking a quick detour through Summer's apartment. It was dark, the light from the back parking lot casting a dim glow on the emptiness. *Where are you?* I wondered. The room was silent and the kitchen was lit only by the glow of the clock on the stove. The roll of paper towels was still on the counter from the impromptu pizza party. Nothing had moved, nothing had changed, and I wasn't sure why I was torturing myself when there was nothing here that could give me any clues as to where she may have gone.

Deciding not to be so melancholy, I continued to the station.

"Hey kiddo, get a load of this headline," Lee said as soon as he saw me coming through the front doors. He was leaning over the front desk where various sections of the daily paper were scattered.

"Man Suspected of Stalking the Perth Paranormal Society Arrested On Charges of Breaking and Entering." This was not really the kind of advertisement the PPS was looking for, but I guess as long as our name stayed in the paper, people wouldn't forget who we were. What's the old newspaper adage about all press being good press, or something like that?

"He's still here, right?" I asked. "They haven't let him out or anything?"

"No, he's still nice and cozy in a cell. Which reminds me, come look. I know you'll appreciate this; Detective Crane is actually doing work for the first time in months." I followed him down the hall towards Crane's office where Thomas was looking through the stacks of paperwork and Crane was typing with two fingers, pounding out some report. Crane never worked late, we needed to mark this date on the calendar.

"Apparently, Chandra completed the rest of her report and they finally charged old Donnie-boy tonight just like I said they would. I don't know how he thinks he's going to weasel out of this. How can he deny that he was there or that he was breaking and entering?" He motioned toward a stack of camcorder cassette tapes in a plastic evidence bag. "Good luck beating that kind of proof," he said.

The tapes were stacked on the edge of the desk next to several fingerprint cards where they had dusted. The crowbar that Donnie had been using was in a large brown paper bag that had already been taped up and labeled as evidence.

"Have they mentioned anything about Summer's break-in?" Was it possible that our police force would put two and two together and come up with three? It wouldn't be the first time.

"Yeah, I watched Crane make a little note on the other page about Donald's possible involvement, but they haven't matched any of the evidence yet. I don't know if they plan on looking at the crowbar closer or what? Trying to sort out the fingerprints in Summer's place was a nightmare since half the town's been in and out of there. His fingerprints being inside wouldn't necessarily prove anything unless they were from up in her apartment. Did you fill Pansy in?" he asked.

"Yep. She's going to call Bagel in the morning and see when his next day off is so they can drive south and talk to the aunt. I'm hoping that they can..."

I was suddenly interrupted by singing.

"In the fields of glory,
where courage stands tall,
we're the warriors united,
we answer the call.
With unyielding spirit,
we face every test.
In the heart of the battle,
we give it our best.

"I can't believe I remembered that song," Thomas ended with a murmur.

"Uh, what was that?" I asked. Had the kid finally cracked?

"The Warriors fight song. Bethel High School, see." Thomas pointed to one of the photos on the desk, a ceramic mug with a white feather and faded writing on its side sat at the top of a pile of kitchen items that had been flung into the kitchen floor.

"That's from Summer's apartment," I told Lee.

"Yes, I gathered that, Watson."

I stuck my tongue out at him before turning my attention back to Thomas. "I've never heard of Bethel High. Where's that at? Why do you know this song?"

"The mug," he said pointing. "The eagle feather was the symbol for Bobby's high school team, the Warriors. All of his yearbooks had that symbol on their covers and he sang the fight song all the time when he was drunk. He used to be a football player when he was in school. He even had the feather tattooed on his arm with his jersey number.

"You're telling me that your stepfather had this symbol tattooed on his arm?" I asked, slightly stunned.

"Yeah."

Lee and I looked at one another. "I mean it's possible that she picked it up at a thrift store, somewhere just because she liked the symbol on it," Lee said.

"Yeah, but now that I hear the fight song it reminds me of something that I know I've heard Summer say. The part about with unyielding spirit we face every test. Although, to be honest, I've lived in Perth my entire life and couldn't sing our high school fight song if you paid me."

"Have you ever actually attended a pep rally?" Lee asked me.

I paused to think back. "Bagel and I almost went to one in tenth grade, but then we saw they'd left the side door open so we ran over to the Firefly for milkshakes, instead." He rolled his eyes, but I continued to think about all of the times I'd seen her use this particular mug. "But this was the mug she drank tea out of while she reviewed videos with Pansy. Like, always. If I had to say she had a favorite mug, it was this one."

"Looks like we've just added something else for Pansy to investigate," Lee said.

"There's no time like the present. Let's go fire up the computer and see what we can find online."

The three of us floated back home and I made Lee and Thomas wait outside while I checked our bedroom to make sure Pansy was decent. I found her pulling pajamas out of a drawer.

"Hey, we have some stuff we're going to need you to look up on the internet."

"Fine, just give me like fifteen minutes to shower and put some PJs on and I'll be ready to look stuff up."

Lee and I went out to sit in the power lines and Thomas

looked at us like we were crazy. "What are you doing?" he asked.

"We're charging up," I told him. "Every time we move something or push an object around it drains some of our energy. So, when we sit here and soak up the extra power from the power lines it kind of recharges us."

"Like an alternator?"

I had no idea what an alternator was but nodded anyway. "Sure, like an alternator."

He joined us in the power line and looked around like he was missing something. "I don't feel any different," he said, holding his hands in front of his face like he expected to see them glowing. "It doesn't feel like anything to me."

"Yeah, it's not supposed to. It doesn't feel like anything to me either but it really does help if you need to move something quickly." We continued to soak up the energy for the next twenty minutes before I saw our bedroom lights flicker on and off twice. This was Pansy's signal to me that she was ready for company.

"Okay, she's ready." We floated back in as Pansy was booting up the computer on my desk. "We might have a clue," I told her. "We need you to investigate Bethel High School in South Dakota. Thomas's stepfather used to go there and he recognized one of Summer's mugs as a symbol for their team."

"Okay, but you know she picked up a lot of her things from thrift stores. It doesn't necessarily mean anything," Pansy said.

"Yeah, that's what I said but then he started singing their fight song and part of the song was 'with unyielding spirit we face every test' and I know I've heard her say that.

"Oh," Pansy agreed. "I remember her saying that a couple of times, actually."

"Exactly. It seemed like a good idea to look it up and see if maybe we can find anything about the town. Maybe go down there and see if there are any old yearbooks in the library."

"That could be really hard if we don't know what year or even what her real name was," Pansy said as she typed the school's name into the search bar.

"Yeah, but we have photos of her and surely she couldn't look that much different could she?"

A result for the school popped up and Pansy clicked it, causing an 8-bit cheerleader to bounce across the screen.

The page had information about the upcoming homecoming dance and a big splashy headline welcoming the seniors class of 1997. There were only two photos on the home page, one was a landscape photo of the school and the other was a close-up of the sign which included the same single white feather next to the name.

"Well, that all goes together," I said looking over Pansy's shoulder.

"I told you," said Thomas.

"Okay, write that address down and we'll look it up in the Atlas to see how to get there."

"No offense but this seems more like a real living person job than a ghost job," she said, taking out her troll pen and scribbling the address in her notebook.

Bethel, South Dakota. The atlas was still laying on the end of my bed and she rolled the desk chair over and began searching towards the back of the book for the state of South Dakota.

She stopped, looking up at me. "Okay, do we go find Thomas's family first or do we go look for Summer?"

Lee and I looked at Thomas and he just shrugged. "I mean it's been twenty years, so another couple of days isn't going to be a matter of life or death or anything," he said. "But your missing friend might need help. I vote we find your friend."

"Or," I said, thinking about the logistics since it was late and Pansy's brain had apparently already shut down for the evening, "You and Bagel can go check out the Aunt tomorrow or Sunday, you know, on a weekend, and then go check out this Bethel place on Monday when businesses like the school board and the library will actually be open."

"Fine. I'll call Dario tomorrow and see if he can take some days off work. And now, if you can all get the heck out of my bedroom, I'd really like to get some sleep."

24

On the way to family therapy Saturday morning, Pansy had dropped off the two disposable cameras she'd used at graduation at the one-hour photo place in Trinidad. She then spent the ride home choosing the best shots to fill up her new mini-album for her purse. 'Best' was a relative term because Pansy was a terrible photographer, but the least blurry shots earned a spot in the new album. Bagel would have done a better job, but he had left his camera at home for graduation, telling Pansy that he "refused to waste film on these people."

Later that day, Randy dropped off two good photos that he'd taken of Summer over the years while investigating, and then spent a good fifteen minutes trying to talk Pansy out of driving all the way to South Dakota. He understood that the trip to New Mexico required the ghost crew, but the search for Summer needed living people and he argued that one or two of the adults should make the trip. Pansy had argued that while she was also an adult, she could spend a few days running all over the countryside while the adultier-adults had real responsibilities—like jobs and kids—that kept them close to home. He didn't like it, but he finally had to concede her point.

Sunday morning, Pansy picked Bagel up at the butt crack of dawn. He swung a cooler into the backseat, the ice rattling in protest, and settled his camera bag down by his feet. Apparently, this trip warranted the use of his precious film.

"Oh, the cooler is a good idea. I didn't even think about packing drinks."

"Honestly, I didn't either. This," he waved a hand towards the back before buckling his seat belt, "this was my mother's idea. I think she thinks we're on some kind of romantic weekend getaway," he said with much eye roll.

"I mean, we can pretend it's a romantic weekend getaway if she's going to make us food. What did she send? Oooh, is it her famous lasagna?"

"Leftover manicotti and a six-pack of Dr. Pepper, because it's your favorite. Not my favorite, but yours. And we have to bring her forks and Tupperware back under penalty of death."

"Awww, my future mother-in-law loves me more than you."

"Oh my god, stop."

"Well, she's way classier than me, I was just going to stop at a gas station somewhere and grab some chips and beef jerky or something." Pansy leaned forward and pulled some folded pages out of the map pocket of the Tracker. "Here, I made copies of the atlas at the library yesterday, enlarged them, and highlighted our path. You're the navigator."

"Great," Bagel muttered, flattening the four sheets of paper across his lap.

"Gerri, you know the plan—go get the boys, locate the auntie, and we'll meet you at the Motel 6."

"O Captain, my Captain," I told her, giving her a salute before I left the two of them to go pick up Lee and Thomas at the police station. After a quick check-in on Donnie who was still asleep in his cell, the three of us flew south so that we could track down Aunt Lulu's whereabouts before Pansy and Bagel arrived.

We took our time, knowing that what should be a six-hour drive for the living was only going to take us about three. We watched the sunrise, inspected lizards and funny-looking cacti, and even checked out all of the businesses in that town where we'd found Summer's VW, just to see if she happened to be out and about somewhere. She wasn't, and Pansy's bright yellow Tracker was still nowhere in sight by the time we'd finished investigating. That didn't surprise me because Pansy had the world's smallest bladder and Bagel would be out taking artistic photos of said rocks and lizards at every stop. It was a good thing that they'd left really early.

"We should start at the hotel," Lee said once we'd arrived in Ruidoso.

We entered the Motel 6 and a good-looking guy was standing behind the counter, his dark, waist-length hair long and unbound. His hair was thick and silky and I was really jealous because mine would never look that good, even if I'd still been alive. "Obviously not the aunt," I said, looking around. Apparently, the hunky dude was the only one working the front desk today.

We flew to the house, which was also empty, but we passed the hot pink Geo on our way back down the mountain. Circling back to the house, we watched in silence as Lulu carried bags of groceries into the house. There's nothing that makes you feel more useless than watching someone else work and not being able to help. She disappeared into what I assumed was her bedroom, returning in a few minutes wearing flowy yoga pants and an old tee, a bandana tied around her short curls. House cleaning began in earnest, which was good because it meant she'd still be there by the time Pansy and Bagel arrived.

I left Lee and Thomas there and headed down the mountain to wait for my sister. It was almost one by the time Pansy pulled into the motel parking lot. The vinyl top had been removed from the Tracker and both Pansy and Bagel were bright pink from the sun. None of us had considered the need for sunscreen. "Finally," I said as I popped into the backseat of the Tracker. "Aunt Lulu is at home doing laundry. I'm sure she'll be happy for a distraction."

"Cool, which way?"

"Okay, turn left back onto the highway, and when you hit the little Tastee Freeze up here, turn right. Then take the second right into her neighborhood."

Pansy followed the directions, hanging a right at the little plywood shack painted turquoise blue with a few picnic tables scattered in front. It was apparently a bazillionty degrees, judging by the sweat soaking Bagel and Pansy, so shaved-ice was doing brisk business. Pansy turned onto the aunt's road, driving slowly up the winding hill to the hot pink Metro. Thomas and Lee must have still been inside because they were nowhere to be seen.

"Hey, are y'all in here somewhere?" I asked as I floated in the front door. Thomas was looking over the wall of photos again and Lee was going through Lulu's record collection. "Pansy and Bagel are here," I said as the doorbell peeled.

I heard footsteps and Lulu came from the back of the house, looking confused. No one liked unexpected company.

"Can I help you?" she asked, pulling the door back a few inches but leaving the storm door closed between her and the two random teens standing on her doorstep.

"I sure hope so. My name is Pansy Bellafini and I..."

"Look, I'm not interested," Lulu said and began to close the door.

"We're here about Annamarie," Bagel said, and the door was snatched open so fast I had whiplash.

"I'm sorry, what did you say?"

"Annamarie. She's your sister, right?" Pansy said.

"She was, yes."

"Was. Oh, is she...well, is she no longer with us?"

"She is not. Look, I've got a lot to do today and I'd really like to know what this is about."

"Well, this is going to sound crazy, I am well aware of that, but I'm just going to tell you the truth. Her son, Thomas, is trying to find his family."

Pansy held two newspaper articles out that I hadn't even known that she'd packed. Lulu gingerly opened the storm door to accept them and I read them over her shoulder. "Teens Find Body of Lost Country Music Star" was the headline of the first one. "Teen Discovers Body of Lost Child." Both articles included photos of Pansy, and Lulu looked very confused.

"Thomas has been dead for decades."

"Yes. 1974. I know. He told us."

"What?" she whispered before shaking her head and thrusting the newspaper articles back at Pansy. "No," she said decisively, "I don't know what kind of ugly joke you're trying to play, but this is beyond cruel."

We couldn't let her close the door. "Tell her that there's a photo on her wall of her and Annamarie. Annamarie is in a yellow dress."

Pansy straightened the copies of the articles. "There's a photo on your wall of you and your sister. She's wearing a yellow dress."

Once again, the door stopped mid-swing and was flung open. Lulu stepped out onto the small concrete porch, shoving the storm door open so wide that Pansy and Bagel had to take a few steps back. "How...how could you know that? Did you little punks break into my house? Are you spying on me?"

"No. Look, I... I'm going to ask you a question and you can choose to say yes and I will explain everything, or you can say no and I will pretend to believe you and we'll leave."

Thomas, who was floating behind his aunt, shook his head. "Even if you guys leave, I'm staying here this time until I find my sister." I relayed this information to Pansy, who shot me some side-eye. I shrugged. It's not like we could ground the kid.

"What's the question?" the older woman asked. Her voice still held a note of hostility and more than a little frustration.

"Do you believe in ghosts? Restless spirits?"

Her deeply tanned face lost at least four shades of color and she looked like she would have fallen over if I'd tried to touch her. "Ghosts?"

"Yeah, ghosts. I showed you these articles because I didn't just happen to stumble onto these bodies by accident like I told the reporters. I couldn't tell them the truth, that I was led there by ghosts. And right now, the ghost of your nephew would really like to talk with you." Pansy neatly folded the articles and put them back into her pocket. "Also, Thomas said that even if you don't want to talk with him, he's just going to haunt you until he finds his sister," Pansy added. "Just so you know."

"He's going to haunt me?"

"Well, that's what he told my sister, but he is just a kid so he might get bored and wander off pretty quickly. We have a church at home that's perfectly willing to let him haunt them, but my biggest concern is that the kid wouldn't be able to find his way back home to Perth." Pansy was talking so fast that she was almost rambling, but Lulu hadn't slammed the door in their faces. Yet.

"Perth? You're from Perth? Colorado?"

"Yes ma'am."

"My sister lived in Perth."

"We know."

She leaned forward and looked around the street like she was looking for the production team for Candid Camera. "I think you two had better come in and explain yourselves."

"Yes, ma'am. We would all appreciate that."

"All?"

"Well, besides my friend Dario and I, we actually have three ghosts with us."

The woman stood in the doorway, staring at Pansy like she'd just offered to stand on her head and bark like a seal.

"Maybe she should have waited until they were inside to break that news," Lee said, floating in the hallway behind Thomas.

Finally, a decision was made and the woman held out her hand, "My name is Lulu. Pansy, was it?" Pansy shook the woman's hand.

"I know it sounds nutty, I am fully and painfully aware of that. But I promise I'm not a fruitcake."

The woman chuckled and shook her head in disbelief. "Well, it's not every day that two random white kids show up on my doorstep, but I'm intrigued. Plus, I can't imagine that you'd drive all the way down here from Perth just to rob me, so come on in, I guess."

Pansy followed her into the entry hall with Bagel hot on her heels. Lulu motioned for Pansy and Bagel to have a seat on the brown leather couch before settling onto the front edge of a matching recliner by the fireplace.

"Is that the photo?" Pansy asked, pointing towards the photo in the center of the wall.

"Yes," said Lulu, Thomas, me, and Lee all at one time.

"She was really pretty. There weren't any photos of her in

the news articles we pulled from the microfiche, so I wondered what she looked like."

"Can we, I don't know, start from the beginning or something?" Lulu asked, her hands flailing in the air as she spoke. "I saw the thing about that country singer on the news, that two teenagers had found his body in the woods. So, what? Am I supposed to believe that his ghost led you to his body?"

"Uh, no, that was actually a different ghost. Lee Bradley. He's here with us now."

"You sound like a crackpot when you say it like that," Bagel said.

"Thanks a lot," Pansy replied. She let out a deep sigh and gathered her thoughts. "Okay, so from the beginning. Last October, my twin sister, Gerri, and I were in a car wreck. She died. Three days later, she came back as... a ghost I guess you'd call it. I'm the only one who can see or hear her."

"Except Christine," I interrupted.

"Oh yeah, actually there was a medium we met recently, but anyway... the gist is, because Gerri can talk to the other ghosts *and* me, a living person who can really do things, we've been trying to help them out with their problems."

"You're helping the ghosts?" Lulu asked, the furrow between her brows deepening the longer Pansy spoke. "What problems could ghosts possibly have?"

Pansy shot a glance at Bagel when he started chuckling. "More than you'd think," she finally said with a shrug. "We joined a group of local ghost hunters called the Perth Paranormal Society because, you know, we had questions about ghosts and Ghostbusters wasn't available to call." She pulled the news articles back out of her purse. "The first article, the one about Christopher Fairchild? We found his ghost while investigating a house south of Perth. He helped us out, saved my life actually, and he accidentally led us to his own body when I was running away from some guys who were trying to kill me. You understand why I couldn't, like, tell the newspaper dudes any of that."

Lulu nodded and moved back in the recliner a few more inches. "And that country singer?"

"Well, one of the other ghosts that hang out in Perth, Lee, happened to find the body in the woods a few years back. He couldn't do anything about it at the time, but he told Gerri about it,"

"And by Gerri, you mean the ghost of your dead sister."

"Yes. Anyway, Lee asked if we'd go 'discover' the body," she said, using air quotes. "We agreed because we figured the family of the person needed to know what had happened to them, but we had no idea when we volunteered that it was going to be someone famous. Honestly, I probably would have just left him there if I'd known what a mess it would be. The amount of people trying to interview me was a nightmare."

Lulu snorted and settled a little bit further back in her recliner. "Well, at least you're honest. Okay, let me get this straight. So, you can see your sister, Gerri, and she can see other ghosts, and my nephew? He just so happens to be one of those ghosts?" Her arms were crossed and her voice indicated her disbelief.

"Yeah, crazy, I know. So, Lee was actually the reporter at the Perth Gazette who interviewed Annamarie after the murders, so he remembered the case, and of course, living in Perth, or, I guess, haunting in Perth would be more accurate, he and Thomas had seen one another around town over the years. So, when we, the PPS I mean, were asked to investigate a local church because things kept moving and they were convinced it was haunted, Gerri found Thomas.

"He wants it known that he was helping to clean things, not messing things up," I said after Thomas protested.

"Apparently he wants you to know that he was helping to keep things tidy, not making messes," Pansy relayed to the woman.

"Wait, he can move things?"

"Umm, yeah. They all can."

We all could *now*. There'd been a few months there where I'd been unable to even make a feather move, but now I was thoroughly juiced up.

"Prove it."

Thomas wasted no time in moving a wooden carving of a horse, sliding it a full six inches across the mantel until it clinked against a clear glass vase of fake sunflowers.

Lulu needed a minute to pick her jaw up off the floor. While she was still staring at the mantel, the horse slid back to where it had originally stood.

"Okay. Well. This isn't how I'd planned my day to go," she said, almost to herself.

"Trust me, I understand. At no point in my life had I ever really thought that ghosts could be real, so the whole 'twin magically appearing right after her funeral' short-circuited my brain for a little bit."

"So, everyone becomes a ghost when they die?"

"No. No, most people move on to wherever it is that souls go. From our months of, I guess you'd call it research, the only people that don't are people who feel too much guilt about something. When they come back, if they're going to come back, they seem to always do it three days after they've died. Annamarie, well, I'm sure she was terrified, but she moved before Thomas came back and he didn't know how to find her."

"Guilt? What could Thomas possibly feel guilty about? Did he tell you what Bobby did to them? How that animal beat them all and would have killed Annamarie if Thomas hadn't stabbed him. Her jaw was broken in three places. When she pulled in that night, her face..." Lulu teared up with the remembrance. "That poor child. I can't imagine what he'd already endured living with that demon. He shouldn't feel any guilt about killing him."

Thomas was looking at the ground. Even though she couldn't see him he still couldn't look her in the eyes.

"Lee told us what happened that night. We uh... we hadn't really talked about it with him. About that night, you know. He was more interested in finding his mom and sister, so we were just focusing on that. He said he'd tried to remember how to get here but he'd been really young and didn't know where to go."

"He was six the last time Annamarie had come to visit. That was when Bobby was still letting her out of his sight. He became more controlling over the years, wouldn't let her come home. He'd even pick up the other line when she called so that he could listen in and make sure she didn't say anything bad about him. Probably to keep her from making any plans to leave." She shook her head again and stared at her hands, her fingers were wound around each other and the knuckles were white. "Annamarie cried for months afterward. We had Thomas's body transported down here to be buried and she'd sit out at his grave and cry for hours. Sister... she was scared a lot. They moved in with our mother. I lived a few houses down then, newly married, a baby of my own at the time, and Annamarie stayed with me more often than not. The nightmares she had..." She seemed lost in thought for a minute and Pansy looked at me, silently begging me for what she should say next.

"Ask her about Bethany. Thomas wants to see her, to see that she's okay."

"Miss Lulu, can you tell us where Bethany is? Thomas really would like to see her, see how she turned out. Make sure she's okay."

She rubbed the back of her hand under one eye and nodded,

her voice catching on the words. "Bethany? Wow, we haven't called her that in years. Annamarie changed her name to Susie to keep anyone from finding her and putting that terribleness together. Yeah, let me call her, she's not that... You know what? Let me just take you over there so he can see for himself what she's done for us. They'll follow us, right? The ghosts?"

"Yeah, they can hear and see everything we do. We don't have to tell Beth—I mean Susie. She doesn't have to know about Thomas unless you think she'd want to know that. He just wants her to be happy."

"Okay, let me call over and make sure she's there and not out running errands or anything." She got up, rubbing her hands down the leg of her yoga pants and seemed like she was trying to psych herself up. Finally, she straightened, nodded her head twice and went to the kitchen to place her call.

"She took that better than I thought she was going to," Bagel commented.

"I mean, it's a lot. I get that, but yeah. She did really well with the moving horse statue," Pansy agreed, wiping a tear from her cheek.

Thomas was still staring at the floor, refusing to meet anyone's gaze and I put an arm around him as best I could. "She's okay, Kiddo. You saved them both."

25

Miss Lulu came out of the kitchen wearing a fanny pack and slipped on a pair of hot pink flip-flops sitting on the rug by the front door. Bagel and Pansy walked out to the Tracker while the older woman locked her front door after shooting the teenagers some side-eye. I figured that she was probably like us and hardly ever locked her door on a normal day. This day was far from normal.

"I've been looking at one of these, but I heard they can tip over," she said as she pulled herself up into the passenger seat. Bagel had already squished himself into the back bench seat with the cooler.

"I mean, I think it's fun, especially with the roof off," Pansy replied as she started up the engine. "Which way?"

"Just head back the way you came, and when you get up to a blue house on the corner, turn left."

Pansy put the Tracker in drive and did as directed while Lulu took stock of all of the crap in Pansy's car. The cooler in the backseat that Bagel was now using as an armrest, the little car-sized box of tissues, and the two identical graduation tassels hanging from her rearview mirror. Lulu ran her fingers through the colored tassels. "You know, my grandmother was a very spiritual woman. She knew things that she shouldn't know, like when my uncle died in Korea. She told us all to expect the letter a month before it came. She died before Annamarie moved to Perth and I often wonder what she would have said to her. If she could have had some sway with my sister to keep her from marrying that..." I knew she probably had some strong words to say but held her tongue. "That man. But Susie, she's going to have a harder time understanding this. She's a no-nonsense kind of girl. I think we need a better story for her. Turn up here." She pointed right.

"Well, I have my camera," Bagel said. "And Pansy is going to study journalism. You could tell her we were here to interview you about... I don't know. The hospitality industry or something."

"I can work with that," Lulu laughed. We'd left the residential areas behind and were driving through a run-down commercial area full of mechanic garages and windowless bars. "This is the place up here, next to the salon." She pointed towards an old shopping center where four two-story shops, each painted a different faded pastel shade, were all smashed together. There was no marquee to advertise the names of the stores, and the painted lines that laid out two rows of parking spaces had practically disintegrated in the sun. The salon was on the right end, and the doorway on the far left had been boarded shut with a sheet of plywood.

"Oh, cool. Our mom works for a salon in Perth doing nails," Pansy said.

"We're not here about the beauty shop," Lulu said as she slipped out the passenger side door of the Tracker and pointed towards the lavender section of the building. As we drew closer, I could see a smaller, hand-painted sign that read, Women and Children's Shelter.

"Oh, does Susie work for the shelter?" Pansy asked, her concern evident in her voice.

"Work there?" Lulu chuckled. "Practically twenty-four-seven. Through a series of grants and donations, she bought the entire building. She graduated from law school two years ago and runs her practice out of one of the top-floor offices. She rents space to the salon on the end here, and knocked down the walls between the other three shops to create the shelter. It's been up and running for almost a year now."

I floated down the covered sidewalk to the other glass door where a smaller piece of posterboard had been taped to the inside, "Susan Sweetwater, Attorney at Law. Ring bell for entry."

There was an oversized doorbell next to the door and I assumed it was some kind of buzzer system like what you saw in movies where people were 'buzzed in' to a place. Two video cameras were suspended from the metal awning overhead, getting a good view of both doors.

"This place is more secure than Fort Knox," Lee muttered beside me.

As Lulu approached the shelter entry, she waved at one of the cameras and we all heard a buzzing sound followed by a mechanical click. Lulu held the door open for Pansy and Bagel.

I watched Thomas as he took in the front desk and small cafeteria-style dining room with brightly colored lunch tables that looked like they'd been donated from an elementary school. His eyes were big, and although his mouth was open, he seemed beyond words. There was a kitchen towards the back and a doorway by the front receptionist was opened to what looked to be a newly refinished hallway.

"Hey Mitzi," Lulu said, leaning an elbow on the chest-high countertop that separated the receptionist from the lobby area. "Susie said she was going to be here and I have some, uh, students that have come down to interview her about the shelter."

"Oh, that's fantastic. You know we're always looking for donations and trying to get the word out. We just had a truck come in so I think she was in the kitchen helping them unload. Go on back, you know the way."

"Thanks, babe." Lulu waved her hand in a come-on motion and was followed by the two teens and all three ghosts like a Momma duck and her ducklings. We made our way past an empty buffet-style table like our school cafeteria used, and into the kitchen area.

The kitchen held industrial equipment that was clean, but definitely not new. "There was a restaurant in Carrizozo that went out of business last year and Susie got a great deal on all of this," Lulu told them. "They started off with donated residential appliances and that makes cooking for twenty people at a time a little more challenging."

A pretty young woman who looked to be in her mid-twenties came bustling through a doorway carrying a stack of empty cardboard boxes. Her dark blond hair was cut shorter than it had been in her graduation photo, just a few inches long, and gelled back into a style that reminded me of Lee's. She wore jeans, and an oversized tee with a smiley face screen printed across it. Her glasses had bright purple frames and I liked her immediately. Her quick smile upon seeing Lulu made me think of Summer for a brief second.

"Bethy." I heard Thomas whisper her name and the look on his face broke my heart. If I could have cried, there definitely would have been some tears.

"Auntie, who do we have here?" she asked, setting the boxes down on the end of the countertop table and dusting off her hands against her jeans. Two other women working with her continued bringing boxes in from an exterior door and stacking them next to a wall of wire shelves full of bulk foods.

Lulu gestured to the teens. "This is Pansy and Dario. They've come all the way down from Colorado because they've heard about what you've done with the shelter."

Pansy didn't miss a beat and stepped forward, holding out her hand. "It is so great to meet you. I've heard wonderful things about what you're doing here." Pansy was becoming a much better liar than she'd ever been before, and I only briefly wondered if that was a good thing or not.

"Hi, I'm Dario," he held up the 35 mm camera that was hanging around his neck. "I promise I won't take any photos with your, uh, clients in them, but I'd love to get one of you and maybe some shots of the building?"

"Oh, I'm not really dressed for a photoshoot," she said, looking down at her outfit. "Some warning would have been nice, Auntie," she said, playfully swatting at Lulu's arm.

Thomas still looked torn up and I hovered next to him, trying to lend moral support. "See, I told you, she's okay."

"You should be proud of her, Kid," Lee said. "Putting this kind of thing together takes a lot of coordination and effort from a whole community. And getting a law degree? It seems like your baby sister is on a mission."

"Dude, she's killin' it," I agreed.

Thomas nodded his head but couldn't take his eyes off of his sister.

"Why don't we have a seat out here," Susie said, pointing the way back out to the cafeteria.

"Lindy, you and Honey take a break after you get done shelving all of this, okay? We'll start next week's menus when I get done with this interview." Susie led everyone back out to the cafeteria where she gestured toward a table.

Bagel and Pansy took seats on one side while Lulu and Susie

sat across from them. "So how did you hear about us? We don't have the money for advertising and I'm shocked you came all the way from Colorado. And I'm confused as to how you know Lulu?"

"Oh, Pansy's mother was a friend of your mom's and after your Momma died, I'd write to her every once in a while, and keep her up to date on how you were doing."

Oh, she was good at this.

"Yeah," Pansy said. "When Mom told me about this and told me a little bit about your story, growing up and all, I felt like this was something that more people needed to be aware of. We're," she gestured to Bagel, "starting at Greeley in the fall and I'll be working on a degree in journalism so I thought, you know, what better time to grab such a great story?"

"I'm sorry, let me stop you right there. I don't have any problem talking to you about the shelter, but if you want to dig up history, well, that can just stay buried, if you don't mind."

"Oh, no. I understand completely. If I had a nickel every time a reporter told my story wrong, well, I'd only have two or three nickels, but still, there's nothing more infuriating. Your brother..." Pansy paused, realizing she couldn't tell Susie what her brother had said without looking Cuckoo for Cocoa Puffs. "From what I read in the original articles, and from uh, what Mom had told me, your brother died trying to save you and your mother from an abusive husband, so I think this," she gestured around the room, "well, it's a beautiful tribute to that loss. A lot of people in this world grow up in that kind of environment, but it takes a special kind of moxy to turn it around and put yourself in the position of a protector."

Lee was laughing on the other side of Thomas. "They're getting better at concocting cover stories, aren't they," he said. He raised an eyebrow at me. "She's going to make an excellent journalist one day."

"I appreciate that," Susie was telling Pansy, "and if you feel like you have to mention my personal life, I ask that you don't use our old names."

"Susie, it's been long enough," Lulu said, laying a hand on the younger woman's arm. "It's up to you, of course, but I don't think you should have to hide anymore."

"They're dead, by the way," Pansy blurted out. "Bobby's parents, I mean. I found an obituary online for another relative and it mentioned them. His dad died a year or two after the... incident, and his mom just died in '91. If that's who you're worried about finding you."

"They're dead?" Susie said, the shock coming through. "I don't know if I even ever met them, but Momma convinced me that we had to use our new names to keep them from finding us. I spent so much of my life with the fear that they'd find me and take me away that I guess it's just a habit now."

"Oh, sweetie. Did you really think that they didn't know where you were? Sister moved you back into her own mother's house, it wasn't like they couldn't have tracked you down if they wanted to. They just didn't want to. She changed your names to keep the reporters away. When some news vulture descended and asked the council if an Annamarie or Bethany Grayson were living on the rez, they could say with absolute confidence, no, you weren't. It was never about his parents."

"We're sorry to even be dragging all of this up," Bagel said. "I feel bad that we've sprung this on you, we should have called ahead first." He looked sincere. I mean, if we'd had the information we needed to call ahead first, sure, we would have done that.

Thomas floated closer to his sister and reached out one hand to touch her on the shoulder.

Susie swatted at her shoulder and continued her conversation. "Okay, but I'd prefer for the article to not be about me in particular. Yes, I had a rough start in life. A lot of people do, there's nothing special about that. I worked hard in school, graduated early, got scholarships, worked my butt off in grad school, and now I'm back home, continuing to work. And these women, some of them make my story seem like a cakewalk. There's a woman, Cheryl, she and her son were here for a few weeks. He reminded me so much of my brother. I don't remember much about him, just the pictures that Mom took with her when we left. She'd tell me stories about him and make sure that I knew how brave he'd been."

"I wasn't brave," Thomas said, shaking his head. "I was so scared. I'd never been so afraid in my life. That is not bravery."

"She cried so many tears over what my father did, what he took from her, and it created... I don't know. A rage I guess you could say. A rage inside of me that makes me want to never see another woman go through that. She lost her son and even her face. It never did heal quite right. She lost that too."

"She was never the same," Lulu agreed, taking Susie's hands in her own. "And you were still so young when the cancer took her. I wish you could have known her before. You have her smile, you know."

"She really does," Thomas agreed. "I should have killed him sooner. I thought about it so many times, every night for years. But I was too afraid."

Crap, I thought, just as I heard Lee's soft, "Oh."

"Pans." I leaned over to whisper to her. "The guilt. It may not be because he killed Bobby, I think it's because he didn't do it sooner."

"If I hadn't been such a scaredy-cat I would have done it years before. I could have saved us all. I'm happy I saved them, but we could have been together. I could have helped her," the loss on his face was killing me all over again.

"You were just a kid," I told him.

Lulu was giving Pansy the side-eye because she was staring at me, so Bagel jumped in to rescue the conversation. "She sounds like she loved you both very much," he said and it took me a second to remember what the living were still talking about. Oh, Annamarie.

"Yes," Pansy said, turning her attention back to the women across the table from her. "How could she be anything but proud of you?"

"You were just a kid, Thomas. I won't debate the, like, moral ramifications of killing someone with you, but let's look at the numbers. You're a skinny little thing even now. Years before you would have been even smaller. What do you think the odds would have been that you could have caused any real damage before he killed you?"

"But he killed me anyway."

Lee shook his head. "Yeah, kid, but this was the biggest you'd ever been before and if an ambulance had arrived before he'd bled to death, he still would have lived through it. The man outweighed you by a good hundred and fifty pounds, plus he was a drunk, and meaner than a snake. A full-grown man would have been hard-pressed to take Bobby out when he was in a rage. He'd been in a fight at the Buffalo Chip the weekend before he died and sent three adult-sized men to the hospital. You were smart to not try anything before then, son."

Pansy was scribbling in her notebook and tapping her pen aggressively so I floated over to read what she'd written. *Did he poof?*

"Not yet," I assured her. "I think it's going to take him some time, which is good. He deserves some time with his family."

"Thomas," I turned back to the dark-haired boy who was still standing next to his sister. "Do you remember what Lee and I told you about the ghosts we've met that have moved on?

About how, once they no longer feel guilty about the thing that's holding them here, they just disappear?"

"Yeah."

"My advice to you is to not think about Bobby or what happened that evening for... well, for a really long time. Hang out here, stay with your family, meet your cousins. Enjoy their lives. And when you feel like you can leave them, then and only then would I suggest that you think hard and logically about all of the reasons you couldn't have done more than you did any sooner than you did it. Okay?"

He nodded.

Lee brushed a hand through his shoulder. "Just breathe, kid. You found her. She's okay. She's going to keep being okay. Got it?"

Another nod. Bagel got up and was directing Susie to stand in front of the empty buffet for their first shots. He stuffed the lens cap in his back pocket and checked the settings on his camera. "If you can stand right here? Yep. Okay, now turn a little more this way. Great."

Lulu leaned across the table to Pansy, "So. What's going on with your, uh, friends."

"As far as I can tell, Thomas is thrilled to know that she's okay and doing good things for her life but he's really mad at himself for not being able to fix everything sooner."

"But he was just a kid. He couldn't have done more if he tried."

"That's what Gerri and Lee are trying to tell him."

"He always was stubborn. So, is he going to stay here? How can I talk with him? Do I need to get a Ouija board?"

"Yes, he's staying. And yes, a Ouija board works, but not because it's magical or anything, it just has all the letters and numbers you need to communicate. Scrabble tiles also work, or even those alphabet refrigerator magnets. Thomas can move things, but not like, 'pick up a pen and write a novel' move things."

Pansy turned to fully face Lulu. "I want to thank you for not kicking us off of your porch earlier. Finding you guys meant a lot to us and I can't tell you how happy I am that this worked out for the kid. Also, this really is a good story so I don't see any reason not to go ahead and write it up. Maybe we can sell the story to some bigger papers and get the shelter some publicity."

"Okay, you know the way back home to Perth, right?" I asked, Thomas. "If you get bored, or lonely, or need help with something, you know where to find us."

"Yeah, I got it. But I think I'll be alright here."

"And don't think about Bobby," Lee told him. "Compartmentalize. Don't think about it until you're ready to leave them."

"What if I'm never ready?"

"That's okay too," Lee said. "Some things are harder to face than we'd like to admit."

26

Sunburnt and exhausted, Pansy and Bagel made it back to Perth shortly before midnight. Pansy had given the parents a five-minute explanation of their adventures before taking a shower. The hot water did her skin no favors.

"Food for thought," I said, watching her apply lotion to her shoulders and face. "Maybe put some sunscreen on or like, leave the top on the Tracker when you guys take your next road trip."

"Oh my god. Like, is the sun hotter down there or something? I've never burned in my life." Neither of us had, actually. Even if we got a little pink, our skin just turned more golden brown the next day. I'd never seen her this red. "Do we even own any aloe?" she asked.

"Not that I know of. I'm going to run over to Trinidad and check on Mrs. Garcia unless you need me."

"God, I hope I don't need you. What I need is ten hours of sleep, but I'm not going to get that either."

"What time are you and Bagel leaving tomorrow?"

"Nine. We've guesstimated that that should get us close to

Bethel by the time it gets dark, then we'll get a motel and have as much time as we need to ask around town the next day."

"Well, I'll certainly be back by then. Get some sleep."

I was busy thinking about all of the things that could go wrong on a road trip, especially one that was going to take them two or three days, and was really surprised when I floated into what had been Mrs. Garcia's room when I'd last been there and some lady I'd never seen before was in the bed. Had they already released her or had they just moved her to another room?

I floated out into the hallway so that I could go search the nurses' station. Surely there would be a patient list or something lying around on the desk. I hadn't gone five feet down the hall when I heard someone say, "She's back." At first, I paid no attention thinking that it was a living, breathing person talking about someone else, but then it occurred to me that it was after visiting hours.

I turned and sure enough, there was a gray-haired older lady and a gaunt-looking balding man who was maybe in his forties, floating behind me.

"This is our floor kid," the man said, looking me up and down like I was invading their turf.

"That's great, you can totally have it. I'm just checking on a friend to make sure she's okay."

"You have friends that are still living?" the woman asked. She put her hands on her hips and looked me up and down. "You must be new."

"I actually have a lot of friends that are still living, and yes, I am fairly new. I just died in October, thanks."

"Well just so that you understand it, we've already staked out this floor. This half is mine, the other half is Gloria's," the man said motioning to the two sides of the hospital floor. "And there's no room for you downstairs either. Joe and Doug have already claimed the ER and the Morgue."

"Look, I promise, I already have a place to hang out and it is absolutely not in a hospital. So, if either of you can tell me where the old woman who was in this room Friday morning went, I'd appreciate it. Then you can go back to hanging around and doing whatever the heck it is that you guys do here on a regular basis. I don't want to join your little ghost gang or anything like that. I promise."

"Ghost gang," Gloria repeated with a chuckle. The guy shot her a dirty look but she just waved her hand at him. "Oh, stuff it, Lester. The old woman, Garcia?"

I nodded.

"Yeah, they moved her down here. Follow me."

Mrs. Garcia was asleep or sedated, I couldn't tell, but she was quiet and none of the machines were making weird noises. It looked like someone had poured purple ink across the side of her cheek and forehead and I could tell her cheek and jaw were swollen and puffy even in the near darkness of her room. She had a bandage wrapped around her forehead and the hair sticking out of the bandage at strange angles looked greasy. She was going to be very upset about her hair when she came to.

"She was awake earlier when her daughter was here," Gloria said. "The daughter told her that they were going to take her home with them whether she wanted to go or not. That she wasn't going to be allowed to rattle around in that big old house anymore."

"Good," I said, patting Mrs. Garcia's hand even though she couldn't feel it. "She's been living in that house alone for years and the ghost that lived with her finally moved on a few months ago. I've been checking on her ever since. That's how I knew that she'd fallen and called 911."

"Oh, that was you," Gloria said with a knowing nod. "All of

the emergency workers were talking about it downstairs. How she'd fallen but the door was open and someone had called 911. And then the old woman was talking about ghosts? It was the biggest mystery they'd seen in a while. In fact, I'm impressed that you could even pull that off since you're so new. It took me several years to be able to move things."

"Yeah, well, we kind of hacked that," I muttered.

"I don't know what that means," Gloria said while she looked at Mrs. Garcia's chart. "Are you from Perth?" she asked.

"Born and raised. And died."

"Is that old reporter still hanging out there?"

"Lee?" I asked, surprised that she knew him. "Yeah, he's still there."

"He was here a lot when his wife died, and then he came back as a ghost looking for her. You'd think with as many people who die here, we'd have more ghosts come through, but they're still pretty rare."

"Well, most people aren't hanging on to so much guilt that they can't move on. But we've helped two ghosts move on to whatever is beyond. Lee and I. And my sister."

"Really?" Gloria asked, moving slightly closer to me. "So, it is possible?"

"Yeah, apparently it has to do with guilt keeping you anchored here. Once that's removed, you can progress on."

"So, if you understand the why, then why are you still here? You haven't worked through your issues yet?"

It was a legitimate question and one I refused to look at any closer. "Yeah, in theory, I understand it, but..." Lester popped into the doorway of the room.

"Sorry to interrupt, but is your name Gerri Bellafini?"

"Umm, yes." *Okay, weird.*

"Yeah, I've got a lady down the hall here who can apparently see and hear me. In fact, she said she could see and hear all of us, and she thought she heard your voice. She wants to talk to you."

"That old bat can see us?!" Gloria exclaimed.

This information narrowed my options to exactly one person on Earth.

"Christine? Take me to her." I followed him two doors down the hall.

"Oh good, Gerri, it really is you. I thought that was your voice I heard." Christine was propped up with about five pillows and looked almost as bad as Mrs. Garcia. Her face was black and blue and her left leg and arm were both in a cast.

"Oh my God, what happened to you? Did you get hit by a bus or something?"

"A semi, actually, but it just sideswiped me." She ran a hand through her short black hair which was showing a good quarter inch of white roots. She'd been on the road for weeks now and obviously hadn't had time to hit a bottle of Lady Clairol.

"Wait, wait, she could see us this whole time?" Gloria asked from behind me. Both she and Lester were floating in the doorway and both looked dumbstruck.

"Well of course I could," Christine said, waving her good hand around, "but I try not to let on or I'll have every Tom, Dick, and Harry bothering me. Now, Geraldine, come sit down with me and tell me what you're doing here."

"Do you remember me telling you about the old lady in the pink house south of town?"

"The house where the ghost of the little boy had been?" she asked, settling against her pile of pillows.

"Yeah. She fell and hurt herself. I was just here to check on her."

"Well, now that you're here you can entertain me. I'm certainly not going to get any sleep with all of these machines beeping. How's Pansy doing? Is she practicing her seance?"

I spent the rest of the night trading stories back and forth with Christine, finally leaving with the sunrise. It occurred to me that when I'd been on my way to the hospital, worrying about all of the things that could go wrong on tomorrow's road trip, being smashed into the guardrail by a semi-truck hadn't even made the list. Now it was going to be all that I thought about. *Great.*

By the time I flew in through our bedroom window, Pansy was already dressed in a sleeveless baby doll dress with bicycle shorts and a pair of sandals with little leather daisies across the tops. She was shoving some papers, more maps, I assumed, into her book bag but she'd crammed so many clothes into it, there was barely room for paper. She managed to get a small note-book and her favorite pen into her purse, which was also bursting at the seams with whatever on earth she'd packed, and pulled the zipper closed with a flourish.

"Do you think you packed enough?" I said, as drolly as I possibly could.

"I hope so. Dario's going to bring his cooler again, and we're going to stop at Foodarama before we leave town to get drinks and stuff to make sandwiches. Maybe some snacks."

Who was she kidding? Of course they were going to get snacks.

I filled her in on Mrs. Garcia and Christine on the way to Bagel's house.

"I'll have to go see her when we get back. See if she needs a ride home or something. Oh look, he's packed and ready."

Bagel was sitting on the cooler in his driveway, reading a book while he waited. He was dressed in his standard Docs, ripped jeans, and an old Ramones T-shirt. His wardrobe just didn't vary the way Pansy's did. They did, however, sport matching bright pink cheeks and noses. I hoped one of Pansy's overstuffed bags held sunscreen this time.

"Are you ready for this?" he asked after tossing the cooler into the back seat once more. The other seat held both of their bookbags and Pansy's purse, Bagel kept his camera bag by his feet. I guess if they passed something interesting he wanted to be able to take pictures from the passenger seat.

I flew through the Police Station to collect Lee while Pansy and Bagel were in Foodarama. "You ready for more adventures, old man?"

"I don't know. They're taking Donnie Boy over to Trinidad for the arraignment today—I'm kind of torn."

"Why, what do they do during an arraignment? That's just where they decide if they're going to try him and when the court date is, right?" Law and Order for the win, again.

"And set bail. I kind of just want to see how he plays it, you know. Stoic and silent or innocent and clueless?"

"Well, it's not like he's going to be able to pay a couple thousand for bail, right? The man pays for gas with the loose change in his cup holder."

Lee sighed and reluctantly nodded. "You're right—it might be exciting for a whole minute and a half, but it's been years since I've been to South Dakota. Lead the way, kiddo."

We waited by the Tracker in the Foodarama parking lot for another five minutes or so until Bagel and Pansy finally came back out with three bags of groceries, a bag of ice, and two packs of soda. Dr. Pepper for Pansy and Bagel's beloved Jolt. As Lee and I watched them sort the candy, chips, cookies, lunch-meat, and finally the drinks into the Tracker I finally had to speak up. "You two aren't going to get anywhere near Bethel before midnight if you don't get a move on. Bagel can sort it as you drive. Go, go, go."

"Gerri's tired of watching us play Tetris with this," she said, stuffing a treehouse's worth of Keebler Elf cookies into the backseat before finally getting into the vehicle.

"I mean, maybe we did go a bit overboard, but if we're stuck in traffic for hours, we'll be set on snacks."

"They know they're driving to South Dakota, right? Where are they going to encounter traffic?" Lee asked. I just shrugged. Having never been there, I had no opinions at this time. "Tell her to fill up the tank before she goes. And go inside and get a jerry can to carry extra gas, just in case. There are some spots where they may go fifty miles between exits."

I passed all of this info on to Pansy and she scooted over to the Loaf N Jug to fill up. Finding the space to cram a big red plastic container of gasoline was trickier, and caused another few minutes delay.

Finally, they were ready to go.

I was loath to admit that Lee had been right, and while I began our trip excited to see all of the sights that Kansas and Nebraska could offer, honestly, I couldn't have told you where one ended and the other began. There were green fields in every direction and huge swaths of land where not a single person could be seen unless they puttered by on a John Deere or a Kubota.

Pansy and Bagel were making terrible time, as expected, and it was already getting dark as they came up to a town in Nebraska touting the World's Largest Covered Porch Swing. Bagel, who was driving at this point after accusing Pansy of purposefully aiming for the potholes, immediately turned on the blinker and exited the interstate.

"Are you kidding me right now?" I asked. The boy was a sucker for roadside attractions.

"Dario, we still have hours to go. What are you doing?" Pansy asked him.

"We need gas, I have to pee, there's something cool to see here, and I saw a sign for a motel. Civilization seems to be few and far between, so I'm not taking a chance and missing out on any of those things."

Okay, well, he had a point.

"Come on Gerri," Lee said, laughing. "You know you want to see a giant covered porch swing."

"Like, who even thinks of these things? Who sees an everyday item and thinks to themselves, 'yes, this, if we super-size it, it will draw people in from miles around?'"

"It's the 'if you build it, they will come' attitude."

"Ugh."

The park where this giant porch swing was located was already closed, but Bagel and Pansy snuck over the barrier and took pictures anyway. "Do you think I could just pee in those bushes over there?" he asked Pansy, eyeballing some low shrubs on the property.

"You absolutely cannot. Come on, let's go find a room."

They didn't have to go far before they found a cheap road-side motel that accepted cash and asked no questions about their age or marital status. Splitting a room to save money, Bagel practically burst through the door and made a run for the bathroom while Pansy was still gathering bags. A vinyl soft top wasn't exactly secure, especially in an unknown area, and she didn't want to leave anything that could be stolen in the Tracker overnight. This required three trips back and forth to bring everything in.

"We may have overpacked," Bagel finally said, flinging himself down on one of the twin beds. The room was clean and relatively modern. The furniture wasn't great but the bathroom was clean and it didn't look like anyone had recently been murdered in it or anything. It was a big step up from the Cowboy Lodge.

"It's good to be prepared. Besides, we needed the exercise after sitting on our butts all day."

"Well, I'm looking at the map," I told her, examining the papers she'd tossed on the scarred dresser. "And I'd say you still have another three hours to go in the morning. You'd better get your beauty sleep now."

Pansy sighed, stretched, and grabbed her book bag. "I'm going to take a shower."

Bagel grunted before rolling over and rooting around in his bag. "Okay, I'll take one in the morning. Wouldn't want to stress out the hot water heater or anything."

As soon as Pansy was in the shower Bagel pulled out his cell phone, his graduation gift from his parents, and hit the speed dial.

I hovered closer.

"Who's he calling?" Lee asked.

"Inquiring minds want to know," I replied.

"Hey, Jason. Yep. Yeah, we made it almost there. Pansy has to pee every thirty minutes so progress was slow." I could hear sounds on the other end but couldn't make out the words, and I couldn't get any closer or Bagel would know I was there.

"Oooh, it's his boyfriend."

"Well, that explains why he's blushing."

"I think that's the sunburn," I laughed. But my Bagel Boy was curled up on the bed with a little smile on his face. It was truly a Kodak moment. He filled the boyfriend in on their adventures for the day and was still on the phone when Pansy came back out of the bathroom dressed in a set of Minnie Mouse pajamas.

"Oh, let me ask her. Pans, Jason wants to know if you'd be willing to be interviewed next Friday. He never got a chance before, after the whole Stuart Mayes thing, and he'd love to have a chance to interview you. He said he'll try very hard to not make you look crazy."

"Gimme," she said, taking the cell phone away from him. Pansy then proceeded to interrogate the poor boy like an over-protective father interviewing his daughter's high school prom date, but apparently Jason had her eating out of the palm of his hand by the time she was done.

"Okay, I approve, and one more quick question. You don't happen to have a brother, do you?"

Even Lee chuckled and I turned to him, honestly surprised by his reactions to all of this. I mean, he was an open-minded dude, but he was old. Like old, old.

"I'm really surprised at how well you're taking this whole gay thing," I told him.

"Kiddo, I lived through the sixties."

He said it like that was supposed to be an answer. "I don't even know what that means."

He chuckled. "That's probably for the best."

I never did get a further explanation.

27

"Do you want to stop for breakfast?" Bagel asked after they'd loaded everything back into the Tracker.

"Absolutely not. This early?" Pansy said, shoving three more Soft Batch cookies into her mouth and washing them down with a cold Dr. Pepper. *Thank God we have good genes.*

It was still dark and very, very foggy when Bagel pulled out of the motel parking lot, but the sun soon burned the fog away and they made good time on the way to Bethel. By the time they pulled into town, the small diner on the corner was looking good to both of them and they decided to stop for real food.

The diner was decorated almost exactly the same as Chandra's Firefly Cafe. Black & white tile floors, lots of Chrome fixtures, and red vinyl booths and chairs. It seemed to be a universal theme in all diners that they all had to look straight out of an episode of Happy Days. This place, however, seemed to be a little worse for wear. The tiles were scuffed and more than one booth seat was held together with duct tape. That didn't seem to deter the locals though—for a Tuesday morning, the place was jumping.

A waitress told them to seat themselves and they settled into a booth by the front windows. While Bagel was studying the menu, Pansy pulled out the photos of Summer from her purse and set them out on the table.

"What are you going to do, ask everybody in the restaurant if they know this woman?" Bagel asked.

"I don't see why not," Pansy said. "It's not like we're on a secret mission or anything. The more people we ask the better our chances."

A long-faced waitress wearing an honest-to-god poodle skirt and her dark hair in a bun finally made her way over to their table. She pulled a pencil from behind her ear. Tapping it against her notepad, she asked, "What can I get you?"

"Hey, I know this is going to sound really dumb, but do you happen to know this woman?"

Pencil poised, the woman seemed taken aback by the question, but once she overcame her surprise she leaned in for a closer look at the photos. "No, I'm sorry," she said, shaking her head. "I've only lived here a couple of years, but she doesn't look familiar."

"Oh, well she's lived in Perth for the last five years, so that makes sense. But we think there's a chance she grew up here and we're trying to find her. Is there anyone we could talk to who has lived here for a long time?"

"If she's your friend like you say, doesn't she know where you live if she wants to find you?"

"Oh, she's way better at this than Donna," I told Pansy.

Pansy gritted her teeth. "Well, yes, Summer knows where we live but we're afraid that she's in trouble and we want to help."

"And you don't think that she has adult friends that could help her?" The waitress eyed the pair of them like she doubted they could find their way out of a wet paper bag.

"Can I get the Country Boy Breakfast?" Bagel asked. "Scrambled, bacon, pecan."

The waitress scribbled it down and cocked an eyebrow at Pansy. "And you?"

"The same thing I guess. That's fine. And orange juice."

"Oh yeah, orange juice for me, too, please."

The waitress walked over to the window and put the order in. As I watched, she slipped up next to another waitress who was working behind the counter and began talking and nodding towards Pansy and Bagel, while the other woman, who looked like she was a hundred and ten, nodded. The older woman put down the dishtowel she'd been using to wipe down the counter and began shuffling towards our table. She was thin as a rail with a beaked nose and thin face, and her hair—dyed an unnatural shade of red—was piled high on top of her head. She reminded me of the women who came to the salon where Mom worked and had their hair washed and set once a week. But maybe, like Fiona, it was actually a wig. I was now suspicious of everyone's hair.

"Good morning," she chirped as she approached the table. "My name's Birdie, I understand you have some kind of mystery you're trying to solve here." I was pretty sure I'd never seen someone with a more appropriate name in my life.

"Yes, ma'am. Our friend took off and we think that she's hiding from a man. He's in jail, and we'd like to let her know that, but she didn't leave a phone number or any way to contact her." Pansy pushed the photos towards the end of the table and Birdie reached one trembling hand down to pick one up. "Have you seen her before?"

"Well, yeah. I *know* I know her, but...what was her name? Who was she kin to? Let me think." she was muttering to herself and seemed to be searching the old data banks for a name.

All four of us were silent, watching the woman struggle to come up with the connection. Was this going to work? It had never occurred to me to go into a restaurant and ask to help identify someone. I had fully expected that we would need to go to the library and look up old yearbooks, and then call around with the phone book. By George, this was going to be way easier than I'd thought.

She clucked her tongue and snapped her fingers, "Come to think about it, seems to me that was Lorraine's daughter. The one that married that no good scoundrel what lived out Deer Creek."

Pansy was busy pulling her pen and notebook out of her purse, so Bagel asked, "Do you remember her name or know how we can reach Lorraine?"

"Well, I don't know that I should be giving out that kind of information, but you all just hang on right here and I'll go give Lorraine a call and see if she wants to talk to you or not. And look, there's Trudy with your food."

Sure enough, the sour faced waitress was bearing down on the table with four large plates of food. Eggs, bacon, biscuits, gravy, and hashbrowns took up all the space on one plate and the other held a stack of three giant pancakes covered in butter and syrup.

For a hot second, Pansy was speechless. She recovered quickly. "What on earth did you order?" Pansy hissed at Bagel.

"Uh, breakfast, what's it look like?" he mumbled as he already had a mouthful of pancakes.

"I can't believe this worked," I said. Assuming the waitress was correct and the mom agreed to speak with us. But it was a promising lead.

"Agreed. Let her know I fully approve of this method of information gathering." Lee leaned forward to inspect the pancakes. "And tell her that I'm jealous that I can't eat food because my goodness, that looks delicious."

"I kind of can't believe it worked either," she replied. "But wow, this was so much faster than I thought it would take. And yeah, Lee, it really is delicious."

"Not to be a Debbie Downer, but this plan only works if the mom agrees to talk to us," Bagel said. "What if she says no and doesn't want to give us any information at all? That means that we've wasted our whole trip up here."

"No," Pansy said before pausing to chew. "That just means that we don't have any information from the mom, but we could still continue with the original plan. We just need to find the library. We know her mother's name was Lorraine and we know we're in the right town. That's more information than we had before we left Perth."

"Okay, but the plan was to find her name and then track down people who knew her," Bagel argued. "If her mom doesn't want to talk to us then that part of The Plan is still kaput."

"Just think positive thoughts," Pansy told him.

I was getting ready to argue that we could still find other relatives or friends, but I spotted Birdie coming back from the back with a big smile on her face. She pulled off the top order form from her notepad and slapped it on the table next to Pansy's pancakes.

"This is Lorraine's address. I just talked to her and she's expecting you so let me give you directions on how to get there. You can drive over there after you eat."

The town wasn't much bigger than Perth and we didn't have any problems following the directions to Lorraine's house.

Pansy pulled into the driveway of a neat little cottage and turned the ignition off. When she made no move to exit the vehicle, Bagel slapped his hands on his thighs. "You ready to do this?"

"Yeah. I'm like, burning up with curiosity to know about Summer's life, but then, I'm also scared that maybe I'm going to find out stuff that I don't want to know, you know?"

"Yeah. Same. But we drove all this way, so let's do it." They opened their doors but hadn't even made it up the two front steps before the front door was thrown open by an older version of Summer. There was absolutely no question that we were in the right place.

"Wow," Lee whispered.

"I'm going to make a wild guess that you are the two kids from the diner," she said, holding her screen door open so that they could enter.

"Good guess," Pansy said, holding out her hand to shake. "My name is Pansy and this is Dario. We're from a little town in southern Colorado called Perth."

"It's nice to meet you. My name is Lorraine, but come in, come in," she said. "We're letting all the air conditioning out."

Pansy and Bagel followed her down a hallway painted a sunny yellow and into a kitchen that was decorated in red Mexican tiles with blue and yellow accents. Herbs and flowers were hanging from drying racks and colorful glass bottles in the windowsills were lit by the morning sun. The place looked like something out of a magazine and there was no question where Summer got her flair for decorating.

"Sit, sit," Lorraine told them, pointing at the round kitchen table inset with more colorful tile work. "Can I get you a lemonade? Or there's water or iced tea if you prefer?"

"Lemonade would be great, thank you," Bagel said.

"Nothing for me, thank you."

After the lemonade was poured, she sat down with them and came to the point of the visit. "So, I understand that you're looking for my daughter?"

Pansy pulled the photos out of her purse and set it in front of the woman.

"This is our friend, Summer," she said, tapping a fingernail on one of the photos. "She runs a store called Wild Harmony where she sells, well, a lot of random things and runs a yoga studio. She's also a member of the Perth Paranormal Society, which we also belong to, and is one of my favorite people. Earlier this year there was a lot of news coverage about a body that Dario and I found in the woods. Because she was part of the PPS, I'm afraid her face got plastered all over the national news along with ours."

"Oh, I see," her mother said. She seemed to be following along but I could tell that she was captivated by the photos.

Pansy continued. "So, after this press coverage, Summer said she had a family emergency and disappeared. She didn't leave a forwarding address, but we all assumed that she would come back or at least reach out to someone. That was in May. Then last weekend, this guy that's been creeping around town, broke into her apartment and trashed everything in her store. I mean, took a baseball bat or crowbar to everything and smashed it all. He's asking everyone he can find if they know where she is, and trying to find information about her. It's suspicious and has us all worried."

"Donnie," Lorraine said. It wasn't a question.

"Yeah. We set a trap for him so he's in jail right now, but we're all worried because nobody's heard from Summer and we assume that he's the reason she ran in the first place. We just want to find a way to contact her to make sure that she's okay, or if she's hurt, or if she needs help or anything. We would love to help her and we really miss her."

"Well, I'm afraid to disappoint you, but I haven't heard from my daughter in over seven years. Not since she left Donnie. Her real name is Janice by the way. Janice Burell. Well, Hankins after she married the brain donor. I haven't talked to her on the phone, I haven't had so much as a postcard from her, but maybe I can shed some light on why she's running."

Lorraine disappeared down the hallway and I followed her into her living room where she pulled a photo album from a bookshelf. Opening it, she began flipping through the pages and seemed to forget for a minute why she'd gone to retrieve it. As I watched, she snapped it closed and wiped a tear from her cheek.

Lorraine carried the album back to the table and set it in front of Pansy. Pansy ran a hand over the white vinyl cover, the embossed gold filigree around the edges faded and flaking. Bagel scooted closer and Pansy arranged it so he could get a better view. Lee and I crowded behind them. The first page was an eight-by-ten photo of the couple, Summer with her waist-length hair and a knee-length white dress with a big fluffy veil. He had worn a pair of blue jeans and cowboy boots with a black jacket over a white tuxedo shirt.

"Is this the man that you saw in your town?" Lorraine asked.

"Yeah. I mean he's younger here and he doesn't have the mullet anymore, but that's definitely him."

"He looked like he's put on a good fifty pounds since the wedding. What year was this?" I asked.

"What year did they get married?" Pansy translated.

"It was 1987. Right after they graduated from high school. I'd told her to wait, it wasn't like she was pregnant and had to get married right away, but she swore that she was in love with him." Lorraine shook her head in disgust. "I told her there were plenty more men out there in the world and she didn't have to just up and marry the first one that she came across, but who listens to their mother?"

Pansy and I gave one another a look. Certainly not us. Although I suppose the bright side of only having 200 people in your high school means that you're not tempted to pick someone you've known since Kindergarten and marry them. Like, eww.

"I'm going to guess that things didn't end amicably with him," Bagel said, flipping through the photo album.

"That's putting it mildly," Lorraine said, tapping her fingers against the sweating glass of lemonade in front of her. "He wasn't a nice kid and he grew up to not be a nice man. Let's just say that my daughter took a lot of grief before she finally got away from him. Thank goodness she hadn't had any kids, that would only have made it that much harder to escape."

I tried to imagine being on the run, sleeping in your car, changing your name, and doing all of the things that Summer had to have done while also dragging a little kid along. That would only increase the difficulty a thousandfold.

"I know that people always ask why a woman stays when a man is abusive, but the number of hoops she had to jump through before she got enough stuff together to be able to run and stay hidden? She knew when she ran that she'd never be able to come back to her old life. I honestly admire how strong she was. And this?" She tapped one of the photos of Summer and Chandra on an investigation before brushing away the tear that threatened to spill over. "Knowing that she was making a life for herself? That she had a community that cared for her? Well, that almost makes it worth it."

"Tell Pansy to ask her if she knows his birthday. He may be listed with some active warrants under his real name."

"Lee wants you to ask her if she knows his birthday so the police can do a better search."

"This will sound weird, but do you happen to know what his date of birth is?" Pansy asked Lorraine. "He's in our jail now, but when we get back home, I'm going to give this information to the police with his correct name and date of birth to see if there's anything else out there so they can keep him in jail longer."

"I actually do," Lorraine said. "It's the 4th of July, which makes it kind of hard to forget. 1969. He was just a couple of months older than Janice. And if there's any other information that I can give you that will keep him in jail, I'm more than happy to help."

"I'm just so grateful that you agreed to talk to us. And if you do talk to Summer, I mean, Janice, can you let her know that we miss her and that we would love for her to come back home? We'll do whatever we need to do to keep her safe."

"I'm glad that she has friends who care. Do you mind if I keep these?" she asked, pointing to the photos Pansy had laid on the table.

"Oh, of course, keep them, please. And here," Pansy wrote down her address and cell phone number in her notebook and tore it out for Lorraine. "Call me anytime that you want to talk. I can tell you all about all kinds of stories."

Lorraine gave both of them hugs as they walked back out the front door.

"Well that went well," Bagel said as Pansy pulled out of the driveway.

"I know. But can you imagine your parents not knowing where you were for seven whole years? That must be really stressful for her."

"It's too bad that Summer got tangled up with such a crap human being in the first place. No one should have to spend their life hiding."

The question was, where was she hiding now?

28

After another night in a cheap motel and living on turkey sandwiches and huge amounts of sugar, both Pansy and Bagel were thrilled when they drove through Trinchera and knew that they were almost home.

Bagel was at the wheel, and as he finally crossed the east bridge at a little after three in the afternoon, he made an immediate right-hand turn into the Perth Police Station. Do not pass GO, do not collect $200.

They stumbled out of the Tracker, holding their backs like old men and each of them performed a few stretches until their legs regained feeling. Bagel held the door for Pansy and she walked straight to the front desk.

"Excuse me, I need to talk to whoever is handling the break-in at the Firefly."

"You know it's Detective Crane," I said. "Why are you pretending it's going to be someone else?"

"Because he hates me," she hissed under her breath after Delacourt, the officer who'd been manning the desk, walked into the back to see who was available.

"Miss Bellafini." Crane's voice came booming down the hallway. "I hear you have some information. This should be fascinating."

"Well, I think it is," she said, pushing her shoulders back and attempting to smooth her wrinkled tee shirt. She probably should have brushed the cookie crumbs off the sleeve before she walked in, but I decided that now was not the time to mention it. "You may or may not be interested to know that we just tracked down Summer's mother in South Dakota, and know her real name, as well as the real name of the guy you arrested for breaking into the Firefly. He's Summer's ex-husband, Donald Hankins. I suspect that was not the name on his driver's license."

Pansy thrust a clean copy of her notes towards him and Crane stared at them for a second before grudgingly accepting them. You could tell he was cueing up some wisecrack, but it died on his lips as he looked over the pages.

"Well, this seems very thorough," he said. "You've even got his date of birth and previous cities of residence." He flipped to the next page, reading it all carefully. "And you said that Summer's mother gave you all of this?"

"Yeah, that's her number," Pansy leaned forward to search for Lorraine's info on the notes before tapping it with her index finger. "Right there. She'll be more than happy to answer any questions. It turns out that Summer's actual name is Janice and she married this human piece of garbage that you've got locked up back in '87."

"Well, see—therein lies the problem," Detective Crane said. "This would have been handy to have on Monday morning, but he was released on bail that evening. We'll still run checks on all of this and see if anything else pops up, but for right now, Mister... Hankins, is it? Well, he's a free man. At least until his hearing next month."

"Bail?" Pansy said, looking to Bagel and back to Crane. "What do you mean he was released on bail? He's broke."

"Well Miss Bellafini, once you've been arraigned then your bail is set and if someone comes in and is willing to pay it for you, then you're free to go under the condition that you come back in time for your trial."

"And you think that this dude is going to come back for a trial? You didn't even know what his real name was. How could you let him go?"

"Look, as far as we knew, according to the state of Kansas where his driver's license was issued, his name was Donald Chojackni. But don't worry about him showing up for trial, that little woman in all the animal print that posted his bail didn't look like someone he'd want to cross. So, thank you for the information, but we'll take care of it from here."

"Well, that narrows it down," Lee said.

Fiona. What could she possibly be up to?

"Firefly. Emergency Conference. Now," I said.

Pansy nodded, taking the keys from Bagel and driving the three blocks to the Firefly before pulling into an empty spot in front of the high school. Neither of them spoke for a moment. They were tired, needed showers with good water pressure, and could probably stand to drink some actual water if I had to take a guess, but there was more to be done before they could rest.

"Come on, cell phones out. You call Randy and Greg, Bagel calls Shawn and Blake. Anyone available needs to get to the Firefly now so you can fill them all in."

Pansy nodded and opened her door, Bagel followed looking completely defeated. "Call Shawn and Blake," she told him as she pulled her purse from the backseat and dug around for her cell phone. "Have them meet us here if they can."

"It's what? Wednesday?' Bagel said, thinking. "Blake only has morning classes on Wednesday so he should be home."

The two dialed as they walked and slid into an empty booth. Pansy immediately pulled her pen and notebook from her purse as she waited for Randy to answer. She left a voicemail when he didn't pick up. She immediately called Greg next, who answered. Bagel was talking to Blake, filling him in.

"Greg's going to track down Randy and get him here."

"So, how did it go?" Chandra asked, placing chocolate milkshakes in front of them both. "Did you find out anything?"

Pansy covered her face with her hands and let out a long groan, which pretty much summed it up, I thought.

"Did you know they let Donnie out of jail?" Bagel asked Chandra.

"What? When? How? I caught him red-handed! How could he be out?"

"Someone, we suspect it's that woman down in Berry that wanted Pansy to do that seance for her, paid his bail. He's out." Pansy said as she stabbed her straw down into the milkshake. "Thank you for this, though."

"Those.... ugh. No, no one even bothered to tell me. How do they even know each other? What if he breaks in again? What if he targets someone else on the PPS? Do they honestly believe he's going to come back and do a whole trial?"

"Well, if he doesn't show up then Las Animas County doesn't have to spend any money for a trial and it's up to the bail bondsman to collect the fees," Lee said with a shrug.

Yeah, that tracked, I thought.

"Blake is on his way," Bagel said. "I'm texting Shawn's beeper now." His thumb flew over the number pad, clicking the buttons multiple times to get to the correct letters. "There," he said, setting the phone down on the table. "Avengers assemble."

My brain was still stuck on something Chandra had said. "How *do* they know each other?" I asked Pansy. "They sort of met that one time at Canyon Lanes, but she didn't seem to recognize him, or even really care that he existed."

"He was really interested in *her*, though," Pansy said. She briefly relayed the interaction at the bowling alley to Chandra and Bagel, including the bit about Fiona pulling out her checkbook and promising Pansy money for the seance.

"And didn't Gerri say he was down at that bar in Berry when you guys went to do the prelim?" Bagel asked. "He was probably following Randy at the time, trying to find Summer, but that means that he knew exactly how to find a crazy woman with money when he needed one."

"Do you think the crazy in him recognized the crazy in her?" Pansy asked, using one of Summer's favorite quotes.

"It's entirely possible. Let me call someone in to take over for me here, I don't want to miss anything." Chandra jogged back to her office, leaving Bagel and Pansy to finish their milkshakes.

Twenty minutes later, the entire team was together, and a four-top table pulled up to the end of the booth to make room for everyone. Pansy and Bagel took turns telling the group everything they'd learned, covering two and half days of adventure in about ten minutes.

"I can't believe that no one even told us that he was back out," Randy said, smashing one fist against the tabletop. "I mean, burglary isn't murder or anything, but you'd think it would get you more than a weekend in jail."

"We obviously chose the wrong career paths," Greg said, crossing his arms.

"Where would he go? If you called Summer's, I... I just can't think of her as Janice, sorry." Chandra said, shaking her head. "If you called her mom, do you think she'd be able to tell us if he'd gone back to Bethel?"

"Or would he go down to Berry with this Fiona woman and hide out there?" Blake asked.

Shawn looked at Pansy. "Is Gerri here now?"

"Yeah. Her and Lee both."

"Can they do recon? See if we can find out where this guy might be hiding? We can all keep an eye out for him here, we know what he drives, we know what he looks like."

"We can even make fliers and print out stills from the videos. Hang them up all over town, warning people to be on the lookout," Chandra said.

"The police still have the videos," Randy pointed out.

"Either way," Shawn said, "we can keep our eyes open if the ghosts can snoop around. Check motels, Fiona's house, heck, search his own momma's house. We're not going to feel safe until we know where this cockroach is hiding."

"And then, when we find him," Randy paused to smack one fist into his open palm. "I think it's time Donnie had a come-to-Jesus meeting and understood, in no uncertain terms, that Summer is no longer his."

"Okay, well, we'll work on that part later," Chandra said, laying one hand on Randy's arm. "But if they can find him, maybe spy on him, see what he's planning... well, we'll have more information to work with."

"I'm game," I said, turning to Lee.

He nodded. "My agenda is clear. Do you want to take the Cowboy Lodge and then every hotel or motel between here and Berry? I'll start checking everything between here and Bethel. We passed several questionable places he could be hiding out."

"It'll probably take a few days, but yeah, we're in," I told Pansy.

"They'll start the search," she told the group. "I'll call Lorraine and let her know that he's out."

"Great. Now, tell us all about Thomas. We haven't talked to you in days. What happened? Did you find his family?" Chandra asked.

Lee and I left them there. We had a single, greasy needle to find and a whole bunch of haystacks to search.

29

PANSY

I took Dario home and was carrying the cooler into the Venturas' garage when Mrs. Ventura noticed that we were home. We were both smothered in hugs, and I had to politely decline, *twice*, her offer to stay for dinner.

"I've got to get home to see my parents. I know Mom is probably worried about us," I told her. I hadn't called home since we'd left, so that was probably true.

My head hurt, and the muscles in my back and legs were so tight from sitting for so long that it was going to take a week of yoga to stretch them back out. I was also going to be separated from my sister while she searched Greater New Mexico for Summer's ex-husband. Besides the time she'd died, had we ever been apart for that long? *Also*, I thought, adding to my internal to-do list, *I need to find a new job*. That was going to be hard when everyone knew I'd be leaving for Greeley in a month. Maybe the library needed summer help.

I was driving home on autopilot, my discomfort growing with every bump in the road. Contrary to Dario's belief, I didn't actually aim for the potholes, they just kind of jumped out in front of me. Either way, if I never had to drive anywhere ever again, I'd be happy. Thrilled, actually. I was thinking about how wonderful it would be to flick my ponytail like I Dream of Genie and magically appear anywhere I wanted to be when my brain registered *danger*.

Unfortunately, it registered this about half a second too late, because a big black tank—some car from the seventies that was about six feet longer than anything I'd ever want to drive—swerved into my lane at the last second, knocking me off the road. My little Tracker didn't even put up a fight, the front end immediately crumpling with that terrible sound of metal on metal. I bounced into the scrub along the side of the road, pushed along by the more powerful vehicle. For a moment, my brain froze and I was back in our red Cavalier, singing along with the radio. The impact. The sounds. The screaming. I'd been here before. I'd already done this. Gerri? Where was Gerri? I had to save her, I had to... I reached out, groping blindly for the passenger seat but there was no one there. Not this time. Why couldn't I see? I wiped a hand over my face but it was all wet and sticky. My hand was covered in blood. My blood? Gerri's blood?

No. Not this time.

The sound of laughter made me turn towards the busted window. My brain didn't even have time to register *danger* this time. The fist came out of nowhere.

Someone was talking. I didn't know who it was, but they seemed to be having a really good time. We hit a bump and my body was thrown up into the air before landing on my side. My whole body hurt. I opened my eyes, finally settling on just the left one as the right eyelid didn't seem to want to cooperate right now. Everything was gray. No, no. That wasn't right. It was upholstery. Car upholstery. Gray velour. I was facing the back of a seat. I was lying across the back seat of a car that was moving and had some dude in the front seat who wouldn't shut up. The headache I'd had earlier was nothing compared to this, and my arms and legs were...*wait, why couldn't I move my arms and legs?* I struggled to move but felt something dig into my wrists and ankles. *Have I been hogtied? What is going on?*

"I mean, can you even believe that timing?" The voice was saying. "I thought for sure I was going to have to kidnap you from your own house because my god, girl, you don't ever seem to be alone. But there you were, all by yourself, just driving and daydreaming." *Was he talking to me? How long had I been out?*

"And that little Hot Wheels toy you drive, the way that thing folded up?" He was laughing so hard that he had to pause to catch his breath. "You know that Chinese-made crap is awful in a crash, right? Well, you do now." He must have thought that was especially hilarious because he continued laughing like a braying donkey.

Geos were Japanese, thank you. But I know this voice. Why do I know this voice?

Donnie.

It hit me all at once, my brain finally coming fully back online with a rush of adrenaline. This... amoeba had run me off the road on purpose, punched me in the face to knock me out, and now had me hogtied in the back of a car. A car we'd never seen and no one knew to look for.

I was mad. So mad. Did I start to cry? Yes, of course, but only because I was absolutely *furious* that this Patrick Swayze wannabe with bad teeth and no deodorant had gotten the drop on me. The drop, that's what they call it in the movies, right? And why me? What had I done to deserve being kidnapped fifty feet from the turn-off to my own neighborhood? In broad daylight, mind you. He wasn't going to get away with it. Surely, someone would have heard the crash. Someone would find my Tracker. The front end had been destroyed. It wasn't like he'd had time to hide it or drive it into a ravine. Someone would be alerted. Someone would come and rescue me. I just had to wait it out.

I settled into the seat and tried to get comfy. I needed to be calm. I could think better if I was calm. From my vantage point, I could only see the blue sky overhead and absolutely no land-marks. Plus, I had no idea which direction he'd gone after he'd pulled away from the crash. It didn't matter, someone would find me. I just needed to take a little nap and conserve my strength.

Pain registered across my cheek and my eyes popped open, or at least the one that wasn't swollen shut did. My brain was on a two-second delay, but it finally put two and two together that Donnie, who was standing in front of me, had slapped me across the face.

Rude.

"What are you doing? I told you to bring her to me, not kill her." That rasp could only be Fiona, and oh look, what do you know, there she was, standing behind Donnie tapping one red stiletto against the concrete floor.

Where were we?

The lighting was dim and my good eye wasn't really focusing that great, but I knew we weren't in the bar. The room was small, smelled like damp concrete, and was completely empty other than some shopping bags.

Donnie shoved a lantern in my face and I pulled back as far

as I could, but I seemed to be tied to a chair. Was he holding a Coleman lantern? Like the kind we used when we went camping? Did this place not have real lights?

"Well, she might be a little concussed, but she's still alive. She'll still work for my purposes."

"*Our* purposes," Fiona said, tapping her pack of cigarettes against her palm before pulling one out.

"Hey, give me one of those," Donnie whined.

"Haven't I given you enough? I got you out, now help me get all of this stuff set up."

He finally negotiated labor for a cigarette, and I realized that I was tied to a chair in a tiny concrete room with two crazy people. *What was the point of all of this?*

"What are we doing here? Where are we and how do you think you're going to get away with it? It's not like I don't know who both of you are."

"You're the psychic, you should already know how this is going to play out." Donnie snarled.

Was he planning to kill me? It was the only way that I wouldn't talk when it was all said and done. I started to respond by telling him that I wasn't psychic, but you know what? These clowns had already pushed me too far, today. "You're right, I am a psychic and you're just dumb. I can clearly see that this is going to fail miserably, and you're probably going to end up shot by the police. I have no idea what Janice saw in you."

"So, you *do* know her name, you little liar. Where is she?"

"Who the heck is Janice?" Fiona asked. "Donald, I told you to get these candles set up in a circle around the room."

"Janice is his ex-wife and she..." I was rudely interrupted.

"Not ex, she couldn't divorce me without letting me know where she was. She's still mine." Donnie said.

"Lucky her," I said. "Did he tell you that he ran me off the road in broad daylight and left my Tracker sitting not fifty feet from the turn into my own neighborhood?"

Fiona seemed surprised by this.

"The police are already going to be looking for me."

"Well, they'll never think to look here, so I'm confident that we have time. Donald, I said a circle, not a rectangle."

"Are you actually trying to do a seance right now? This still isn't going to work. We can't do a seance with three people." I had no idea if that was true or not but I said it really confidently. "You need four to complete the circle.'

Fiona thought about this for a second, and I almost thought I had her, but she was a stubborn old bat. "We'll try it with three. If that doesn't work, I'll call one of the waitresses from the bar."

"It'll take 'em twenty minutes or more to even get here and I'm already sweating in here," Donnie whined again.

Where the heck are we?

Donnie moved some of the candles to make them more circular and lit them all. With the extra lighting I could see three unpainted concrete block walls with no doors or windows. Were we in a basement? The entrance must be behind me but I couldn't hear any traffic from outside.

I was also sweating, and I thought back to health class and the signs of a concussion, sweating and nausea. Check and check. But I could see that Donnie's chambray shirt was soaked through between his shoulder blades, so it was just hot in here and the heat from the candles wasn't improving the lack of air conditioning. By the time they were all lit, even Fiona was fanning herself with her hands.

"We need to crack this door just a little," she said.

"Just a little, we don't want anyone snooping," Donnie moved behind me and I heard the unmistakable sounds of a garage door being pushed up. A storage unit. We were in a storage unit. Well crap, the old bat was right, no one was ever going to find us here. "There, that should let some air in at least."

They were both smoking and we had about fifteen candles burning oxygen, so I was at least grateful that we weren't all going to die from carbon monoxide poisoning.

"Okay, now hold her hand," Fiona directed.

"Her hands are tied behind her back."

"Well, stand behind her then."

This was like the world's worst comedy routine. Smothers Brothers look out, your replacements are here. "I'm not going to say the words. We've done this before. Your husband is not on this plane. He is literally not here for me to talk to."

"Well, I don't need you to say the words. I have them right here." As they were both behind me now, I couldn't see what she was doing, but after some shuffling and rummaging I heard a click and some static before they both grabbed onto my hands tied behind my back.

The sound of a bell chimed from behind me, and then my own voice. "Spirits, we call upon you and ask that you lift the veil between worlds to speak with us. Our circle is protected by goodness and light. We ask that no harm should fall upon those within the protection of the circle."

She had recorded me. This crazy old loon had recorded me.

"I ask that any available spirit come into the circle." Fiona said, modulating her voice to sound as soft and musical as she was physically capable.

She sounded stupid.

"We would like to talk to you, oh ghostly ones."

Was she for real? And this was a dumb idea, calling on any old random ghost. Who knew what would show up? How would that even work?

But what if it did? I had a secret weapon, one that Fiona and

Donnie didn't know about. Plus, I had the added advantage of being smarter than them. The trick was to find a ghost roaming past wherever the heck we were who was also willing to be helpful. That part could be tricky.

I closed my eyes and concentrated on requesting someone who could make this situation better and not worse. "I beseech you, spirits, bring forth a helper, someone to assist with a great task."

"That's the spirit," Fiona said from behind me.

I kept my eyes squeezed tight and repeated my entreaty, wishing with everything in me that someone who would be willing to help me would appear. Another Doctor Welling would not be a value-add right now. "Where's Casper when I need him?"

"And what is it, exactly that you need?" I heard a man's voice drawl from across the circle. He was a cowboy, like a real one, with leather chaps and a bandana around his neck. But he was just floating there, his wiry body relaxed. He wasn't being held like ghosts I'd called by name. He seemed to be there of his own free will.

"Who are you?" I asked.

"I don't see anything," Donnie complained.

"I don't either, just hush," Fiona hissed.

"*You* called *me*, little lady. I was just wandering through when I felt it, and as I ain't never felt anything like it before, I figured I'd better head on over and check it out. Who are these knuckleheads?" He stepped closer, out of the shadows, and I could see that he had a salt and pepper scruff like he hadn't shaved for a few days. He took in the entire scene, walking closer to Fiona and Donnie and waving his hand in front of their faces.

"Spirit," Fiona said, "I'm going to need you to go find my husband, Gene Dale. He's from Berry, just east of Raton. I need you to bring him here. This little girly doesn't seem to be able to find him."

I rolled my eyes. How was I going to communicate with the ghost without these two knuckleheads, as he called them, hearing me? Morse code? Unfortunately, I didn't know Morse code. But wait, I did know SOS, I thought, thinking back to the SOS Scrubbing Pads commercial. I tapped out the rhythm with my foot, dot dot dot, dash dash dash, dot dot dot.

The cowboy looked down at me with a smile. "Uh, yeah, little chickie. I didn't really need the SOS. I already," he swirled a finger around me, "you know, gathered that there was an issue."

He stepped back and walked around the candle circle. "Is this some kind of seance or something?"

"Or something," I replied.

"Who's she talking to? Tell us what's going on little girl," Donnie demanded.

"There's a man. A cowboy. I don't know his name."

"Well tell him to go find Gene. We'll wait."

"Speak for yourself, it's hotter than blazes in here," Donnie complained some more.

"Tell her I said no. I'm not an errand boy."

"Understandable. But what about a favor for me? Do you know where the hospital in Trinidad is?"

"They didn't take Gene to Trinidad, why would he be there?" Fiona asked.

"I do," the cowboy replied, crossing his arms like he had all day. The movement made the light glint off the star pinned to his chest.

I hesitated. The extent of my knowledge of Morse code was exhausted and my head was splitting. If there was a way to make my request without Tweedle Dee and Tweedle Dum catching on, I couldn't think of how to pull it off. Instead, I spoke quickly. "Christine Hermance, she's there now. Short, black hair with white roots. She can talk to you. I need her to call the police and tell them where I am."

He opened his mouth to say something, or maybe to ask a question, but Donnie smacked me in the side of the head so hard that I almost blacked out again. My cowboy disappeared the second Donnie let go of my hand. I guess a three-person seance was a thing that could be done after all.

"Ain't nobody going to tell anyone where you are, little girl. Not until we're done with you, anyway."

"I don't even know if I believe her." Fiona said, "What if she was just pretending to tell someone, how would we..."

The garage door behind us slammed to the ground, followed by the clank of metal on metal.

Fiona and Donnie were quiet for a full thirty seconds before they began yelling. One of them tried to open the garage door but it wouldn't budge.

"Hello? Who's there? We're locked in!"

"It won't budge. Someone's closed the hasp for the lock. I can't open it from this side."

I drew a few calming breaths, trying to meditate even though my bladder was about to burst. I wanted to let them panic a little bit first. "Miss Dale," I said, interrupting their shouts for help. "Do you remember when I talked about vengeful spirits coming through the protective circle?"

"Vaguely. A bunch of hooey if you ask me."

"Mmm-hmm. Well, the reason you don't just call any old spirit, the reason you ask for the particular ghost that you want to speak with and no one else, is because you cannot predict who is going to answer. A named spirit, one who is specifically called to the circle, is under the control of the caller. But what we just did? The spirit we just called? Well, I hope your life insurance is paid up." I was completely making this up as I went, but it sounded really creepy, right?

"I don't have time for these games, little missy. I need to know where Gene hid the money. I need to talk to him now!"

"Wait, wait, wait," Donnie said, kicking over candles as he began to pace. "You promised me a hundred thousand dollars to kidnap her. Are you telling me that you don't actually have the money?"

"Well, not on me, no one carries that kind of money around with them. But I have it. Gene had it. Somewhere."

"I thought you were rich—that you actually had access to money. You paid my bail."

"I put up the deed to my house for your bail. I don't have that kind of money."

"So, you were planning on paying me out of the money from the bank robbery? Money that is hidden and probably marked even if you find it?"

Fiona gasped. "Who told you about the bank robbery?"

"The internet cafe," I said.

Donnie stopped his pacing, "How did you know about the internet cafe?"

"Umm, psychic, remember?" I mean, let's just go with it at this point. Maybe I could get them to believe me and predict a gruesome death for both of them if they didn't let me go.

Donnie was silent for a moment as he resumed his pacing, kicking over candles and sending them crashing into the walls of the storage unit. "And you were going to pay me off with stolen money? They trace that stuff, you know. Write down all those little serial numbers and things like that."

"No, no. Roger, Gene's partner, knew a guy at the bank. It was an inside job. The friend is the one who filled the bags when they came in to rob it. He made sure there were no dye packs, no serial numbers were written down anywhere. The money is clean—I just don't know where he hid it."

"And this was your plan? Promise me money that you don't have, to snatch some psychic kid off the street, to contact your dead husband so that he can tell you where the money actually is? This was the grand plan?"

"Yes. I just need her to try harder."

"Try harder? Are you kidding me? This is ridiculous. What was supposed to happen after that? Did you think she wouldn't tell anyone?"

"Well, I thought that you could just, you know, take care of her."

This sent Donnie into some kind of crisis mode, waving his hands around in the air and mumbling to himself while he continued stomp-pacing.

"You know, this reminds me of an old saying by Benjamin Franklin," I told the group. "You both know who Benjamin Franklin was, right? Founding father, glasses, flew a kite in a storm."

"He's the one that invented electricity," Donnie said with complete confidence.

"Invented it. Yeah, sure. Anyway, he had a famous saying about keeping secrets. It was 'three may keep a secret if two of them are dead'." I looked at Donnie. "So, if her plan was to get the money, only give you a fifth of it, and then have you kill me, well, that would still leave two people alive."

I was watching Donnie so when Fiona backhanded me, I didn't have time to pull away. "Hush your mouth," she hissed at me.

I spit a mouthful of blood onto the floor. One day I'd learn keep my mouth shut. Today was not that day.

Donnie looked shocked and maybe Fiona's reaction was what kept him from immediately understanding what I was saying, or maybe he was just bad at math. Once my meaning filtered through, though, he swung around towards Fiona with the meanest look I'd ever seen on someone's face. He'd made it three steps towards her when I heard the first siren. Followed closely by a second. And then a third.

And then, Donnie reached behind him and pulled a gun out of his waistband.

Great.

The hostage situation, however, was short-lived. As soon as the police arrived, they flung the garage door open, even as Donnie was trying to tell them that he had a gun. My back was to the door, so I couldn't see exactly what was going on, but my guess was that they had more than one. In response, Donnie immediately scrambled to squat in front of me, pointing his gun directly into my face.

I may or may not have peed a little.

"Come any closer and I'll shoot her."

Fiona, who'd been standing on my left when the door was opened, began to cry big crocodile tears. "Oh, I'm so glad you're here to rescue us. Arrest this man, he's crazy." Donnie's attention turned to Fiona and he yelled, while entirely too close to my face, I may mention, "She's lying, she's the one who's crazy. She's behind all of this."

"Look," said an unfamiliar man's voice from behind me. "Put the gun down and let's talk about this. There's no reason for anyone to get hurt."

"I'm not putting my gun down until someone finds my wife. That's the whole reason I even made this trip. It's what I want. That's my demand. I demand that someone bring my wife here. Janice Hankins." He was nodding and muttering to himself and while yes, there was a gun to my head, I felt like he was making all of this up on the fly. Then, I noticed the gun he was swinging around in my face was a revolver. Which I could see had no bullets in it.

"You've watched too many movies, Donnie," I told him. "But so have I. There aren't any bullets in his gun," I yelled. Donnie turned his attention to me, eyebrows raised, but before he could say anything he'd already taken a beanbag to the face. Knocked out of his squat and lying flat on his back, Donnie took aim at one of the two cops who were rushing around me with their bullet-proof shields.

The gunshot was deafening in the enclosed space.

What do you know? I, in fact, could not see well with only one eye and was also not really psychic. There actually had been a bullet in that gun.

I definitely peed myself then.

30

Dario and I met his very special not-boyfriend friend at The Buffalo Chip Friday for lunch. He had floppy blond hair and a preppy look to him, but Gerri was right, he was super cute.

Dario had picked me up because I was sans mode of transportation at the moment, and as we walked toward the table where Jason was waiting, I had to nudge Dario in the ribs. "Are you sure he's not a Jehovah's Witness?" He wore a white dress shirt and skinny black tie and looked completely comfortable in both. Dario was wearing a Hawaiian print shirt that I was certain belonged to his father, but at least it wasn't a black tee shirt.

"When I said I wanted to interview you, I didn't mean go out and get yourself kidnapped," Jason said, holding out a chair for me.

My left eye was still swollen, although makeup helped disguise the bruising, at least from thirty feet away. I looked like I'd been in a fight and lost. I pulled some of my hair over that side of my face but when our waiter came bouncing over to ask what we'd like to drink, he'd paused in what could only be described as horror when he got a good look at my face.

"You should see the other guy," I told him. Dario and Jason both laughed, but the waiter, mortified at his faux pas, apologized profusely. "Iced tea, please," I told him.

"So, Pansy, let me tell you what I know, and then you interject whenever you need to correct me or add something. This Donald Hankins, alias Donald Chojakni, alias Donald Bisbee, alias Donald Sunderland, he was married to Summer, whose real name was Janice Hankins, née Burell."

"That sounds overly complicated and one hundred percent correct."

"Great. He was an abusive husband, she ran away seven years ago, and landed in Perth five years ago with a new name, where she opened a business called Wild Harmony."

"Also correct."

"Then, we have the other player in this drama, Fiona Dale, recently widowed and living in some place called Berry, New Mexico. Her husband had died after getting into a bar fight with his cohort in crime, presumably over the five-hundred-thousand dollars they'd stolen in a bank robbery. According to the tape, Gene hid the money but didn't tell his wife where it was."

"What tape?"

"Oh, you hadn't heard? The Fiona woman, she had one of those little micro recorders in her purse, you know, the ones that take the little tiny tapes?"

I nodded.

"Well, the recorder was on the floor when the Raton police collected evidence, and when they pressed play, what do you know? It was a full confession. She must have accidentally hit the record button while they were arguing, or it started to record when she dropped it, but it caught everything that she admitted to on tape, including the part about her trying to hire

Donald to kill you. That's like, something they take seriously in New Mexico."

"It caught everything?" I asked. Had it been an accident or had the Cowboy given it a little help?

"Oh yeah. With her confession and Donald shooting at a cop, not to mention all of the aliases they now know, who knows what else they'll dig up. Either way, it's going to be a while before either of them see daylight again."

"That's the best news I've heard all day," Dario said.

We ordered food and continued to talk about my experience, our hopes for college life, books we loved, books we hated, and even our favorite musicians although Dario's taste in music was never going to reconcile with mine, or apparently, even Jason's. And every time they snuck little looks at each other or 'accidentally' brushed their hand against the other's, my heart went a little gooey.

Jason was telling us about one of his professors when I heard a voice behind me screeching across the room, "Oh my god you are not going to believe what I found!"

Gerri was back. I pretended that I'd heard my cell phone ring and grabbed my purse, pulling the phone out. "I'm so sorry, I've been waiting on this call and I'm going to take it outside."

"Oh, of course. I'm sure you're getting calls about everything, all day long."

Dario made a little shooing motion with his hand. "We'll be perfectly fine without you. Take as long as you need."

"Mmm-hmm. I bet. I'll be right back."

I pulled the cell phone out of my purse and held it to my ear so I could talk to Gerri without everyone in the restaurant thinking that I was a nutjob. I mean, sometimes I felt like I was, but not today.

"Well, I can tell you what you didn't find," I said into the phone as I walked past her. I pushed through the front doors and into the parking lot. It was steal-your-breath hot outside and I'd worn long pants because my legs were covered in bruises. I regretted that.

"Dude, I looked everywhere for Donnie, including places I wish I had never seen because good grief if I could wash my eyeballs out, I would, but what I…" when she finally floated around to where she could see my face in the daylight, she stopped cold.

"What happened?"

"Donnie happened. Well, Donnie and Fiona. That woman wears rings and doesn't pull her punches," I said, rubbing my still-busted lip with the memory.

"Dude. Start from the beginning."

"Short version, he ran me off the road, kidnapped me, she tried to make me do a seance asking for any random ghost to stop by because she thought they'd just go get Gene for her because she wanted them to or some nonsense. Anyway, some cowboy ghost did show up and I sent him to get Christine and have her call the cops. Cops showed up, and Donnie and Fiona are both in jail. You should have seen Mom's face when I told her that a seance saved me."

Gerri was speechless, which was a state I preferred her in.

"Wait, wait, so Christine called the cops and they actually believed her?"

"Yeah, I talked to her last night. They just moved her into a rehab place to recover, but thankfully she was still there at the hospital when the cowboy arrived. Apparently, she's worked with the New Mexico state police so often that when she says go, they go. No questions asked."

"Wow. That's like, a lot."

"Oh, there's lots more to tell you, but those are the highlights. So what did you find?"

"Okay, but first, you're not grounded, are you?"

"I mean, the parents weren't happy when they had to come to collect me from a police station, but they *were* happy that I was still alive, so no, I'm not grounded. Or, at least I won't be once I get another car."

"Good. Okay, so, you know I told you about the baby raccoons?"

"Raccoons? You came flying in here all excited about the baby raccoons?" I hissed into the cell phone. I probably looked like I was having a breakdown in the parking lot. I mean, I'm sure they were cute and all, but clearly, my story was winning.

"So, I hadn't been to Fiona's in the daylight, and while I was there, I went to check on them. There was a loose piece of latticework that wasn't fully set back in correctly, and that's how the Momma was getting in and out."

"And...?" Good grief, she loved to drag a story out.

"And, when I floated under there, imagine my surprise when those fluffy little suckers had wallowed a nice deep hole out of all the loose dirt under the porch. And do you know why that particular patch of dirt was soft and loose, and not as hard as an oven-baked rock like everything else in the Dales' yard?"

"You found the money," I whispered. I was so stunned that I almost forgot to keep holding the phone up to my ear.

"I found a whole Rubbermaid tote full of money. Tell Bagel to go get a shovel."

"We can't steal it," I whispered.

"Oh, that's not what we're going to do with it. I mean, we are—technically—taking it, but we're not keeping it."

I went back inside fairly buzzing, and as I sat down, Dario was telling Jason about how he'd always wanted to take a long road trip but now that we'd done it twice in one week, he was firmly in favor of sitting at home for the next month.

"About that," I said, smiling at him in a way that no doubt concerned him greatly. "You have tomorrow off, right?"

We were flying down the open highway, the wind in our hair, well, the wind in Dario's hair, mine was back in a braid, but there was definitely wind. And heat, because the air conditioning in the Bronco didn't work. We'd just passed Las Vegas when my cell phone rang. I didn't recognize the number, but I also didn't want to have to check my voicemail.

"Hello?"

"Pansarooni? Is that you?"

"Summer? Oh my god!" I smacked Dario in the arm a few times in my excitement.

"Dude, I'm driving here."

Gerri's face appeared right next to mine so she could listen in. "Oh my god, you don't know how worried we all were when you didn't come back!"

"Worried about me? You're the one out here with your face plastered all over the newspapers again."

"Well, you see one of my very best friends just up and disappeared, so I figured I'd better make a lot of noise if I wanted her to notice and come back. Where the heck are you?"

"Eh, I don't know if I'm ready to give away all of my secrets, yet. But I came to town to hit the laundromat and saw the papers. Is he really in jail?"

"Dude ran me off the road, kidnapped me, held me at gunpoint, and then tried to shoot a cop. Yeah, he's in jail and won't get out until he's like a hundred and thirty. Actually, if he hadn't tried to shoot a cop he'd probably already be back out again, but they've denied him bail this time around. So, if what you're really asking is if it's safe to come home, then the answer is yes."

"That's good, because yes, that's really what I was wanting to know," she said laughing. I'd missed that laugh. "It says here in the paper that he tore my whole apartment up. Was there anything salvageable?"

"Yes. Sort of. You're going to need a new mattress and a couch, but Chandra cleaned all of your clothes and we all cleaned up the apartment, and Sarah had the window replaced. But the downstairs? There was no saving all of your stuff, I'm sorry. Sarah was going to check with the insurance company but they needed to talk to you. Honestly, I don't know how any of that went so you should call Sarah. Also call your mom, Janice. She worries about you."

"Janice? My mom? How on earth did you guys figure that out?"

"See, people underestimating us always gets them in trouble."

"Agreed. Are you going to be home tonight? If I leave now I can be back before dinner."

"As much as I'd love to meet you for dinner, Dario and I are about five hours from home right now. But I promise, I'll stop by first thing in the morning to see you and give you a hug."

"Good grief, what are you two doing so far away?"

Gerri and I both looked towards the back seat where a beat-up Rubbermaid tote sat next to the cooler, leaving dust and dirt all over everything. "Oh, we were just cleaning out some old things and had to make a donation to the women's shelter. But I'll see you tomorrow and tell you all about it."

"That'll be great, see you tomorrow. Oh, and Pansy?" her voice had turned serious.

"Yeah."

"Thank you. I am so sorry... I'm sorry that I ran away and

left everyone else to deal with my problems. I'm sorry this happened to you and I'm glad that you're okay, but thank you. Tell Dario and Gerri and even Lee. Thank you all."

"You know I'd do it all over again if it meant you were safe."

"Yeah, I do know that."

I disconnected the call and tossed the cell phone back into my purse. "Pick up the speed, Bagel Boy."

"Oh my God, do not tell me that you already need to pee again," he grumbled.

"Okay, I won't tell you, but it looks like there's an exit about three miles up the road and I suggest that you take it if you value your upholstery." I batted my eyelashes for effect.

Behind me, Gerri cackled.

EPILOGUE

"There, how's that look?" I asked, standing back to admire my handiwork. Plastic shopping bags covered my hands, each dipped in a cream-colored paint I was sponging over the peach color we'd applied the night before. No one had ever trusted me to help paint their walls before, and I blushed when Sarah began clapping.

"That looks so much better. Summer is going to love it! Once this gold paint dries, we can move these shelves over and put the books in," Sarah said, waving her brush around as she spoke. The shelves—rescued from a thrift shop in Trinidad earlier that week—had already been painted in a swirl of blue and purple. While I'd been working on the walls, Sarah had been stenciling a series of moons, stars, and suns over the surface to complete the look.

Over the last few weeks, Summer had been dragging furniture and shelving back into Wild Harmony, making the empty space come alive once again. Since Donnie hadn't deemed the yoga studio worth destroying, she'd been able to resume classes almost as soon as she'd returned to Perth. And, as I was still unemployed, Summer had hired me to help her and Sarah restock and repaint the shop while she taught. Her students had flocked back, eager to resume their stretching and straining. She'd even had to add more classes because of all of the news articles written about her after Donnie was charged.

Call it fame or infamy, either way, there was no more hiding for Summer.

A little blue S10 with a jumble of furniture in the back pulled in front of the shop and Sarah groaned. "Dear Lord, what junk has she scavenged, now?"

"You're going to be a professional sponge painter and stenciler by the time this shop is reopened," Gerri told me before floating out of the large plate glass window overlooking the street to check out the haul. I removed the plastic bags from my hands, turning them inside out to keep from smearing paint everywhere.

The bell over the front door rang out as Summer pushed inside, her arms full of shopping bags. "Oh my gosh, guys, this looks amazing. I can't thank you enough for helping with this."

"Don't the walls look great? I was just telling Pansy what a great job she was doing," Sarah said. She scooted paint cans together on the canvas-draped countertop to give Summer some room for the bags. "I think we're almost done."

"Good, because I stopped at the thrift store while I was in Trinidad, and found a set of CD racks that could use some love."

I could see the racks, as well as another shelf and what looked like an end table or something in the back of the truck. She'd traded her VW bug for the truck while she'd been on the run, and it had proved to be useful now that she was home.

"Looks like you found more than CD racks," Sarah said, nodding towards the truck. "Are we going to start selling furniture, too?"

Summer laughed as she emptied the bags. "No, but I found

some extra shelves on a curb and thought they'd work for the candles I ordered. And there are two tables for upstairs that I found in a second-hand shop."

"So? What did the lawyer say?" I asked. The whole reason she'd gone to Trinidad this morning was to meet with an attorney and the curiosity was killing me. Gerri floated back over toward me while we waited for the answer.

Summer ran a hand through her dark curls. A pixie cut had been part of her disguise when she ran, all of her locs cut out. It had taken a few days to get used to, but the look really suited her. "It was good news. He thinks I can get out of this without sharing too much money with Donnie. Maybe even none, if we get lucky."

Lee had been correct about Summer paying cash for the building when she'd moved to Perth, but fortunately, she hadn't robbed a bank to get it. What she *had* done was win a small lottery. It wasn't a bazillion dollars or anything, but it was enough that she could take the winnings anonymously and run away. It had given her her freedom. However, since she'd technically still been married to Donnie, there was a chance he was entitled to his share of the winnings.

"You'd think that being an abusive piece of crap would be all the court would need to hear," I said. The man had held me at gunpoint, there was no love lost there.

"Honestly, it's the shooting a cop that's really going to work against him," Summer said. "The court couldn't care less about what he did to me. The statute of limitations is up on all of that."

"Well that's dumb," I mumbled.

"I want to go haunt him some more," Gerri said. "I think I can break him."

I snorted.

"And—more good news—the attorney is going to start on

the paperwork to change my name to Summer Hopkins. The legal way," she chuckled.

"At least you're free now. Even if everyone knows more about you now than you ever wanted them to," Sarah said, wiping the paint from her sponge. "I think it's worth it."

Summer sighed. "Yeah, it's weird, you know. I feel...vulnerable I guess. Like I'm a gazelle out in the open savannah. But knowing that the lion is locked up makes that a little less scary."

I nodded. To the best of my knowledge, both of the men involved in the scheme I'd accidentally uncovered last winter were still in jail, as well as Donnie and Fiona. All of them hated me, and all of them knew exactly where to find me. So yeah, that bit about the gazelle standing in the open savannah hit a little close to home.

I glanced over at Gerri, who was staring me down.

"I've got you," she said.

I nodded again, knowing she did.

"Oh, also, the furniture company should be here this afternoon. They're finally bringing me the new bed and living room suit I ordered."

"We could have helped you carry it up," Sarah said.

We? We who? She'd seen those stairs, right?

"No, the pullout couch weighs a ton. I'll let the professionals deal with the stairs on that one."

"A pullout?" Sarah asked, one eyebrow arched. "Did you make new friends while you were on the run that I don't know about?"

Summer rolled her eyes. "No, it's for my mom. I mean, for me, while Mom's here, anyway. She's taking some vacation time. She's driving down this weekend and plans to stay for about two weeks."

"Ohhhh," Gerri and I said at the same time.

"I'm so glad you two can spend time together. When Dario and I went to visit her she said that she understood why you couldn't see her, but I could tell that she really missed you."

"I kind of can't believe how fast she forgave me for disappearing. I've missed her so much over the years, but was afraid she'd be mad at the way I handled things."

I tried to imagine not being able to see Mom whenever I wanted. Or Dad. I looked over at Gerri, knowing full well that her guilt—the whole reason she stayed with me—was because I couldn't let her go. "Yeah, I can see how being separated would be miserable, but she knew you had to avoid her to keep her safe. You did what you thought was best for everyone."

"Well, I can't wait to meet her," Sarah said before pointing toward the truck. "Do you need help moving that stuff in?"

"Let me clean my hands off," I said. Summer and Sarah headed out the door while I ran upstairs to the kitchen sink. Gerri was looking through Summer's purchases on the counter when I came back down.

"She's got a box of plant food in the bag, Pans," Gerri said. "Obviously she needs to baby the snake plant so it can recover from your tender loving care."

"It's still alive," I hissed, hoping Sarah didn't notice me arguing with myself through the window.

"Barely."

"Hush. I was, like, busy and stuff."

Gerri's hair swung over her shoulder as she started back in with that annoying laugh of hers. I mean, I'd tried to keep the plant alive. It obviously hadn't received enough sun, or water, or enough Enya being played at it, or something. The long green leaves had been droopy and little more yellow than was probably healthy for it by the time I'd returned it to Summer.

I opened the door just as the two women carried the first item in. "You'll be moving furniture of your own soon, won't you? When are you guys leaving?" Summer asked as she set a wooden CD rack down on a drop cloth.

"We're leaving Friday morning. I am, at least. We predict that Dario will 'be leaving,'" I made air quotes with my fingers, "over the better part of two hours while Mrs. Ventura finds a thousand more things that he absolutely needs to take with him."

"And that's what, a four-hour drive to Greeley?" Sarah asked.

"Yeah, about that. Robbie does it in like three and a half, but he's not two car wrecks in," I said, rolling my eyes. Not that either wreck was my fault, but I was certainly not pressing my luck. Plus, the Four-Runner dad had found for me to replace the Tracker got awful gas mileage. Doing the speed limit was in my best financial interest.

"Are you afraid people will recognize you?" Sarah asked.

"Not really. It's a big campus, and it's not like people my age watch the news or anything. My goal is to just blend in and be Pansy Bellafini, normal freshman teen."

Gerri found that hilarious and I shot her a dirty look.

"Girl..." Summer said, closing her eyes and shaking her head. "I will never be the one to advocate for being normal, but I wish you luck."

"I think it will be fine. Even if there are other kids from Perth there, it's not like they're going to care enough to tell the whole school about me or anything. I probably won't even have class with anyone I know. I'll be starting out fresh." Those were the words I said out loud. Inside, I could feel my anxiety begin to bubble. I pushed it down. It was going to be fine.

"Well, starting fresh is a great feeling, I've got to tell you," Summer said. "Speaking of, after we bring this stuff in, I need you two to help me pick out afghan's from this new catalogue I got. I'm not sure which ones to order."

I made the appropriate noises of interest as I followed them back out to the truck. *College is going to be fine*, I thought as I stuffed the anxiety down further. I had tasks. I had friends. I had family. I could pretend to be normal. It was all going to be fine.

ACKNOWLEDGMENTS

I want to thank the Kickstarter supporters first. That faith you show in supporting this indie press does not go unnoticed, and it is a go-to when I need motivation. We can't thank you enough, and I hope the end product does all of your faith justice.

Second, I want to thank my fellow IGW writers, especially Sheila and Tobi. The support you provide, the retreats, the games, the conferences...it goes a really long way in reducing my imposter syndrome. You share knowledge, snacks, and most importantly, love.

And last, I want to thank my Henlo family. Never once in this journey have I regretted stalking you to find a publisher. You're good at what you do, you keep me in line, and I'm sorry to say, you're just stuck with me now.

ABOUT THE AUTHOR

Author A. B. Hooser lives in Huntington, WV with her family and two dogs. Artist, gamer, writer, she lets the ADHD lead her into every new adventure. She tells people that she has mastered the art of procrastinating by creating an entire sticker business to avoid nishing the multiple books she has half- written.

READ INDIE. STAY AWESOME.
MORE BOOKS FROM THE HENLO PRESS

Glass Mountain by Laura Treacy Bentley

These Old Familiar Rooms by Mike Hornyak

Orphan Poetry by Alexis Cremeans

Extreme Human Overload by Diana Johnson

The Mother of Monsters by M.A. Elliot

The Wonderfully Wild Adventures of Kana and Charlie : Montrous Mo and the Stolen Apples by Josh Taylor, Illustrated by Jeremiah Morgan

304 Monsters by Stephen Bias

West By God by Tyler Bell

Deadly Choices: Will You Survive? | Camp Meltaway by Tiffany and Caitlyn Pace

Old Bones:Volume One by Various

A Shade of Winter by A.B. Hooser

Nora the Narwhal and her Curly Horn
by Alan Maynard, Illustrated by Soma Cather

Mumblings: West Virginia Horror Stories by Caitlyn Pace

Afterwords by Stephen Bias

The Dictionary Game by Mike Hornyak